One Woman—In the Hands of a Madman

It was apparent that he knew the river, or at least knew what to be looking for. "Get out," he ordered.

She didn't move very fast, a little act of defiance at his tone, but it was wasted on him.

"Why are you doing this?" she asked, trying to keep her voice even.

"Better to travel after dark."

"No, I mean why did you kidnap me? I'll just slow you down."

The finger raised again, while he swallowed. "You were a gift from Providence . . ."

Gently Down the Stream

ALSO BY JOAN BANKS

Death Claim

"A terrifying page-turner . . . compelling . . . unpredictable!"

—Judith Kelman

Edge of Darkness

A frightened and desperate woman returns to a roadside diner . . . where her husband mysteriously disappeared. A shattering novel of suspense.

GENTLY DOWN THE STREAM

Joan Banks

B
BERKLEY BOOKS, NEW YORK

GENTLY DOWN THE STREAM

A Berkley Book / published by arrangement with
the author

PRINTING HISTORY
Berkley edition / March 1991

ISBN: 0-425-12347-2

A BERKLEY BOOK ® TM 757,375
Berkley Books are published by The Berkley Publishing Group,
200 Madison Avenue, New York, New York 10016.
The name "BERKLEY" and the "B" logo
are trademarks belonging to Berkley Publishing Corporation.

PRINTED IN THE UNITED STATES OF AMERICA

10 9 8 7 6 5 4 3 2 1

To Diana,
who, when we ran aground, said cheerfully,
"Well, here we are!"

My thanks to Lt. David Cook, Missouri Highway Patrol; my sister-in-law, Phyllis Fredrick, L.P.N.; Patti Johnson, R.N., and James Welch, M.D.

GENTLY DOWN THE STREAM

Thursday Evening

1

No ONE LIKED traffic stops, Delano Smith not excepted. He'd go out of his way to overlook small infractions, but there was something menacing about the Chevy van he was following now. Its black paint was tattooed with primer, and the windows were obscured by dark film. It begged to be stopped.

"Eight twenty-one, my ten-twenty is Highway CC and Bass Road—vehicle stop, no taillights. License Zebra-Paul-Paul six-four-one."

The dispatcher acknowledged the message while Del, as his friends called him, followed the van at an interested distance designed to intimidate its driver. He reached over and turned on his flashers.

For the most part, he liked his work as a state trooper. When he was growing up in East St. Louis, he'd fantasized about being a policeman; around his neighborhood a kid saw enough cops to either hate them or idolize them for the power they seemed to have. Del fell into the latter category, maybe because he didn't have a father to look up to at home. After four years in the army, he was still undecided about a career, until the day he saw a notice in the paper announcing a recruitment test for the highway patrol. After that, things just kind of fell into place. He signed up and passed the exam with flying colors, aceing the physical agility test and the personal interviews as well. His mama, who'd brought him up by herself, had encouraged him, then died before he completed the six-month training. She'd have been proud oi her son.

Del took his Smokey the Bear hat off the seat and settled it on his head, then opened the door of his car, ducking slightly as he got out.

His bright headlights cast an intimidating shadow before him as he walked up to the van, unsnapping his holster just in case. He couldn't see any passengers, but the windows were obscured by that damn brown film. "May I see your operator's license?" he asked when he came abreast of the driver's open window.

To Del, the man inside, not over thirty years old, looked a little too clean-cut, with ultrashort blond hair trimmed close around the ears.

The driver tried to pass his wallet out the window, but Del refused it. Once a man had accused him of lifting a ten-dollar bill in a similar situation. He'd known better, but a rookie has a lot to remember. Later, things like that became second nature.

"Take it out, please." Out of the corner of his eye, Del saw a patrol car pull up behind his. Why had they sent him a backup?

He turned his head very slightly and saw that it was Clarence Ray; they'd just had a cup of coffee down the highway at the Quartz Café. But why had they sent him? Del's glance cost him.

The door of the van flew open, knocking the trooper backward and off balance as the driver came out of the seat, a submachine gun clasped to his side. He rolled expertly away from the van, firing before Del could draw his gun. Clarence started to fire, but not before the driver turned on him with another volley. He crawled under the car. As Delano Smith staggered to the van, trying to find cover, the driver shot again. His Kevlar vest, which was now standard issue, didn't do any good; the bullets penetrated his unprotected side, his head, his belly.

From his vantage point lying stricken under the second highway patrol car, a semiconscious Clarence Ray, bleeding from multiple wounds, saw the young blond-haired killer flee into the nearby woods.

Susan Morrow sighed and played with a curl that corkscrewed in front of her ear. "Are you sure we won't need a skillet?" She was peering into the top of a paper grocery bag which sat on her kitchen table.

Her friend Jan, who was sitting at the table, laughed. "No. We're going to make this simple. We're trying to get away from it all, not take it all with us."

Susan shoved the bag aside. "Would you like a soft drink?"

"Diet?"

"Yeah."

Jan made a face. "No, thanks, I'm not putting any of those weird chemicals in my body."

"I'll remind you of that when I'm slim and trim, and you're fat and have rotten teeth. I have some cranberry juice. Want that?"

"Sure."

"You know," Susan said as she dispensed ice cubes from the door of the refrigerator, "I'm nervous about this trip. I've never gone camping without Ted." She knew as she said it Jan would rise to the bait. It was exactly the sort of thing Jan Spencer hated to hear. *So then why*, Susan wondered, *did I say it? Am I looking for an argument?*

"That's why you need to go! Imagine being forty-five and—"

"Forty-four, thank you."

"Forty-four, and you've hardly ever been anywhere without Ted."

Susan looked a little sheepish as she opened the refrigerator door and moved some things to locate the cranberry juice. "I'm kind of old to start now."

Jan glanced at her. "That's the point exactly. Your attitude." She made a sound of derision. "We're not too old, and I don't want you to talk like that. It's ridiculous for a woman in this day and age to be so dependent on a man. I mean, what if something happens to him?"

Susan preferred not to entertain the possibility aloud, so she remained silent, wondering why she'd allowed herself to get caught up in this crazy idea of a canoeing trip. What business did two women have going out into the . . . the wilderness, for goodness sake—alone?

The plan had been made three weeks ago, and actually, she'd been the one who mentioned it, although not with the idea that they would actually go. Just casually. "I'd love to go canoeing," she'd said, "but I can't get Ted interested. All he wants to do is watch television." It had really been in the nature of a complaint; Ted was becoming such a frump. She could remember when they'd indulged in all sorts of outdoor activities with the kids, but not anymore.

Jan had jumped right on the idea, embroidering it into a weekend adventure. And, Susan admitted, it had been fun planning it—she liked planning—but now here she was, confronted with the reality of going off into the wild. It was probably just pretrip jitters—she always felt them the night before she went somewhere—so it was best just to shut up about it.

"Here you go," she said to Jan, handing her a glass. "Ohmigosh. I'm about to forget the matches." She looked at her friend with a wry grin. "I can take matches, can't I?"

Jan wrinkled up her nose and shook her head. "Naah. We're gonna rub sticks together."

"Maybe I'd better put in some aspirin and some—"

"*Susan!* Picture this"—she put her hands out in front of her in a dramatic gesture—"picture a canoe with two women in it, floating down the river . . . and sinking from the weight of everything they're carrying."

"It's not that bad," Susan said, smiling at her friend's histrionics. She went ahead and tossed the aspirin in the bag as Jan rolled her eyes in mock exasperation.

Susan stood there a moment more, looking uncertain, then uncapped a partially empty two-liter diet cola bottle which sat on the ceramic tile countertop. Only a faint fizz erupted. Flat, but she had no one to blame but herself; Ted never drank the stuff. She poured some into her glass anyway, asking Jan at the same time: "What else do you suppose we've forgotten?"

"The guy we're renting the canoes from is an outfitter—at least that's what Noreen's husband told me when he gave me directions." Noreen and Jan worked together. "So relax. I'll bet we can pick up what we forget there."

"Well, I'd like to have everything—no point in buying it if we have it here." She looked around distractedly, one hand scratching her head, the other holding her drink. "Where'd I put that list?"

"Try your pocket," Jan said with a good-natured laugh.

Susan looked down and saw the folded paper sticking out of her jeans pocket. She shook her head slowly as she pulled it out and began to run through it systematically. "I'm getting so forgetful."

"Aren't we all," Jan said.

Later, Jan backed out of the Morrows' driveway, dwelling on the fact that she resented the hell out of Susan's dependence on a husband. She used to be the same way. Then her husband Clive had dealt their marriage a death-blow, leaving her disgusted, dismayed, and on her own. He'd always run around on her—she knew that, but had ignored it because there were compensations. For one thing she'd liked the security of being married. And for another, Clive definitely knew how to show Jan a good time. But every woman has her limit. Jan's was finding Clive in bed with some sweet young thing, a teenager. In Jan and Clive's own bed! After all, even in the worst of circumstances, there was such a thing as propriety.

Her anger mounted just thinking of the scene that day, and she took a few deep breaths to calm herself as she slowed for a speed bump at the edge of Susan's housing development.

It drove Jan crazy to see a woman so dependent on marriage, which she now considered to be a rather tentative state. Especially when the woman was her best friend, and the marriage was with Ted. He looked like a heart attack waiting to happen: stressed out, overweight, and inactive.

She shook her head and sighed as she enumerated his liabilities in her head. *Boy! What would Susan do if Ted kicked off unexpectedly?*

Susan had it so easy. Her husband brought home a good salary. She had two decent kids who'd weathered adolescence with only minor storms. And she had time to dabble in all her little hobbies like painting and counted cross-stitch.

Shame on you, Jan told herself, as she recognized her depreciation of her friend by her use of the word *little*. It wasn't Susan's fault that Clive had been a philanderer and ol' Ted was steady as a rock.

Jan laughed aloud. Steady as a rock and about as boring—an accountant who fit every stereotype she had of them. He was parsimonious in deed and spirit. Maybe ten years with Clive was better than being saddled with Ted for a lifetime.

But why my resentment? she wondered. *Am I a little envious?* It would be nice, sometimes, just to relax and let someone take care of her again, without worrying about the next rent payment.

She drove down Fifteenth Street and turned into her apartment complex, two rows of one-story units facing each other across a driveway. She pulled under the carport, opened the door, and stepped out, catching her breath sharply. There was someone standing there.

"Why in hell don't you look before you get out of your car? I could have been anyone."

"Eric! You scared me to death." She leaned against the car, her palm against her chest.

"You should have your doors locked when you pull in here and then take a look around before you hop out. You're too trusting," he said as he fell in step beside her. He was carrying an empty wastebasket.

"I'm not going to become paranoid, always looking for the bogeyman." They had reached her porch. She turned and leaned against the wrought-iron railing which flanked it.

"Wanna come over to my place for a drink?" he asked.

"No, I'm going canoeing early tomorrow, so I need to get some sleep. Another time, okay?"

"Sure. Must be nice to be a teacher and have the summer off."

"You're not going to make me feel guilty. This is the first summer I haven't sold encyclopedias or something since I was in high school. Besides that," she said, making a face at him, "being with thirty fifth-graders for nine months is worth about two years of your data processing."

He guffawed. "I'll give you that one. How long you gonna be gone?"

"Just till Sunday."

"Well, hey, I guess I'll see you later, kid. Have fun."

"I plan to." She closed the door behind her, then leaned against it, wondering why she couldn't be interested in Eric. Just because he was short, balding, and overweight. She laughed aloud again. Who was she to talk? She reached up and pulled a strand of her fine, blunt-cut hair in front of her eyes. She couldn't focus that close any longer, but it was obvious that the hair was no longer dark brown.

Eric had a good job. That was an asset. But there was a liability. Something was missing between them—that intangible something. Would she ever feel that for someone again?

Lee Newton crashed through the woods, heedless of the noise he was making. Time, not quiet, was his main ally now. The air was close, a combination of the high humidity and a daytime temperature that had reached ninety-eight, typical for July, and hadn't dropped much, although the hour was nearing midnight. A full moon peeked through the branches, giving enough light to allow Lee to put some distance between himself and the site of the shooting.

He cursed under his breath. *That black son of a bitch swaggering up to the van like he was someone, demanding to see my license.* Even now, the thought of it made Lee seethe with anger, sending the blood roaring through his head.

He needed to calm down; it was behind him. His main

focus had to be getting through the woods in the semidark-
ness with all his faculties in high gear so he'd be able to
outrun the authorities. He paused for a moment to get his
bearings and remembered something he'd forgotten. He
dropped to his knees. "Almighty God, lead me as I go forth
into the wilderness. Watch over my steps and guide me so
that I may fulfill my mission. . . ." His prayer continued
for several minutes, then he stood up feeling clearheaded.

The Colonel would fault him for leaving the van full of
ordnance behind. It wouldn't matter to the old man that he'd
had no choice but to get out of there as fast as possible.

*There's no way I could've gotten down the highway in
that van. And if the next wave of troopers had caught me in
it, I'd have been a goner, and then where would the plan for
Wednesday be?* He was, after all, the one who would lead
the operation. The Colonel sure as hell wasn't going to
participate.

And he knew there *would* be a wave of law-enforcement
people—wave after wave probably. They'd be crawling all
over this area, combing the hills, searching people's private
property because he'd killed one of their own. They'd pull
out all the stops to apprehend Lee Newton. A slight grin
turned up the corners of his mouth, but it immediately
faded.

To his way of thinking, he hadn't had a choice, but that
wouldn't keep the old man from criticizing him. He'd
accuse the younger man of not showing enough restraint, of
acting first and thinking later. Hell. He had no right. Old
man sitting out there on his can giving orders. He wouldn't
praise Lee for exterminating one of their enemies. No, he'd
focus on the van and make Lee look bad to the others,
dressing him down. He liked to do that. Lee would suffer in
silence, knowing the old man wouldn't be calling the shots
forever.

Lee almost hated to go back to the Compound. At the
conference from which he was returning, he hadn't felt the
conflicts that seemed to be rampant in the group he was in.
Instead, it was like his old group with everyone on the same
wavelength. The sense of camaraderie was high, because

the Revolution was at hand. They all felt it. The Zionist Occupational Government was about to be brought to its knees. The brothers were going to declare Judgment Day.

And he, Lee Newton, was going to be one of the leaders when it happened. He shivered, remembering the sense of well-being he'd had, being surrounded by all the energy of the brothers at the conference. There were so many of them, alive and well and living all over the country, not just in compounds, but right out there like normal people. *Like* normal people? They *were* the normal people. It was the Jews, the niggers, the spics, and all the mongrels who were abnormal, who needed to be expunged—who *would* be expunged. The New Order was imminent, and like it or not, he needed to get back to the Compound to take part in the first strike of the new phase of operations. It was going to go like dominoes set up in a pattern on a table. His operation was number one.

At a clearing he looked up and found the North Star to orient himself. Ahead, out there in the wildnerness, deep in the hills and hollows, was his immediate destination. To the casual hiker or hunter who wandered that far into the forest, it appeared to be a dank hole beneath a protruding rock at the base of a hardwood-covered hillside like hundreds of others in the area. But if a person took the time to get down and investigate, he could feel air coming out of it, quietly sighing. Sometimes it even made sounds, kind of like nature was moaning.

He'd learned about it from a member of the group who'd discovered the hole as a young boy and investigated it, as any kid would. Years later, when the boy grew to manhood and joined the group, he oriented them to this area and the breathing cave became one of their survival-training sites. Just last summer, eight of them had squeezed through the mouth and bellied along the throat for three hundred feet before it opened up so they could stand. Before them lay a network of caves and tunnels that riddled the underground for miles, waiting to be explored.

Passages south, he thought, passages toward the river. There'd always been tales about how all the caves inter-

linked. Well, a lot of them did, and the breathing cave was
one entrance into one of the longest systems he knew. Once
through it, the river would take him the rest of the way to
the Compound, where the others were waiting.

His immediate problems were two: getting a flashlight
and finding the cave again.

He'd covered several miles before he discovered a house on
a dirt road. There was a mercury-vapor light in the yard; no
farm seemed to be without one anymore. One bit of good luck,
however: his approach didn't seem to rouse any dogs. He
scouted the perimeter and noticed there were no cars, just
one truck, up on blocks. No one appeared to be home. He
approached cautiously; still seeing no signs of life, he tried the
doors. They were locked, but a window in the kitchen was
open, and he thought he could gain access there. Standing on
a cinder block, he sliced the screen along the bottom of the
frame, then reached in and unhooked the latch. One boost took
him over the sill, through the opening, and headfirst into the
kitchen.

His heart was pounding as he righted himself. The house
was almost silent. Night sounds drifted through the window, and he could hear the hum of an electric clock over the
stove.

Quickly, he relatched the screen, smoothing the wire
mesh back into place, then with just the light from outside,
he jerked open the kitchen drawers, one after another,
looking for what his mother would have called the "junk
drawer." What was the matter with these people? Didn't
they have a junk drawer? He took a box of utility candles
from a cutlery drawer and stuffed them in the big pocket on
the side of his camouflage pants. A flashlight would be
better, but in a pinch . . .

He went in a small room at one end of the kitchen and,
knowing it was risky, flipped on the light. No flashlight on
the shelves there. He was about to leave when he noticed a
rechargeable one plugged in above the clothes washer.
Perfect, he thought. No dead batteries, a full charge. He
jerked it out of the wall socket.

Before he turned off the utility room light, he looked

around the kitchen to see if there were any signs of his entry, then went out the door, pushing the little button in the center of the knob so it would lock behind him. Hadn't these people heard about deadbolts? When the Revolution came and there were roaming bands of counterinsurgents everywhere, they were going to be in serious trouble. Look how easily he'd broken into their house.

He'd just slipped into the woods again when car lights appeared coming down the road. He stopped and watched as the car turned in the driveway and braked to a stop. It was an old couple. He could tell by the stiffness of their movements as they walked to the house, their inviolable castle. Ha! Lee shook his head at such naïveté, turned his back on the scene, and plunged into the woods.

To find the cave entrance he'd first have to locate an old bridge which crossed Sherman Branch, a clear-water creek with a railroad track running alongside it for about five miles. His best reckoning told him it was eight to ten miles to the creek, so he began making his way through the thickening tangle of forest to the south. The flashlight made the going much easier.

He'd misjudged the distance, and after only an hour, he came to the tracks. Walking along the rails was much faster. Occasionally, he'd pause, look around, then set off again, following in the shadow of a ridge until one particular hollow looked right, the way he remembered. He cut off straight south again.

The pulse of the night enveloped Lee as he went farther and farther from civilization; he was alone in the wilderness and on his way to the river.

The pretrip jitters blossomed, and Susan couldn't sleep. Ted, as usual, had dropped off the minute he was horizontal. Susan felt a moment of resentment as she wiped the cleansing cream off her face and listened to her husband's heavy breathing. It wasn't fair; men didn't have to go through all the rigmarole women did just to go to bed.

She chided herself for aiming her resentment at her husband, something that happened more and more often lately—she felt hostile toward him about such little things. The other morning it was the way he put his socks on. He made such a ritual out of it. He'd stretch each one out, always twice, then run his hand down inside, then begin to roll them systematically toward the toe. She'd wanted to scream just watching him, but realized it was irrational, so she'd turned away, gritting her teeth to keep quiet. He had a right to put his socks on any way he wanted to, so why did it bother her?

The resentments felt like cracks, and she kept applying invisible tape to keep them from growing, to keep her marriage together. Ted seemed to think they were happy. And maybe they were. Certainly they were comfortable. Perhaps she was examining their life too closely.

A bitter look crossed her face as she stared in the mirror. *You look old*, she thought. Her permed hair was pulled back from her face with a headband to keep the cream out of it, and it accentuated a haggardness that astonished her. In her head, she was about thirty. Where had this aging body come from? She wiped the tissue across her forehead and looked away from the reflection. Thank goodness for makeup, she thought, glancing at the dresser, which was covered with an assortment of creams, lotions, and concealers.

She put the lid back on the cleansing cream, straightened up the dresser a little, unleashed her hair, and fluffed it up. The perm was easy, but maybe it was time for a new style. She fingered one of the tight curls, deciding to let her hair grow out and then see what her hairdresser suggested.

Susan stepped back from the harsh vanity lights and studied herself. That's a little better, she thought, then murmured aloud, "Confucius say, 'Mature woman should stay out of strong light.'" The words brought a slight smile to her lips.

She turned out the bathroom lights, then went into the bedroom, decorated in a soothing blend of gray and mauve. Ted had carefully folded back the heavy bedspread and laid it on the bench at the foot of the bed. Susan pulled back the summer-weight thermal blanket—it was too warm for that tonight—and slipped between the sheets. The attic fan rumbled monotonously, pulling in a warm breeze.

Well, this is it, she thought negatively, reaching over to turn off the bedside lamp. *Probably the last night I'll ever spend in this bed. Jan and I will probably have an accident on the way down there or we'll drown, and I'll never get to meet my grandchildren and. . . .*

Ted stirred and mumbled something in his sleep, momentarily distracting her from her thoughts. She looked over at him. Dear Ted. Why was she so critical of him? She could just see the tiny bald spot at the crown of his head protruding from the sheet, which he'd pulled up around his neck, even though his legs were sticking out.

"Bald spot?" he'd said one day when their son Jeffrey mentioned it. "I have a bald spot?" He'd hurried off to the bathroom to look. "I don't see anything," he'd yelled to them. "Someone come show me what you're talking about." They'd gotten a good laugh out of his consternation. Tears sprang to Susan's eyes remembering it.

The house was so quiet now, with the kids gone, and it seemed to be missing something. Was it just the absence of young people? Jeffrey wasn't financially independent—that might take years—but his loyalties were shifting. He'd just finished his sophomore year at the university, and she'd selfishly expected him to be around this summer. Instead, he and a friend had gotten summer jobs at Estes Park hauling garbage. Garbage! That was better than being home? And this was the boy who never could remember to empty the trash.

Jennifer, though, was really on her own; she'd graduated in May with a degree in public relations and had landed a job in Senator Grindstaff's local office down in Marshallville. It seemed odd to have her living out-of-state. Susan and Ted had visited once since their daughter had gotten settled, and she'd proudly shown them around her office and introduced them to the senator, who wasn't there very often, but had dropped by that day.

"You've got a lovely daughter, Mrs. Morrow," the senator had said, patting Jennifer on the shoulder. His bald head gleamed under the fluorescent lights. "We're glad to have her on our team for this election coming up."

Jennifer beamed. She'd already impressed upon her parents how exciting it was to be working for a U.S. senator. Susan remembered the day Jen had called with the news about her job.

"Guess what, Mom," she had said, an undercurrent of excitement in her voice. She didn't wait for Susan's reply. "I've got a job in Senator Grindstaff's office in Marshallville. Isn't that great?"

Susan had to dredge up who the man was, but after a moment she remembered hearing his name on television. "Congratulations, honey. What will you be doing?"

"I'm going to be organizing his campaign on the west side of the state this fall—the nitty-gritty stuff like volunteer coordination, helping with the media, things like that, so I'll get to learn all the ropes. Isn't it great?"

Might be a short-term job, Susan thought with middle-aged cynicism, then stifled a remark to that effect. Instead she asked a more neutral question: "How're his chances?"

"He's been senator just about forever, but the governor down here is running against him, so it'll be an interesting race."

Was that a roundabout way of saying his chances were not too good? "Well, I hope he wins, honey."

Ted looked up from the front page and frowned when Susan told him the news. "Grindstaff, huh? He's not my brand of politics, but I guess it'll be good experience for her."

After visiting the senator's office and their daughter's cubicle in it, and getting the grand tour of Marshallville, the Morrows went back to Jennifer's for dinner. She seated them at a tiny, painted table, then served spaghetti and salad to them with a first-time-on-her-own flourish.

"I'd have made lasagna," she told them as she poured red wine into glasses scrounged from Susan, "but I didn't want to heat up the apartment."

Ted grinned and pushed up his bifocals. "Very practical.

Sounds just like you," he whispered to Susan as Jennifer went into the kitchen to get the bread.

Susan disagreed. "More like you, if you ask me. Maybe like both of us."

It had been a pleasant evening. And getting the kids out on their own was the name of the game—it meant she was a successful mother—so why didn't she feel great?

She wiped the tears away with the corner of the pillow-case. Her moods were so inexplicable these days. High one moment, low the next. In the course of the last five minutes, for instance, her hostility toward Ted had changed to a wave of love. A deep sigh escaped her. She glanced over at Ted to see if the sound had disturbed him as she pushed the back of her head deep into the pillow and clung to the sheet with clasped hands above her breastbone. Maybe she'd wanted it to awaken him—so they could talk—but he was still sawing logs. She reached over and started to touch him lightly, but stopped and withdrew her hand.

She turned over and tried to relax, then tossed over to her other side and flexed her ankles several times. The trip had her keyed up. For thirty minutes, according to the digital bedside clock, Susan tried to relax, then, disgusted, she turned the lamp back on and reached for the paperback mystery on the bedside table.

Neal Lassiter dreamed of the silence. It was always like that. The complete silence when you knew the enemy was right there next to you, hiding in the saw grass. He recognized it as the beginning of the dream now, after twenty-five years, and he willed himself awake.

His body was sweaty. The humidity in the room re-minded him of 'Nam; maybe that's what had triggered the nightmare. The steamy wetness of it. There was even a damn mosquito in the room with him; he could hear its high-pitched whine. He slapped at it as it came near his ear, his hand smacking the pillow. There'd been lots of mosqui-toes over there.

The demons of the night wouldn't flee—they were playing at the edges of his memory—even though he was now fully awake, so he sat up and turned on the bedside lamp. A spot of blood and the scraggly, disarranged insect lay on the pillow.

He flipped the pillow to the cool side, then reached over and took a cigarette from a pack which lay on the night-stand. He rarely smoked these days. Funny, he always wanted a cigarette after sex and after the nightmares. The nightmares were growing infrequent—the doctors had helped that—and, he thought with an inward laugh, so was sex. Pretty soon I'll be a nonsmoker, he thought drily.

He leaned back against the headboard and bent his knees, resting his wrists on them and watching the smoke drift up toward the ceiling fan in a swirl. He tried to focus on the here and now, to banish the ghosts. He thought about tomorrow.

Let's see. Should be able to finish putting the siding on the building; that's about a day's worth of work—maybe two, if I have any business.

Hauling canoers back to their cars took a lot of time, but his canoe rental wasn't very busy; he'd be lucky to have customers at all. *One of these days,* he thought, squinting and taking a long drag on his cigarette, then stubbing it out, *one of these days they'll come in droves.*

His river—that's how he thought of it—just hadn't been discovered yet. It flowed through some of the most beautiful country he'd ever seen, pristine in its loveliness. The location just wasn't as convenient as its sister river, which it joined downstream a ways; you could tell by the number of people who *didn't* spend their weekends floating it. But as the other river became more congested, the canoers would gradually discover the Upper Fork. *Count on it.* He was torn between wanting to keep it to himself and needing to keep the wolf from the door—he still owed money on his place.

He gave his beard a good rub, then lay back and turned out the lamp, dwelling on the improvements he needed to make. Finally, he drifted off into an untroubled sleep.

* * *

Lee Newton found the cave. Its opening grimaced at him from beneath a flat ledge on a hillside, silent tonight, no moan of air escaping it. He squirmed under the rock, then began to inch along on his stomach. There wasn't even enough room to raise his head, so he turned it, putting one cheek down against the cold rock, then drew a knee up to one side like a frog and pushed with his other foot. He had to extend his arms and shove his gun and the light ahead of him in order to get through the crevice.

He'd never been claustrophobic, but he was nevertheless relieved when the passage enlarged enough to allow him to stand. He flexed his muscles, tightened like piano wire from the strain, then relaxed them systematically. After a moment, he panned the passage ahead with his flashlight, hoping to see the markers still in place from his last trip in here. The cave was a labyrinth of twists and turns, passages going in different directions, crawl spaces and pits. Great for exploring with other people, but a nightmare alone. You could get lost in here for months, going in circles, except you'd die first from exposure. The cold, which was already penetrating his sweaty shirt, was a stark contrast to the heat outside.

If the markers are gone, he thought, momentarily panicking, *I'm sunk.* It was the first time since the shooting he'd felt any physical fear, but he quickly corrected his thinking. *No, I'll just go back out the way I came and think of something else.* He mumbled a short prayer.

Just then his light caught a bit of Day-Glo red in its beam. He smiled, adjusted his gun confidently around his shoulder, and started toward the flag.

The farther he intruded into the mountain, the more exhilarated he became at his cleverness. *I've eluded them,* he thought. *I'll come out of the cave just north of the Upper Fork, get some food, make contact with base operations, then follow the river.* He saw no problems.

Friday Morning

2

"HERE, LET ME get that." Ted Morrow shoved his glasses up and took the plastic sack containing a sleeping bag and pillow from his wife, thinking how good she looked in her red mid-thigh-length shorts and a red-and-white-striped top that had belonged to their daughter Jennifer.

"Okay. I'll get the food," Susan said.

"Are you about ready to take off?" He'd just come down from the bedroom, ready to go to work, and was already noticing how warm the day was. They didn't use the air-conditioner at night, and the lower floor was beginning to get stuffy. He ran his finger around his lightly starched collar.

"As soon as Jan gets here. You look handsome this morning," she told him.

"Thanks." Ted went out through the kitchen into the garage and pressed the door opener. As the door ground upward with labored squeaks and groans, Jan wheeled into the driveway in her 1982 Mustang. "Here she is now," he shouted over his shoulder to his wife.

Jan saw Ted and hollered out the window of the car, "Where shall I leave this?"

"Just pull over beside the driveway there, on the grass." He pointed. "If you'll leave the keys, I'll put it in the garage later."

She backed the car up and came in again, angling it onto

the strip of lawn flanking the concrete. The women were taking the Morrows' family car on their outing because Ted thought it was more reliable. He didn't want them breaking down somewhere out on the highway.

"How are you, Janice?" Ted asked, walking toward her, still carrying the plastic bag. He liked to use a person's full name, not a nickname. He was the one who'd insisted they call their children Jennifer and Jeffrey, not Jenny and Jeff. The kids' friends had shortened the names, of course, but at home it was Jennifer and Jeffrey. Maybe he felt that way because he was a Ted, not a Theodore, not an Edward. Just plain Ted. Always and forever.

"I'm fine," Jan replied. "Beautiful morning, isn't it?" She was getting her things out of the car, and he noticed she was wearing olive drab canvas shorts and a white T-shirt. *She's in good shape,* he thought. "Can I help?"

"I've got it," she said.

Ted went into the garage, opened the back door of the car, and deposited the bag he was carrying. "Here, put those in," he told Jan, who set one of her plastic bags on the seat, then hoisted the other across it.

"My old crate won't know what to do in a garage," she said. "You'll spoil her."

Susan came out of the house just then, struggling to walk with a cooler hitting her on the legs with each step. "Hi," she hailed her friend. "We ready?"

"As ready as ever."

"Honey, do you want to take my revolver?" Ted asked, taking the cooler from her.

Jan spoke up. "Aw c'mon, Ted. She'd probably end up shooting me."

"Really, Ted," Susan said. "I'm more afraid of the gun itself than I am of anything happening."

He shrugged, his habitual frown growing ever so slightly deeper.

Susan reached up and pecked him on the cheek, and he put his arms around her automatically and squeezed. "Now don't you worry," she said.

"It doesn't seem right to me—two gals going off alone."

"You're just old-fashioned," Jan said good-naturedly.

Ted snorted. "Ha! A person's not even safe in his own home with the doors locked, let alone out on a river." He shoved his glasses up on the bridge of his nose.

"Why didn't you say something earlier?" Susan asked in an exasperated tone. "It's a little late now for all this concern."

He shrugged. "Well, you have a good time this weekend," he said, glancing at his watch. "And be careful. Do you want me to get the rest of your things?"

"There's just one more bag. I can get it."

Ted glanced at his watch again, as if he hadn't seen it the first time. "I'd better hit the road or I'm going to be late." He got into his car and backed out of the garage, rolling down the window as he did so.

"Don't forget to lock up, honey. Janice, why don't you go ahead and move your car in, then you can keep your keys."

Jan nodded, thinking she'd leave the keys on the floor of the car rather than have them on a canoeing trip.

"You girls be careful now."

"Don't worry, we won't talk to strangers or anything," Jan assured him.

The cardinals and chickadees woke Neal Lassister. Their cheerful tidings and the cool morning air energized him, but he momentarily remained still and thanked his Maker for putting him here in this time and this place.

He'd been an angry teenager who'd gotten drafted, and Vietnam hadn't helped the anger go away. Once back from his hitch and out of the army, he'd wandered around for two years doing this and that. It was the early seventies, and most of his friends were drifting, too. He'd spent eighteen months at a commune in California, but it dissolved eventually. Then he'd had a series of dead-end jobs in seven different states.

Into his thirties, though, the allure of wandering began to pale, so he got married to the first acceptable woman who came along, and she worked while he went to college, still not knowing what he wanted to do. Teaching beckoned mainly because he had no other idea for a career. He was familiar with teachers, knew what teachers did, so he became one.

He taught junior high school science for four years and loved the kids because they were all just beginning to unfold into adulthood, feeling their way with tentative steps. One moment they would be children, erupting with enthusiasm on the school grounds; the next they were embryonic adults, so cool and calculating—but always he saw an attitude of discovery in their behavior. He felt sorry for the parents who couldn't see that these feelers toward independence the kids were putting out were what parenting was all about—letting go—right from day one.

He accepted the kids and their sometimes strange behavior, but his tolerance for the administration was just above zero. Finally he could no longer hack all the artificial rules and regulations. The home administration—his wife—wasn't working out so well either. She had her own rules and regulations. Eight years, no kids, and they called it quits.

Feeling lower than ever, he'd gone into therapy for a while at the veteran's hospital, and they'd come up with a name for his adjustment problems. Delayed Post-Traumatic-Stress-Syndrome, though the other day he'd read in a magazine that it was no longer a syndrome; it was a disorder. Just like the big boys to change the rules in the middle of the game.

His big problem, he and the therapist had decided, wasn't that there was no brass band, no hero's welcome when he got back from 'Nam. What he couldn't deal with was the loss of his integrity. He hadn't believed in what they were doing over there, but he'd done it anyway. Shot dozens of people, even one woman who obviously wasn't a V.C.

Now he just wanted to be left alone to be his own man. And he'd found his little bit of heaven on a river in the mountains in which to do it.

He stood up and extended his arms above his head, flexing his powerful back muscles, yawning. He took a pair of cutoff jeans from a chair and stepped into them, then sat on the bed and put on his ragged canvas shoes.

His place consisted of only two rooms: the bedroom and a living room–kitchen combination. It was more a cabin than a house. He strolled over to the apartment-sized range, put on some water for instant coffee, and poured himself an oversized bowl of cereal.

His dog, a Rhodesian Ridgeback, heard him from her post on the front porch and pawed the screen door several times until she managed to let herself in. She usually started the night at the foot of Neal's bed, but finished it on the porch after a little midnight prowling through the nearby woods. The cabin was so remote that Neal never locked the door; he did, however, sleep with a revolver under the bed.

"Hi, Brandy," Neal said, patting her. He heard the water boiling and stopped eating to prepare the coffee. He poured some dog food into Brandy's bowl and finished his now-soggy cereal while the dog crunched away.

After he'd eaten, Neal took a mug of coffee out on the front porch and draped himself into an old wooden rocker, feet on the porch rail, sniffing the heady aroma until the coffee cooled enough to drink. The dog joined him.

"Gonna be a hot one, ol' girl." Her tail wagged.

The temperature outside was about seventy-five, he judged. Pretty warm for this early in the day, but perfect for comfort. He'd liked the climate better on the California coast, but something had drawn him home, to the deciduous forests he'd known as a boy. Hot in the summer, cold in the winter, but wonderful in the autumn and spring.

Adjacent to the house, some fifty feet away, was a slightly larger, half-finished building. It was his office, from which he ran his canoe rental and his guide service. He kept a small amount of essentials—bug spray, sunscreen, matches, and the like—for paddlers. The interior was complete, but it was waiting for an outer skin. A stack of cabin-grade cedar siding lay on the dry grass of the side yard.

He sipped the coffee, scratching his shoulders because it

felt good, then his leg where a mosquito had gotten him the night before. Maybe the one he'd done in.

Thirty minutes later, his dishes in the drainer, he was on a ladder, nail apron draped around his middle, baseball cap on his head, putting the first piece of siding on the building. Brandy lay at the foot of the ladder having her first nap of the morning.

Lee Newton emerged from the cave with his stomach hollering for food. He vaguely remembered a house about a half mile across the timber, so he set off to find it. His memory served him well.

At the edge of the woods he squatted down to take stock of the situation at the farmhouse. A gray Mercedes waited near the front door. A man came out of the house just then. He was no farmer. He looked more like a stockbroker or a banker in his conservative gray suit. Moments later a woman in a stylish outfit followed. Yuppies, fixing up a farm house. Lee figured by their clothes they worked in Springfield. He wondered how long before they would flee back to the city to live.

After they left, he approached the house, wary even now in case someone was still there. A dog began to bark.

Lee ducked behind a toolshed and waited, but nothing new developed, so he moved quickly to the side of the house, safely out of view from any window. He worked slowly alongside it until he came to sliding glass doors. There was a dog, looking out, barking at him intermittently in a high-pitched voice. But no one else came. Lee tried the door and found it open.

The dog, a classy little rag mop, stopped barking the moment he got inside, begging for attention instead. It danced around his feet, then dropped back with its chest flat on the floor and its rear end up, tail wagging, then lunged forward again. He had no use for lap dogs and finally muttered to it in a mean voice, and it disappeared into the other room, tail and ears down.

His entry had been into a garden room which reminded him of the glassed-in breezeway at his parents' home. There were plants everywhere, some he immediately recognized: a jade, a Norfolk pine, a spider plant. His mother had been real big on plants, except she'd always made him water them. It hadn't made a lot of sense to him: having them, but not wanting to take care of them.

The inside of the house was decorated in contemporary style, sleek and expensive, a far sight from its humble beginnings as a family farm. The oak floors were finished to a high luster.

He glanced out the kitchen window. An enormous patio spread out over the backyard. Whiskey barrels billowed with begonias. A glass-topped table and four chairs with plump, pastel plaid cushions sat a short distance from a smoker.

Everything was beautiful and just right. And those two who'd just left were as blind to the realities of what was going on in this country as nearly everyone else. They were content to have material things and ignore the internal rot. Little did they realize how threatened their oh-so-perfect life-style was.

Lee ran his hand through his short-cropped hair. Enough daydreaming. He moved away from the window and found the pantry, where he took two cans of tuna, a can of stewed tomatoes, and a can of pork and beans from the back of the shelf, thinking they probably wouldn't be missed.

At the sink, he swigged some orange soda from a two-liter bottle, then dumped the remainder down the drain and filled the container with water. He added the bottle to the cache he was accumulating on the table.

The utility room was a picture of well-stocked neatness, straight out of a home-decorating magazine. A column of plastic bins held all sorts of odds and ends, including a rope which he promptly took and coiled neatly around his shoulder bandolier-style.

A bit of rummaging turned up a piece of cord, and Lee used it to tie the two-liter bottle of water to the coil of rope; he didn't want the container dangling at his waist, hindering his movements. He put the cans in a garbage bag and fastened it to the rope, too.

He lingered a moment at the kitchen table, taking a mental inventory of what else he might need. His hollow knife handle was outfitted with waterproof matches, a fishhook, and nylon filament line. It also held a length of wire, an all-purpose sort of item.

He looked around for a phone and spied one on a kitchen desk.

"I'd like to make a collect call," he told the operator after he dialed. He didn't want a number showing up on these people's phone bill. An old man's gravelly voice accepted the charges from a nonexistent Mike Drum, then said, "Bo here." That was their code for base of operations.

"I've had a slight hitch in my plans," Lee said.

"What is it? You should be back here by now."

"I skinned a bear." He could just see the man's skin flushing at the news.

The old man let out an audible and disapproving sigh. "Let me think." Another sigh. "This will change our plans for Wednesday. I'd better notify—"

Lee's eyes widened. "No," he said. "There's no reason to change our plans. I'm on my way in now."

"And you may not make it."

"I'll make it, don't worry about that."

"How long will it take you to get here?"

A long-haired cat jumped up on the desk next to Lee. He hadn't seen it approach, and the movement startled him. The voice on the other end of the line started to repeat the question, but Lee interrupted. "I'll be there Wednesday morning. God willing." He shoved the cat onto the floor. She hissed in protest.

"That's cutting it too close."

Lee noticed a sack of dog food on the floor and picked it up. "It'll be okay," he assured the man on the other end of the line. "Everyone is ready." The truth was, he liked cutting it close. It was more exciting that way. No sitting around, waiting to begin an operation. After all, they all knew what they were supposed to do. The Colonel's way, by contrast, was slow and methodical. Lee smiled to himself, thinking how this change would be rankling the old man. Maybe he'd have a heart attack over the whole thing, and then Lee wouldn't have to deal with him.

"I said it's too close. I'll have a pickup waiting for you at Site Ten after twelve hundred hours on Tuesday. That'll give us almost twenty-four hours."

Lee knew the place he meant. It was more commonly known as River's Bend, a place where they held rappeling exercises off the bluffs. He sighed, giving in. "Yes, sir."

After hanging up, he crumpled the sack of dog food into a tight bundle, unfastened the plastic bag, and added it to the things he was taking.

The refrigerator was full of food, so he made a sandwich and ate it greedily, then helped himself to some grapes from a bowl in the refrigerator.

Picking grapes off the bunch one at a time and popping them into this mouth, he went into the master suite. The bath had been converted from an adjacent bedroom. It had a huge whirlpool tub.

"Ver-r-ry fancy," he said to the dog, who was following him around. His reflection in the wide expanse of mirror caught his eye, and he reached up to rub his sprouting beard. He didn't fit, that was for sure. But he could have had all this if long ago he hadn't realized there was a higher purpose than just acquiring *things*.

Just then the dog took off like a shot toward the garden room, yipping excitedly. A moment later, between the yips, Lee heard the sliding door glide open; then a voice.

"Well, good morning, Mitzi," it said in a high pitch reserved for babies and animals. "Did 'um miss Lacey?"

Lee silently crept to the bedroom door, dropping the grape stem into a wastebasket he passed. He could hear the jangle of the dog's tags coming back toward him.

"What do you want to show me, girl?"

Damn dog, Lee thought, *thinks she's Lassie or something.* Sure enough, the dog appeared just then at the bedroom door and gave an excited yip when it saw him.

Lee scooped it up and without a moment's hesitation plunged his fingers into its neck and pressed till the dog went limp in his hands. Immediately he set its body on the floor, seized his knife, and took the wire from it.

The woman's voice still came from the other room. "Well, hello, Miss Kitty. I didn't forget you. Here's a yumyum. What do you think Mitzi's up to? Huh? Where'd she go?" She had stopped momentarily.

At the sound of her footsteps starting down the hallway, Lee drew the wire tautly between his hands, holding his breath. Just then the phone rang, jangling his nerves, and the footsteps retreated.

"Hello . . . Oh, hi, honey . . . Are you sure you've looked everywhere? . . . ." An exasperated sigh. "If you'd put your keys in the same place every time . . . Okay. I'll be right over."

Lee sank back against the wall, relieved. Had he killed the woman, whoever was on the other end of that line would have been looking for her by the end of the day. Anyone who turned up missing in the next several days would be like a red flag to the authorities, pinpointing his route.

A dog? Well, that was different. He picked it up carelessly, planning to throw it somewhere out in the woods. It might never be found out there.

The trepidation of the night was behind Susan now. Broad daylight always laid her fears to rest. There was something about the clear harsh sunlight that illuminated the recesses of her mind where the dark things dwelled. She was a daylight worshipper. Funny to think she'd once considered herself a night person. That was in high school and college, when she'd liked being dramatic and melancholy.

The sunlight was warming the car now, especially where it was hitting her left arm. "I'm going to turn on the air conditioner, if it's okay with you," she said.

They'd been driving with the windows down, but the noise was bothering her; conversation was impossible. She fiddled with the fan control, keeping one eye on the winding road.

They'd left the plateau of home behind and had moved

into the highlands an hour south. The hills marched before them into mountains as they crossed the state line.

"You want me to do that?" Jan asked.

"I think I've got it. Is my driving making you nervous?" she asked with a smile.

"No, but the road's getting kind of twisty." Jan reached out and adjusted a vent so the air wouldn't blow into her face, then said, "Did you bring your bird book? I think I forgot mine. I don't remember packing it."

Susan nodded. "I remembered." She'd known Jan for years, since college when they'd lived in the same dormitory. Their interests had been dissimilar at the time and their acquaintance casual, but as adults they'd run into each other at an Audubon meeting and had soon formed a bond of friendship. The newly divorced Jan was looking for new alliances, people who didn't know her ex-husband, and Susan helped her through the emotional trauma. The experience had reinforced their friendship. Susan sometimes wondered what would happen if Jan married again. What if she didn't like her friend's new husband? Surely their relationship could still survive.

"Look there," Jan said, pointing at a shop alongside the road as they came around a bend. "Handmade baskets. Let's stop."

Susan was driving slowly because of all the curves, so she managed to slow down and pull over onto the gravel parking strip before they passed the place.

They both stretched when they got out of the car. Jan bent over and touched her toes a couple of times, then twisted at the waist till her back popped. "Ah, much better," she sighed.

"Good morning," the elderly man who sat behind the counter called as the bell on the door jingled. His face was a map of wrinkles, broken by bushy gray eyebrows as thick as wire brushes and a mop of similarly textured hair. "How are you ladies this morning?" He was weaving strips of white oak.

"Fine," Jan said. "Do you make all the baskets?"

"Some of them." A grin crinkled his face even more.

"This is a co-op crafts store. We got people participating from all over this part of the country." He pointed to a square oak basket with a handle. "That's one of mine. And there's another next to it. You'll see my initials burned into the bottom of 'em. R. C. Ralph Charles."

"This is really beautiful work," Susan said, turning one around in her hands.

"Thank you. It's a living."

"Are you a native?"

"Nah. Retired down here from Michigan. Too cold up there, and the property taxes got too high for my blood."

"I thought you sounded like a northerner."

"Guess I'll never lose it. You vacationing?"

"We're going canoeing," Jan said.

"Just you two ladies?" He glanced toward the car to see if there were any men there, waiting while the women shopped. "I thought maybe your men were outside."

"No, it's just the two of us."

The elderly man shook his head. "You young ladies sure are independent these days." Susan smiled and glanced at Jan. *Young.* She wasn't feeling young. Her kids—now *they* were young. And independent? This weekend was just for show.

The two women picked out baskets, each with an R. C. on the bottom, and went to the counter. Mr. Charles licked the end of his pencil and began to write a ticket. "Shame about that trooper, wasn't it?"

"What?" Jan asked.

"Some fellow shot a state trooper just up above the state line and over east of here last evening."

"That's terrible," Susan said. "Did they catch him?"

"No, he's still on the loose, but I guess they have half the law officers in that part of the state out looking, so they'll get their man." He finished up one ticket, took the money, made change, then started on the second. He worked slowly, but finally they were ready to go on their way.

"Thank you, ladies. And you have a nice day."

They both thanked him, wished him the same, and went back to the car.

"Shall I drive for a while?" Jan asked.

"Sure."

Susan stashed the baskets in the trunk, and they pulled back out onto the highway. "You know," Jan mused, "some people think saying 'Have a nice day' is part of some sort of left-wing conspiracy."

Susan rolled her eyes. "You don't mean it."

"Really."

"Well, some people can find conspiracies everywhere."

"They're bound and determined to make life more complex than it already is."

Susan nodded in agreement.

An hour later they were nearing their destination. The gravel crackled beneath the tires and a great cloud of dust blew up in their wake.

"Uh-oh," Susan said.

"What?"

"Look at those clothes hanging out there." They were passing a ramshackle house with two lengths of line strung between trees, sagging in the middle from the weight of the wash.

"So?"

"You wouldn't believe the dust we're stirring up behind us, and it's going to blow right over those clothes."

"*C'est la vie,*" Jan said.

"Very cavalier of you. You apparently never hung clothes out on a line."

"Nope. Started out with a dryer."

"I'll never forget this flock of starlings that used to nest near our place. Every morning, splat, splat, splat—right on the diapers. It was a real nuisance. That was before the city did that starling removal program."

"That was a long time ago now." They were well past the house now, passing through a virtual tunnel of trees. "Do you think we're on the right road?"

"I think so."

"Read those directions again," Jan said. They were written on the back of an envelope.

"Turn right at the red house. Then it's about a mile and a half on the left,"

"Have you seen a red house?" Jan asked.

"No, not yet."

"Maybe they painted it."

They drove a few more minutes. "There it is," Susan said. "They *need* to paint it." The red was flaking off, leaving the house with a disheveled look.

"This is really off the beaten path."

"You could say that."

Jan grinned at her. "I did."

"Smart aleck."

The road surface changed from pea-sized gravel to brown creek rock, badly washed out in places. Jan slowed down, trying to avoid the obvious gullies, but they were still jounced around, even through the car was barely moving.

"Thank goodness! There it is." Jan said. "I'm not sure my kidneys can take this much longer." She was pointing to a half-finished building with a van and two canoe trailers in front. There was a sign: CANOES FOR RENT.

A shirtless man on a ladder turned to see who was driving in, then started down. His dog accompanied him across the yard, barking a warning, but not straying from his master's side. The man silenced the dog with a command.

Jan emitted a little sound of appreciation at the sight of the man, which Susan noticed. "Down girl," she said, laughing. She eyed her friend with amused suspicion. "I don't suppose Noreen's husband told you there was a good-looking hunk out here in the woods, did he?"

"Nope. Cross my heart." She traced an *X* over her heart with her index finger.

Susan opened her door, reacting to the sudden heat with a grimace.

"Hi," the man said as he approached, the dog tagging along, tail wagging, tongue hanging. Hunk or not, Susan thought, he's funny looking in his tennis shoes, shorts, nail apron, and ball cap.

"We need to rent a canoe," Jan said, stooping down to the dog's level and extending her hand to it, palm down.

"Well . . . I'm pretty busy," he said with a crooked smile, "but I just happen to have one left." He glanced back at the two trailers, both fully loaded.

"Boy, are we lucky," Jan said, grinning at him. "Good thing we got here early, before the rush. What's your dog's name?"

"Brandy." The man lifted his ball cap and rubbed his head. "You need portage?"

The women nodded.

"We want to spend tonight on the river," Jan told him, "then tomorrow night at the campsite here, before we start back home."

"Great. Come on inside while I get you all taken care of." Behind his back, Jan rolled her eyes and grinned at Susan, who suppressed a laugh.

The building was warm, but a ceiling fan stirred the air.

"The husband of a friend of mine—Hugh Thompson—told me about your place."

"Oh, sure, I remember Hugh. He and his buddies have been down a couple of times. They start out up above here. That what you have in mind?"

"It's too low right now, isn't it? Hugh said we could put in here and float on down."

The man nodded and handed over a clipboard with a form for her to fill out. "It's low all right; you'd be walking about half the time. And when there's water, it's tricky. You seasoned canoers?"

"We've both been a few times," Jan said. "Never together, though."

"Don't let her fool you," Susan piped in. "She's an experienced canoer. I'm the novice. I've never been without my husband, and I usually just follow his instructions."

"Notice she said *usually*."

He smiled. "You won't have any trouble from here down to where I pick you up. It's a good float. You get to run a few gentle rapids. Nothing harrowing." He looked at the names on the form. "I'm Neal Lassiter, by the way."

"I'm Susan, and she's Jan. We need to eat before we start. May we just go down by the water?"

"Sure. You'll put in down there, too, so just pull your car down and we'll unload your things, then you can leave it by the house." He untied his nail apron and pulled on a T-shirt that had been hanging over a chair.

Jan glanced around. "Uh, do you have a bathroom we could use?"

"There's an outhouse down by the campground, but why don't you come over to my house. It's a little nicer. No flies."

"Nice place," Jan said when they went in. "Did you built it?"

"Yeah. Lived in a travel trailer while I did it. There's the bathroom. I'll meet you outside."

"You first," Jan said, looking around.

Susan emerged from the bathroom a few minutes later, wiping her hands on her shorts. "No towel," she said.

"Isn't this place cute?"

Susan appraised it and shrugged. "A little too primitive for me, but . . . I guess you could call it cute."

"I like it," Jan said, disappearing into the bathroom.

Neal was waiting by their car. They drove to the water's edge, where he helped them unload their gear.

Susan began taking sandwiches and soft drinks out of the cooler. "We've got plenty. Why don't you eat with us?"

"Thanks, I'd love too. Haven't had such a good offer in ages."

They settled down on the gravel. Jan rummaged in a bag and found some chips to add to their meal.

"Where have you canoed?" Neal asked, noticing at the same time that the dog was making a nuisance of himself in front of Jan. "Sit, Brandy."

"She's okay," Jan said, reaching out to pet the dog. "Mainly on the Current and the Buffalo, but last summer I went to the Chattooga for a few days with a friend."

"Did you do Bull Sluice?" he asked.

"Nope. Call me gutless." She crunched into a chip. "Have you?"

"Yeah. I was there a couple of years ago."

A common interest bonded the two strangers as they

continued to talk, unconsciously excluding Susan. She was used to it. In gatherings of people she often seemed to fade into the background, with no one interested in what she had to say.

She took a bite of her sandwich, gazing into the trees overhead. Several birds darted among the branches, and she tried to follow their movements, but couldn't tell what kind they were. The cover was too dense.

The river turned here, washing against the rock for centuries and cutting away a bluff on the other side. Their side, the inside of the meander, was a gradual slope down to the water.

Neal swilled his soft drink, then wiped his upper lip with his hand. "This part of the river'll be pretty tame for you."

"We're doing this for relaxation," Jan said.

"She's doing it for me," Susan amended, still feeling like the odd man out. "Doesn't want to scare me to death." Active people made her feel inadequate.

"Down past the convergence of this fork and the Big Pine—quite a way—the channel cuts between two bluffs. The Narrows. It's a Class Three there." He looked at Jan. "You'll have to come back sometime and do it. Takes a couple of days to get down there from here."

"Whoo! Heavy-duty white water," Jan said, scratching Brandy behind the ears and offering her a chip.

"But we aren't going that far, right?" Susan asked, with mock concern.

He shook his head, taking another drink. "Down here about two miles there's a nice shoal, give you a good ride, then just beyond it you hug the left bank, get out of the current, and pull into the hollow there. There's this nice deep little spring where you can go swimming."

"Skinny-dipping," Jan said.

"Well, uh, it's plenty private," Neal said, sounding almost embarrassed. He stood up. "Mighty good sandwich. Thanks for inviting me. Give me your trash, and I'll carry it up to the house, then I'll bring a canoe down. You can drive back up. C'mon, Brandy." The dog was still hanging closely around Jan, begging for attention.

"I'll help you," Jan said, following him. The dog scampered beside her.

"Want to ride?" Susan asked getting in the car.

Jan shook her head. "I'll walk."

Neal was already off the gravel and on the path to the house through the narrow band of woods.

When Susan reached the house, Neal motioned where she should park. He was getting a canoe off the trailer with Jan's help. Neal handed Susan two life preservers and two paddles to carry, then he and Jan shouldered the canoe and started back toward the water.

They make a pretty good team, Susan thought with an indulgent smile, following along behind them. *Maybe this will lead to something.*

The three of them strapped the provisions into the boat, then the two women took a few minutes more to put on some sunscreen. Susan waded in, pulling the canoe off the rocks. "Cold," she said, sucking in her breath as the water filled her tennis shoes. Neal held the boat back while they both climbed in, then gave them a shove into the current and sent them on their way.

Neal had watched the straight-haired one—Jan—slather her arms and legs with sunscreen. She'd sat on the gravel, her legs extended, her hair falling forward, obscuring her face. Her hands had moved sensually up her calf, spreading the white cream with overlapping strokes, massaging it in. He'd had a hard time not being obvious about watching. Next the thigh, then the other leg. Good tight muscles. He wanted to volunteer to help—and might have—but her friend was there. The friend was okay, too, but she was wearing a wedding ring.

On the way up to the house, he'd suggested to Jan that she come back another time, and they could do the Narrows together. She looked at him steadily for a moment, then shrugged and gave him a noncommittal maybe. She probably thought it was a standard line. It wasn't. The river wasn't something he wanted to share with just anyone. There was a quality about Jan he liked—besides her body.

As he watched them float away, his thoughts returned to the way she had looked rubbing in the sunscreen. *Better get to work, boy,* he said to himself, *get your mind off of that.*

He bent over to get a stick, then tossed it down the bank for Brandy, who was dancing along beside him.

Brandy was just a year old and still loved to play. She retrieved the stick and raced back to Neal.

"You thought she was a nice lady, too, didn't you, Bran? Damnit." His earlier feeling of satisfaction at his life here had momentarily been sidetracked by an ache of longing.

He threw the stick for the dog again—into the water this time. Then he plunged in after her. The cold water would fix him right up.

Friday Afternoon

3

LACEY, THE CLEANING lady at Diane and Tom Kendry's house, made the ten-mile round-trip to her house and back, and drove five more miles to the sawmill to deliver her seventeen-year-old son to work. His carelessness exasperated her, but she didn't want him to lose that job. The family depended on the money. It was bad enough that he was late.

And now she was running late, too, and would have to step lively to make up for lost time. She was due at the Lawsons' this afternoon. The Kendrys were only one of her ten employers, and she worked at their house for half a day, every other week. Their place was always so tidy, it just took vacuuming and dusting. Didn't take her long at all.

Lacey noticed when she returned that Mitzi didn't meet her at the door. That was odd. When the dog didn't eventually appear, she began to look for her.

Finally, she called Mrs. Kendry at work and told her she was afraid the dog had accidentally gotten out.

Mrs. Kendry said not to worry. Mitzi wouldn't wander far, and maybe she would have an exciting adventure in the woods.

Lacey hung up, glad that the woman was so understanding, but still feeling anxious. She took a plastic trash-can liner and started through the house emptying wastebaskets, including the one in the master suite with the grape stem lying on top of the other trash.

* * *

With Jan in the stern and Susan on the bow seat, the two women paddled with vigor for the first fifteen minutes. It was the elation of actually getting underway. Then, out of the blue, Jan said, "What are we doing? We'll get to the takeout hours early if we keep this up. Besides, this is supposed to be relaxing." She dropped her paddle in the bottom of the canoe with a thump, sprawled backward onto the end of the boat, and slung her legs up over the gunwales. "Keep a steady course, matey."

"I keep thinking about the calories I'm working off," Susan said, letting the canoe drift now. They were in a clear, deep stretch with no ripples. "I can already feel new muscles." She rubbed her upper arms.

"It's hot," Jan said, cupping her hand over the boat's edge and splashing cold water on her legs. "When we come to that spring—uh, what's his name? . . . Neal was talking about, let's go swimming." She flicked cold water at Susan.

"That feels good. Do it some more." Jan splashed her again as Susan stuck her paddle back in the water and drew on it, just to keep them drifting straight. In a moment she repeated the movement on the other side. "That man couldn't take his eyes off of you," she said over her shoulder.

"Who?"

"Don't be coy with me, Jan Spencer. You know who." A colorful dragonfly landed on her arm, and she flicked it away. Snake doctors, her grandmother had called them. She wondered why.

Jan chuckled. "Too bad he lives so far in the boondocks. I noticed there were no signs of a woman about his place, and he seemed nice. He must be about our age; there was some gray in his beard."

Susan realized she felt a little pang of envy. It wasn't that she wanted to be single, but sometimes she regretted that there would probably never be another romance in her life, never again the delicious finding out about another person.

"When you mentioned skinny-dipping, he turned red and changed the subject."

"Well, my goodness," Jan marveled, "a shy one in this day and age."

"More likely he was embarrassed by what he was thinking."

Jan's robust laugh echoed across the water. She was leaning back, soaking up the hot sun, her eyes closed against the glare. Her life vest lay under her head like a pillow. "He asked me to come back and go canoeing."

"Really? What'd you—?" She stopped in midsentence, and Jan's eyes popped open to see why. Susan's attention was riveted on a log that had fallen into the water. She was pointing. A yellow and brownish bird was perched on it. The canoe drifted on by, both women silently watching.

"A warbler," Jan said. Both of them were looking back. "What kind? Do you know?"

"I get my warblers mixed up," Susan said as she swiveled around to face the stern and began undoing one of their bags. She pulled out the bird identification book and thumbed through it. "I think it must be a female hooded warbler." She handed the book back to Jan. "Top of the page."

They'd moved into a shady bend of the river as Susan sat up and waited for Jan to confirm what she thought the bird was. Neither of them was paying attention to their progress. Suddenly, an overhanging branch smacked Susan in the head sending her toppling sideways out of the canoe. The cold water hit her like a sharp pain, and she shrieked.

Jan jerked upward, and the same branch almost caught her, but she managed to duck as she grabbed her paddle and began backstroking to maintain the boat's position. "Are you okay?"

Susan was standing waist-deep in the water, rubbing her head. She grinned and wrinkled her nose. "I'm all right." She managed to climb back into the canoe without upsetting it. "I'd better start paying attention. And I wasn't wearing my life vest."

"It could happen to anyone," Jan said. "I'm the one who

should have been paying attention. I know the potential hazards."

They floated in silence for a while, enjoying the solitude. Occasionally one of them would point out something along the bank. After about forty-five minutes they rounded a bend and saw some turbulence ahead. The first.

"Oh, good," Jan said, repositioning herself to paddle. "Fast water. This is the shoal Neal was talking about."

Both women buckled on their life vests, while Jan sized up the rapids. "Looks like we should try to stay over to the left of that big rock and over in between those other two," she said. "You see where I mean? See how the current's going?"

Susan nodded. Her heart was revving up as the canoe began moving faster now, plunging toward the white foam breaking over and around the jumble of boulders.

"Backpaddle," Jan shouted over the noise.

Susan knew they'd have more control if they were moving slower than the current. She reversed the direction of her paddling. The bow was slipping sideways. She pulled, but the stroke didn't seem to make any difference against the power of the current. The front of the canoe jolted upward on an unseen rock, then took a nosedive. As they emerged from the foam, the bow careened perilously to one side.

"Brace," Jan shouted.

Susan leaned out, using her paddle like an outrigger. The canoe stabilized and shot into the main current.

She heard Jan give an encouraging cheer behind her as they hurtled forward again, plunging down a funnel of water between two submerged boulders. Immediately a blockade of rocks loomed in front of them, and Susan couldn't even see a passage through them.

"To the left," Jan yelled. The water sprayed across them as they maneuvered the canoe into what appeared to be the best channel. The boat shot past the rocks, slowing briefly, then the current pushed it forward again into an open stretch where the ripples gradually diminished and the river calmed.

"That was great," Jan said, wiping the droplets off her face, "but too short."

Susan was grinning from ear to ear. She let out a whoop. "We did it!" She was feeling a profound sense of accomplishment. It was especially exhilarating after her earlier tumble into the water, which had left her feeling rather foolish.

"Well, of course," Jan said matter-of-factly. "Hey, there's the spring Neal was talking about. We're about to miss it."

Susan looked over and saw a curtain of cottonwoods, one leaning down over the water. The branches almost concealed the entrance to the cove. *A hidden grotto*, she thought. *What fun!*

They paddled over and ducked under the leafy curtain, grasping the branches and pulling their way through it hand over hand.

"Look over there," Jan said. She pointed at a snake lying along a limb.

"Ugh!" Susan jerked her hand off the branch she was holding as she involuntarily shuddered. "What kind is it? Can you tell?"

"Looks like a water moccasin to me."

They were through the branches now, and a pool spread out before them as the canoe slid through the placid water. It was flanked by high bluffs on three sides. The water was a deep, clear green. Fish could be seen beneath the surface, probably begrudging the intrusion, Susan thought. Right now, just past midday, a slice of sunshine was hitting the pool, although under the bluffs it was shady.

They pulled the canoe up on a gravel bank. "We can dump this water out," Jan said.

"I thought we were going to swamp back there," Susan said. "Look at all the water we took on." She began to untie their provisions. "If that one was easy, I'd hate to see a Class Three."

Jan grinned. "Grab the gunwale, and we'll roll it over. That's it, right there. Now heave." The water they'd taken on in the rapids came rushing out. "Let's leave it like that

a moment to finish draining." She was unbuckling her life
vest as she spoke, then began peeling off her clothes.
Moments later she stood, naked, in only her canvas shoes.
"I'm going swimming."

"I kind of took that for granted." Susan snickered. "Your
shoes look nice," she said wryly.

"Listen, these rocks are hard on my tender little feet."
She was crunching across the gravel to the water.

Susan reflected on how little modesty her friend seemed
to have. "What if someone else comes in here?" She
glanced nervously toward the trees they'd passed under.

"I'll be in the water." A moment later she splashed into
the chilly pool. "Ohmigosh. It's so cold."

Susan had always been a get-wet-gradually person, and
even though her clothes were still wet from her earlier
tumble into the water, she waded in only to her knees.

"C'mon. You can't do it like that. Just jump in."

Well, why not? Do something different. She held her
breath and threw herself forward in a shallow dive. She
dog-paddled around in the center of the pool, which was
about four feet deep, then lay on her back, drinking up the
sunshine with her eyes shut. She was still wearing the life
jacket, so she bobbed there, relaxing. In the woods on top
of the bluff she heard a cardinal's *what-cheer,* then a less
familiar bird song. She opened her eyes, squinting against
the brightness.

Swallows were soaring toward the bluff face, then diving
into crevices high above her; she recognized their distinctive silhouettes against the bright sky.

The sun blinded her momentarily, and she glanced away,
but looked back quickly, a movement catching her attention. There was someone on top of the bluff. What would
someone be doing up there? Could Neal Lassiter be following them? After all, he'd told them about this place. She
scanned the rimrock, then put it down to imagination; there
was no one there now.

*Law-enforcement officials are calling for residents of Pres-
ley County to be on the lookout for Lee Newton, a white*

male with blond crew-cut hair, approximately five feet nine inches tall, weighing one hundred and fifty pounds, wearing camouflage pants and a T-shirt. The man is wanted in connection with the slaying of Highway Patrolman Delano Smith Thursday evening. Newton allegedly shot Smith, wounded a second officer, then fled on foot into the heavily wooded area west of Bass Road. He is armed and dangerous. Persons with information as to his whereabouts should notify their local law-enforcement officers.

Friday Evening

.

4

As THE SUN dropped below the tree line, the air began to cool perceptibly. The stretch of the river seemed languid, its boldness buried somewhere in its depths, waiting perhaps to surprise canoers around the next bend, but for now content to drift.

Susan was sitting flat in the wet bottom of the canoe, leaning lazily against the bow seat, eyes closed, while Jan paddled intermittently. If the truth be known, Susan was ready to go home; she'd had enough of this. Right about now she could be sitting in a lounge chair on the patio, a glass of iced tea in her hand, watching the lightning bugs twinkling out on the lawn. She'd splurged this spring and thrown away the old aluminum lawn chairs with their multicolored vinyl webbing, replacing them with an expensive set—two chairs and a lounge—with cushions. Maybe Ted would be suggesting a trip to Braum's ice cream store right about now. Ummm! Rocky Road. She could almost taste it.

"We'd better look for a good campsite," Jan said, interrupting Susan's reverie.

Susan opened her eyes, murmured her assent, and began to scan the bank. Here the edges of the river were choked with water willow. Unable to find a place they'd want to pull over, let alone camp—not after seeing that snake earlier—they continued to drift. Change on the river came with each curve, and what looked like a perfect gravel bar presented itself soon enough, jutting out of the green tangle as the river swung around in a careless meander.

"Look good to you?" Jan asked.

Susan nodded, took her position, and picked up her paddle.

The two of them, working well together by this time, steered the canoe firmly, and it met the shallows with a gentle scraping.

While Jan steadied the canoe with her paddle, Susan got out in the water and dragged the boat up a few more feet onto the gravel, then Jan got out, lifting one of the plastic bags out with her.

"I'll look for firewood before it gets any darker," Susan suggested, eyeing the gloom of the woods.

"Okay," Jan said. "I'll unload."

Susan walked over to the bag Jan had already taken out of the canoe and began to rummage through it. She found the bug spray, pulled it out, and aimed it at her legs. "Want some?" she asked Jan, shuddering as the fine mist hit her.

"No, not yet. I hate that smelly stuff." She waved her hand in front of her nose.

"I'm not exactly crazy about it, but it's better than being eaten alive by chiggers and ticks." Susan put the can down. "I'll be back—soon, I hope." Her soggy rubber-soled shoes squeaked as she walked across the rocks, studying the undergrowth marking the edge of the gravel bar until she saw a beaten-down place, an animal path to follow into the trees.

Twilight had filled the woods with menacing shadows and hiding places. The snap of a twig nearby made her jump as she picked her way rather timorously through the dense network of branches which stretched upward for the vestiges of light leaking through the leafy canopy above.

For a moment she lost her fear and experienced a sense of connection to an earlier time, a time before the white man's invasion. She moved silently, visions of Indian women with papooses darting through her mind.

The deepening fantasy was sharply interrupted by the

sight of a beer can, half-exposed beneath some dry oak leaves. Civilization had preceded her to this spot.

She shook her head in silent regret as she carefully picked up the can and held it upside down. A drizzle of dirty liquid ran out.

She waited until it was empty, then continued her search for firewood, the earlier spell broken. Her trepidation had returned, and she moved with a caution born of fear rather than respect.

"I found some token trash in the woods," she told Jan a short while later when she emerged onto the gravel bar. "I was daydreaming about what a primitive place this was until I found this." She dropped the can.

Jan nodded, adding a grimace. "They're everywhere. I'm surprised there wasn't a disposable diaper, too."

Susan laid her load down, picked up the can, and put it in a plastic bag they'd brought for trash. "We need some bigger wood. I couldn't carry enough."

"I guess it's my turn," Jan said. She picked up the insect repellent and sprayed a mist around her.

"Thanks," Susan said, eager to let her friend do the rest of the gathering. She really didn't want to go back into the forest gloom. "There's sort of a path over here." She walked with Jan to the woods edge and pointed it out. "It leads to a clearing."

As Jan left, Susan squatted down beside the gravel bar and gathered some dry grass for tinder. Back near the water, she knelt and arranged the rocks to make a fire circle. She then selected a forked stick from the ones she'd gathered for the fire. She held it in front of her, examining it as if it were some sort of talisman, and perhaps it was to be that: a charm against the night. She ceremoniously placed it with two other sticks balanced against it and put the dried tinder under it. The tepee foundation began to grow, with the other sticks and twigs placed carefully so as not to cause the fragile structure to collapse.

Years of being a brownie leader for Jennifer and a den mother for Jeffery had given Susan expertise in at least one area, she thought with satisfaction. She recalled with nostalgia all the stews she'd concocted over open campfires and tin-can stoves. And s'mores for dessert. A graham cracker, a piece of chocolate, and a toasted marshmallow to top off a sometimes good, sometimes burned, sometimes half-raw meal. She smiled to herself. Those had been good times.

By the time Jan returned, a small pillar of smoke was rising from the sticks in front of Susan. "Good job," Jan said, carefully adding more wood to the fire. She sat down next to Susan to watch the flames grow.

"Oooh, kind of lumpy," Jan said, shifting her weight on the rocks, trying to get comfortable. "We may have to sleep in the woods."

"I think I'd rather put up with the lumps than sleep in those woods," Susan said. "They're kind of creepy." She shivered, partly at the thought of the woods, but also because the air was turning chilly. They'd dipped in the river several times in the heat of the afternoon, and Susan's clothes weren't completely dry yet, especially where she'd sat in the bottom of the boat. She moved nearer to the fire, but then the smoke began to bother her eyes, driving her back again.

"I'm kidding you. I brought two brand-new cheap air mattresses."

"Good for you!" Susan said thrilled. "I didn't even think of that. I'm glad we don't have to sleep in there." She looked over her shoulder at the woods, which were beginning to look sinister as the shadows deepened.

Jan yawned. "Do we have to wait for that fire to die down, do you think?"

"It's good enough for our purposes. We'd better get this show on the road before we fall asleep," Susan said, catching the yawn. "I'll open the beans." Carefully, she arranged some rocks so she could put the can right at the edge of the fire.

"Did you bring those aspirin?" Jan asked.

"You mean the ones you said I should leave at home because I was taking too much stuff along?"

"Yes, those," Jan answered with a sheepish smile.

"I did. You can't keep a Virgo from trying to be prepared for any emergency." She rummaged in one of the plastic bags and pulled out a small tin, then poured some water out of a thermos for her friend.

"You mean you brought other extra stuff?" Jan asked, swallowing two of the tablets.

She smiled. "Nah. Just the aspirin. You have a headache?"

Jan pressed on her forehead. "Just starting."

Susan frowned in sympathy. "Well, I hope those help it."

Jan pulled some trail mix out of a bag, then some cheese from the cooler, already cut in chunks, and two apples. "This is my kind of meal—no muss, no fuss."

"Amen. Sometimes I think I may go crazy if I have to plan one more meal. But I feel guilty, since I don't work, if we go out more than once a week."

"Stop feeling guilty. You've put in your time. Just think, you've been married—what, twenty-five years?"

"Twenty-four."

"Well, think of all the meals you've fixed in that time."

"No wonder I'm tired of it."

"But I guess its no worse than putting a rivet in a car coming down an assembly line."

"No. Especially if you have to tighten rivets all day *and* fix the meals when you get home. Even so, I think I need a change."

"I've been thinking the same thing. It's our age—raging hormones again. It's seems like a dirty trick to have to go through adolescence, then have to reverse it all in your forties." She paused a moment. "I tell my kids at school not to think they'll have only one career in their lifetime. If they make a mistake, they can change their minds. I should listen to my own advice," she added.

"I haven't had my first," Susan said, pulling her wet shoes off and wiggling her toes, thinking maybe that would warm them up.

"Yes, you have. You've been a parent."

"You know what I mean."

"And all I'm saying is you're entering phase two."

"Maybe so."

"Why don't you take a couple of classes to update your credentials and get a teaching job?"

"The truth?"

"Yep."

"Well, I *say* it's because I don't want to spend the rest of my life with kids. I want to do something with adults. But"—she hesitated—"I'm also in a rut. I just can't seem to make a move. It's as if I'm stuck where I am."

Jan nodded. "It's hard to change—if there's no push. I mean, if Ted left you, now that'd be an incentive."

Susan pondered that for a moment, a flutter of panic rising in her chest. Is that what it would take? Was she so dependent that she'd have to be pushed out of the nest like a child?

"But why can't I just be happy staying home, doing the things women have done for centuries? Why do I feel uneasy about it?"

"You tell me."

"Maybe because housewives don't get much respect, and maybe because there are so few women at home these days that there's no support. I'm the only one in my neighborhood in the daytime; I'm like the last dinosaur."

Jan leaned forward. "It isn't the times; it's the dependence. From the time I was little I was taught that I couldn't cope with all kinds of things by myself, that Mommy and Daddy would take care of it. I was the *real* princess. I could feel the pea under a hundred mattresses. It's always been easier for me to let someone else take care of things."

"That doesn't sound like you at all."

"My current independence was hard won."

"You handle things so well now."

"I guess. But I still find myself wanting to be taken care of at times. The best thing that could happen to me would be to find a partner who refused to let me be dependent. Because dependence makes for insecurity. And it's addictive."

"How can a person break out of that, I wonder," Susan

said. "I mean, without getting a divorce," she added quickly.

"Take responsibility for yourself." Jan, using the one towel she'd brought, pulled the can out of the fire by the lid, then spooned the beans onto two paper plates.

"That sounds so simple, but when you're part of a marriage . . ."

"I guess you have to start with little things. Make some decisions about your life by yourself."

"I don't know how Ted would react."

"You could tell him how you feel, how you're going to make some changes."

Susan mulled that over, trying to think of what decisions she could make on her own that wouldn't have an impact on Ted.

"I'm about ready to quit my job," Jan said, her mouth full.

"Really? How come?"

"Because I've become dependent on it, just like you are on Ted. I'm tired of what I'm doing—have been for two years—but it feels so secure that I haven't been able to leave. I think I'm going to have to push myself on this one."

"What do you think you'd like to do?"

Jan shrugged and shoved another bite in her mouth. "I could be a counselor with just a few more hours at the college, but I'd really like to get out of the school system altogether. I just want a change."

They both fell silent for a few minutes, mesmerized by the fire, then Susan said, "Well, here we are. Where's the entertainment?"

"Bring on the entertainment," Jan agreed, flourishing her plastic fork. Almost as she said it a chuck-will's-widow started its monotonous song. The two women laughed at the coincidence.

"Uh-oh," Jan said. "Someone's watching us."

Susan caught her breath, remembering when she'd thought someone was on the bluff earlier. "Where?"

"An owl is sitting in that tree just across there, staring at us." She pointed. "Can you tell if it's a barred?"

Susan laughed with relief and zeroed in on it. "I can't see any horns, and the size is right for a barred."

Just then it gave a rising crescendo of hoots ending with a fluttering purr, and the two women looked at each other with satisfaction.

A mist was beginning to hover over the river, and the current seemed asleep, making the bluff's reflection on the black mirror of the water's surface almost perfect.

"Pretty nice out here," Susan said.

"Glad you came?" Jan said.

Susan hesitated only a moment, then nodded. "It's been fun so far."

"Always cautious."

She shrugged sheepishly. "I can't help it."

Just then they heard sounds, two voices floating downstream with the mist. Soon a johnboat came drifting along, one of the two men inside nonchalantly rowing it. He hailed the women with a "Howdy," then murmured something to his companion, a light-haired man dressed in overalls and a T-shirt whose pale features seemed to blend together in blankness. The rower, a bearded man who had the look of a redhead even in the dim light, was clad similarly. He leaned into his work and started pulling the boat toward the gravel bar.

"Oh, Lord," Jan said under her breath.

Both men were drinking beer; one finished off a can with a satisfied sigh, then crushed the can with one hand and tossed it onto the opposite bank.

"He Tarzan, we Jane," Jan said, again under her breath.

"Now we know why the wilderness is so full of trash."

Jan put down her paper plate and stood. Susan followed her lead, the same cold fear she felt crossing a deserted parking lot to her car after dark washing over her. Only now the danger was manifest.

"Where're your menfolk?" the blank-faced one asked with an inane grin that exposed missing front teeth, but at least gave his face some definition. Their boat scraped the bottom and came to rest.

"They're up a ways fishin'. Be along soon," Jan said.

Good, Susan thought. *Jan's quick*. She herself would have probably told them the truth, that they were alone.

"Didn't see no one."

"Hmm. That's odd," Jan said, frowning. "Wonder where they could have gotten to. Must be in some backwater."

"You fishing?" Susan asked, to change the subject.

"Nope."

"Oh." Silence.

"You seen anyone out here?" the bearded man asked.

"No," Jan said. Susan shook her head.

"Well, you want to ask us over for a bite to eat?" The blank-faced one gestured toward the fire and chortled. "We could use some of whatever you got."

"I'm afraid we don't have enough," Jan said. Her voice was tense.

The bearded one stood up and stepped out of the boat, using an oar to balance himself. "C'mon, Three-Fingers," he said to his buddy, then said to Jan, "We ain't big eaters."

"Just stay right there," Jan ordered.

"You ain't very hospitable." He grinned and started to advance toward her, motioning for his friend to join him.

"That's right. We're not," she agreed.

"Please," Susan said, "just leave."

The bearded one walked over to her, grinning, and reached out as if to touch her face. "You don't want our company?"

"Don't touch her," Jan said.

He ignored the order, letting his fingers brush Susan's cheek. "We're kinda hungry, ain't we, Three-Fingers?"

His touch set the whole scene before her in action. Jan dived toward their supplies and thrust her hand deep into her rucksack.

"Watch her, Eugene," the man in the boat yelled as he came leaping out, carrying a long pole with a hook on one end. "She's got a gun."

Eugene whirled on Jan and lunged, wrenching her up by the arm. They struggled for a moment, and the man threw Jan to the ground. As the gun clattered to the rocks, Susan grabbed a long, sturdy branch which lay halfway in the fire, swung it over her head with both hands, and brought it down solidly over the bearded man's back. It splintered, spraying out glowing fragments. She pulled the branch up, ready to strike the other one if he made a move toward them.

Eugene let out several yipping howls of pain as the fiery embers from the stick shattered over him. He danced around to get the sparks off.

Jan scrambled for the gun, then jerked herself to her feet.

Except for the expletives pouring from Eugene's mouth, things settled down as quickly as they'd started. "Hellfire, bitch," he said to Susan, his eyes narrowed. "You 'bout burnt me to death. You're gonna pay!"

"Outta here," Jan yelled, motioning with the gun, which she was holding with both hands.

"We get the message, don't we, Three-Fingers?" But he didn't move for a long moment.

Susan quit breathing as they all stood frozen in place, the man's hostility charging the air.

He moved then, saying to Jan, "Better be careful carrying a gun, lady. You could get hurt."

He pushed the boat off the gravel, carefully climbing aboard while the other man, who'd already gotten in, steadied the boat with an oar, then the pale one began to row into the current. A can exhaled as one of the men popped a tab on another beer. The sound carried loudly across the water.

"What do you suppose they're doing out here if they're not fishing?" Susan whispered as the men moved out of earshot downstream.

"Frogging and looking for trouble," Jan replied. "That was a gig the one was holding."

"Oh."

"My father was a frogger. He didn't use a gig, though—he did it by hand. But his friends used them." After a moment she turned toward the fire, came back to it, and stared at the flames. Her voice was tight with anger. "Those damn creeps, coming in here like that. I'm going to talk to the sheriff about this when we get off the river. They aren't going to get away with it." She touched her side and winced.

"Jan, are you okay? Did he hurt you?"

"I'm okay." She lifted her shirt and strained her neck to look at her side. "I imagine I'll have some bruises, but I seem to be in one piece." She touched her side and screwed up her face again.

Susan came over to look. "I don't see anything. Maybe one of your ribs is cracked."

Jan pulled her shirt down and examined her arm, which had a scrape from elbow to wrist. "Did you bring any antiseptic?"

"No. Sorry." She sat down and picked up her abandoned paper plate. "I brought almost everything else."

Jan smiled slightly and joined her friend on the ground.

Susan took a bite of her food, but it no longer tasted good. "Hey, what are you doing with that gun anyway? I thought you told Ted—"

"I didn't want him to think we were scared, but I always carry it with me when I travel. Maybe if I had a man along I wouldn't, but—"

"Well, I'm glad you had it."

"I'll put it under my pillow tonight, in case they get the foolish notion to come back."

"Good. That'll keep me from accidentally shooting you." She gave a dry laugh, remembering Jan's words to Ted. Then her eyes opened wide. "Pillows! We forgot pillows!"

Jan shrugged. "Oh, well, we can use our life jackets."

After a quiet moment Susan asked, "Do you think those men know we're alone? Or do you think they just have a lot of gall?"

"I think the fact that only two sleeping bags were spread out was a dead giveaway."

"Don't say that word." Susan shuddered, adding her plate to the fire.

"What?"

"Dead."

Jan laughed. "How about some toasted marshmallows? That fire's just about right. And look here." She reached into a bag and pulled out a small plastic sandwich bag with several graham crackers and a Hershey bar inside. "S'mores!"

"I can't believe it!" Susan said with a laugh of delight. Her laughter, however, couldn't lift the mood. The conversation kept reverting to the earlier incident.

"Do you think we ought to go on tonight?" Susan finally asked.

"No. We'd just get to the takeout way too early. And besides, those two might be right around the next bend."

The fire had dwindled to a glimmer of coals before either woman wanted to move away from its safety.

"How's your head?" Susan asked.

"Worse. The aspirin didn't seem to help."

"Maybe it's this dampness," Susan said. Her clothes seemed to be clinging to her.

"Getting thrown around didn't help. Anyway, I know I'm ready to turn in." She pulled out the unopened air mattresses, handed one over to Susan, then began to blow into the opening. After a moment she stopped, her thumb over the opening. With the other hand she pressed on her temples. "Wow, this is *really* helping my head."

"I'll do it. You just relax."

"No. I can manage."

Susan put one hand on her friend's arm. "Come on, Jan. Letting me blow that thing up won't compromise your independence. I promise."

Jan smiled sheepishly, plugged up the hole, and thrust the air mattress at Susan. "Here."

When Susan had finished inflating the mattresses, Jan took hers and stood up. "I think we'd better go into the woods."

Susan glanced around uneasily. "You think they might come back?"

Jan shrugged. "I wouldn't bet my life on it either way."

She reached down for the insect repellent. "Better use some more of this." She handed it to Susan.

Together they moved into the woods, carrying their sleeping bags, life jackets, and air mattresses, the smell of Deep Woods Off in their nostrils, following the reassuring beam of Jan's flashlight.

There was a bluff just upstream from where the women camped. It exposed itself abruptly as the river turned, then dropped away from the water, changing its profile to a steep hill with no exposed rock. Trees massed thickly there where the soil had gathered deep and rich in a delta, moving inexorably down from the high ground over the eons.

Lee Newton watched the panorama below him like a movie. Two women camping together. He branded them lesbians almost before thinking. Enter: two men in a johnboat, their paths soon to cross. The light was fading fast down there, but he could see clearly enough to watch the altercation developing. Even the angry voices carried through the valley. He squinted his eyes for a better view. One of the women had a gun. It was odd to see two women out canoeing alone, odder still that one should carry a gun.

Indignation bubbled up inside him. Women out of their place. It was one of the many things wrong with the world today. He thought of Ruthie and Joanna waiting for him back at the Compound. They were his helpmates and knew their roles.

He ripped open a can of tuna with his knife, said a blessing, and pulled the chunks out with his fingers, sucking each one clean of the briny liquid running down them. It tasted good. He'd not taken the time to stop and eat during the day. Not that he was running scared; his indoctrination had freed him of that.

He'd spent sixteen years scared—well, maybe half that, because he wasn't really conscious of the outside world until he was eight—before he suddenly realized that the planet teetered on the brink of doom. He remembered when he first became aware of it. Everywhere the world seemed to be exploding into chaos. Right there on television there were pictures of dead bodies heaped high, of protesters, people rioting. He'd go to bed nights and hide his head under the pillow.

When he was sixteen he'd tried to commit suicide, that's how much it bothered him—being scared all the time. Death would be better than waiting.

He'd been out earlier with a girl from his school—he couldn't even remember her name now—and they'd gotten to drinking, and he'd started telling her about the hellish state of the world while she fondled him. The alcohol had made him verbose but little else, and when he realized he wasn't going to be able to perform, he fell into a drunken despondency.

Thick-tongued, he tried to talk her into a death pact. It would be a noble end to the evening, he'd said. They could compose a note to leave behind. She'd called him crazy.

It turned out she was just a slut on the make, no more interested in the state of the world than most people. The girl disgusted him, and he never spoke to her at school again.

After he took her home that evening, he pulled into his own garage and left the car running, figuring he'd end it by himself. But his parents heard the car come in, and after a little while they came out to check on him and foiled his suicide.

His dad had yelled at him and told him never to pull a stunt like that again. His mother had suggested that perhaps Lee needed some counseling, but the old man put the lid on that idea.

"You want people to think he's crazy?" he'd asked.

What kept him from trying again was meeting Carroll Smith. Carroll had a hole-in-the-wall survival store where he stocked everything from freeze-dried foods to weapons. Lee had chauffeured his mother to an antique store in a run-down part of town, and there was Carroll's place, right next door. Lee knew now it wasn't chance that took him there; God had intervened in his life.

The place looked like an army surplus store from the

outside, but it was more. That was obvious to anyone who wandered in.

Carroll was sitting behind the counter reading when Lee entered, looking like a college professor. He had graying hair, thin eyebrows, and was rather slight.

Lee looked at various weapons, thinking about alternate ways to commit suicide, the idea still very much on his mind. He didn't say much, but the older man, who was probably trying to pass the time, soon drew him out.

Before Lee knew it, he launched into his speech about how you might as well be dead as alive in the world today. He even told Carroll about his attempted suicide.

The man stood up, leaned toward Lee, and said, "There's something you can do about it, son." He handed Lee a book to read. It was a novel, but it painted a specific and brutal picture of the future which made Lee's imaginings seem rather tame.

Over the next several days Lee read it, then returned to visit Carroll again. This man understood. The store became like a sanctuary to him over the next month, and he was taken into Carroll's inner circle.

The turning point came when the man invited Lee to come to a prayer meeting at a friend's house. He realized that his life before had been godless, but from that night, Lee had something to hang onto. He was accepted by the people there and he liked what they had to say: that all the problems had started with the Jews, who mistakenly thought of themselves as the Chosen People, when in fact it was Christian Americans who were the true Israelites, descended from Isaac's sons. That's who the Saxons were. It all made sense, and it was a great comfort to know the truth.

The brothers at the prayer meeting were zealous in their belief that there was holy work to be done and with that work would come salvation. From that time on Lee got over his fear.

Forcing himself back to the present, he surveyed the river. The drama below had dissolved. The two men in the johnboat had floated on downstream out of sight now, and

the two women were once again alone. Somewhere an owl
hooted.

Lee massaged his shoulders, pressing his fingers into the
taut flesh. He wasn't a tall man, and his muscular build—
wide at the shoulders, trim at the hips—made him appear
shorter than he was. He had high cheekbones under clear
blue eyes and light lashes and eyebrows, bleached white by
the sun. He was in top physical shape, trained first courtesy
of the military, later at a commando camp. When the
Colonel was setting up his camp, he'd asked Lee to serve as
a trainer. Lee's reputation attracted survivalists, and some
stayed on to form a permanent "family." Lee had not only
trained the men in guerrilla warfare and survival techniques,
he also converted them to Christianity, much to the Colonel's chagrin, he thought.

He felt no remorse about the patrolman he'd shot. It was
God's instruction that he and his fellow patriots cleanse the
earth of the enemy in order to pave the way for the New
Order. He was simply carrying out the imperative. The state
patrol—and all the state and federal bureaucracy—were part
of the Zionist conspiracy, a bunch of Jew bankers trying to
take over the chosen country: The United States of America.

He'd followed the women's progress since he'd first seen
them swimming, staying well out of sight, but following
them along the river. Now their fire had almost gone out;
just a red glow of coals remained. The talking had stopped,
and the women were carrying their sleeping bags into the
woods, vague shapes in the dark, slipping away. Good.
They'd be out of his way when he slipped down and
commandeered their canoe.

Susan's husband Ted had gotten home at the usual time. He
rifled through the mail the way he did every day, but found
nothing of interest.

Gordon, a guy at work, had given him a hard time about
letting Susan go canoeing without him. Even the normally
reserved Hal Martin had clucked over it. "Women can't
handle themselves out in the wilderness," Hal had said.

Gordon had taken the conversation off on a different track. "Well, since she's gone, what are you going to do? Got big plans? I could slip out, and we could maybe go down to that topless place on Grand. You ever been there?"

Ted had begged off. He saw no reason to make a drastic change in his normal routine just because Susan was out of town. Besides, Gordon wasn't someone with whom he cared to associate socially. It was common knowledge that the guy ran around on his wife.

Ted went upstairs to change, fully intending to go out and mow the lawn, which needed it. After a good rain on Tuesday, seed heads had popped up like stubble on a man's face.

Ted pulled a baby blue Izod shirt over his head, tucked it in, and zipped up his shorts, then sat down on the bed to lace up his running shoes. He padded down the stairs unenthusiastically, and as he passed through the den, he decided to sit down—just for a few minutes—to catch the news. The next thing he knew it was ten o'clock. He'd slept the evening away.

"I'll mow the lawn tomorrow morning before it gets hot outside," he said aloud, a little startled by the sound of his own voice. He got out of his recliner and went into the kitchen to the refrigerator.

Susan had left him a plate with meat loaf, some kind of a rice conglomeration, and green beans, all ready to pop into the microwave. There was also a bowl of salad. He prepared the dinner, ate it, and set the dishes in the sink, unrinsed.

The dead bolt was in place on the kitchen door, so he got a beer, turned out the light, and went back to his chair. He settled back in front of the television, then pulled the beer tab.

Why was it so different with Susan gone? Sometimes they'd spend an entire evening with little conversation, so why did the house feel so strange now? It must be the sounds, he decided. She'd be puttering around the kitchen, then would join him, usually to bury her nose in a book.

Another person's sounds must make a subtle but noticeable difference in the atmosphere of a house.

He began to wallow in his loneliness, his mind darting and shifting to reinforce his mood. She was really important to him, but he didn't show it very often. When was the last time he'd surprised her with a gift? He snorted. Who was he kidding? He never thought of bringing gifts. Hell, his gift was bringing home the bacon. Wasn't that enough for her?

The thought was tinged with vehemence, but he softened immediately. He really couldn't complain; she was a good wife. Sometimes she'd bring him a new book he'd been wanting, or a magazine she knew he liked. Or just cook his favorite kind of food. Little things that showed she cared. She'd always done her part.

He took another swallow of beer. Sometimes, he'd lie awake at night and worry about his part, about the fact that this household, this family, all depended upon him. Was the money going to stretch far enough? Would they be able to afford a new car? Was there enough in his retirement account? Always there was something nibbling away at their income. It was better now that Jennifer was out on her own, but worrying had become a habit.

He hadn't ever wanted Susan to know it bothered him, because she'd have felt she should get a job. And he never wanted her to feel that way. Times had changed, but he still thought the head of the household should be the breadwinner.

Ted's mother, Clara, had worked outside the home for as long as he could remember, just to make ends meet. He'd been a latchkey kid from the day he started school. When he was little he'd had to go home with the Holcomb brothers, Tim and Rusty, and they'd made his life miserable. Finally, in third grade, he got a key which went around his neck on a chain. It was a relief to be free of the Holcombs, but the house was a lonely place after school, until five-thirty when his father got home.

He didn't want his family to be like that; he'd always wanted his wife to stay home. For Jennifer and Jeffrey.

He punched the buttons on the remote control, running

through the channels, stopping momentarily at this program or that, not really seeing. He was remembering how much trouble he'd had sleeping when the Unidyne plant had closed. Good friends his own age suddenly were out of work. It'd been a real nightmare for them and their families. He'd opted, just out of college, for the security of government work; he was still glad. It might not pay as much, but a man knew it was going to be there.

About 1 A.M., he went upstairs. He turned down the spread neatly, shut off all the lights, and climbed rigidly between the sheets. He forced his eyes shut, but they popped right back open. The house was too dark and silent.

He got up and took his gun out of the dresser drawer, then turned on the bathroom light and crawled back in bed. He didn't like that either. If someone came in, they'd see him before he saw them.

He hadn't bothered with the attic fan tonight and now he wished he had. It would mask the strange sounds he kept hearing. A sharp clunk came from downstairs, and Ted tried to pinpoint what it could be. The cold metal of the gun comforted him as he waited and listened.

Lord, this house is big.

No one came up the stairs, so he turned out the bathroom light again and crawled back in bed once more. Sleep still didn't come, so he padded barefooted down to the family room, gun in hand, and turned on the television to some shouting evangelist. A little hellfire and damnation preaching could focus the free-floating anxiety Ted felt.

Saturday Morning

5

THE MOON WAS up and almost full as Lee began his descent to the river valley. The flashlight's charge had died, so he was dependent on the intermittent moonlight and his instincts. His movements were quiet now, and he was aware of things most people would miss: the pattern of sounds, the feel of the air, the sense of the earth under his feet. For years he'd been pitting himself against nature, testing his abilities, until she was no longer a foe but an active instrument in his survival.

His toughening up began just out of high school when he'd joined the army at the suggestion of the brothers, and for almost four years he'd recruited for the brotherhood, right under the nose of the federal government.

He'd found plenty of guys who understood his message. Some of them were from poor families who saw jobs being eaten up by what he and his friends considered to be all the garbage civil-rights legislation. Other were more like Lee, looking for a way to make sense of a world that felt out of control.

In his second year in the army he'd developed a network of men who supplied him with munitions to funnel outside—everything from lightweight portable rockets to rifles and ammunition to C-4 plastic explosives.

And from his civilian friends, there was a steady supply of money coming in. Lee didn't know where that money came from until several of his buddies were arrested for a string of armored-car robberies. Their conviction pretty much put an end to the big flow of equipment to the outside, but the guys who were committed ideologically still managed to filter some stuff to him.

He kept a low profile and didn't run into any trouble until one of his earlier sources, a druggie, turned on him and informed. There was enough evidence of Lee's activities to get him discharged, but to avoid publicity the army called it honorable.

After that he'd gone to the West Coast, where he'd taken part in his first fund-raising: he and four other men had robbed a string of banks. There'd been nothing to link them to any of the crimes, and they'd wisely stopped before their luck ran out.

The money from the jobs was divided up among many different groups, one being the fledgling Compound the Colonel was starting. Lee felt he'd been instrumental in getting the group going, both with the money and as a trainer, and Wednesday would be the first payoff. It gave him a warm sense of satisfaction.

The way became steeper now. Lee held onto saplings to keep his footing, moving carefully to avoid dislodging any rocks. He caught hold of a blackberry bramble and stopped a moment to suck the wound, then started off again, down into the hollow that ended at the gravel bar, increasing his caution. His path would lead him near where the women were camped, and he didn't want to alert them with any sounds.

It was undoubtedly the most uncomfortable night Susan had ever spent. And it seemed interminable. Perhaps she had slept and perhaps not. If so, it wasn't very deep, just a thin veneer of unconsciousness, never taking her completely away from an awareness of her surroundings and the possibilities that lurked in the dark.

The clearing in the woods where they'd thrown down their sleeping bags, while perhaps safer and definitely less lumpy than the gravel bar, was unforgiving in its own way. The thin skin of soft soil barely masked a rocky soul.

Overhead, popping and cracking sounds pierced the night. *Are there animals in the trees chewing through branches? Will a branch come crashing down on us at any moment?* Something hit the ground nearby. *A snake?*

Susan shuddered and considered getting up and moving back near the water. Surely those men wouldn't come back. But fear trapped her right where she was.

Her clothes were bunched uncomfortably around her, and the crotch of her shorts had gotten twisted as she turned over. As she lifted her hips and tried to shift the material, she realized the air mattress was completely deflated. *No wonder I'm miserable,* she thought crossly. Still, she was reluctant to get out of the security of the sleeping bag to blow the thing up again.

"What am I doing here? she wondered as she struggled to turn over again. Her hip bone ached where she'd been lying on it. *I could be at home on my own wonderful mattress, a gentle breeze from the attic fan skimming over me. It could have been a day trip.*

This was one of those decisions Jan was talking about, she thought. A way she could take more responsibility for her life. A trip without Ted. She grimaced comically for her own benefit. Did it have to be such an uncomfortable beginning? And did they have to encounter those awful men? Anyway, what did she think this proved? That she was independent? Ha! She wouldn't be here if it hadn't been for Jan's prodding. As usual, she was just being swept along.

She mulled over her adult life. That was the pattern: being swept along. She never took the initiative. An opposing voice inside her asked: *In what ways do you want to take the initiative?* Good question. It perplexed her. Nothing seemed worth the effort.

A mosquito buzzed around her head, and she pulled one arm out of the sleeping bag to swat at the sound. There it was again. She pulled the bag over her head to escape the insect.

Her inner voices started up again. *You were a scout leader, weren't you? That took some initiative.* The other one countered: *You only did it because most of the other mothers were working. Would you have done it if there'd been anyone else? No. See? No initiative.* The voice was belligerent.

Could it be that some people could go through their entire lives and never make an opening gambit? Susan wondered. Never acting, only reacting?

Okay, now, she thought, *this is just a game. Try to think back to a time—anytime—in the last twenty-five years when you've initiated something.* She reviewed the years in her head. Well, it had been her idea to get pregnant. Of course, Ted had agreed that it was a good time for it, otherwise she'd probably have been willing to wait. Okay. But she had taken the initiative with the kids. Yes, that was it. She was a good mother; no one, not even an inner voice, was going to say otherwise. The kids were her territory, and she had strong mothering instincts. Maybe that was why she was feeling so lost with them gone. Parenting had been the one area of her life where she'd felt competent and necessary, and Jennifer and Jeffrey were evidence that she'd done okay.

She must have dozed. The next sound she heard was a familiar one—retching. No mother could mistake it, and Susan reacted instinctively. Her head popped out from its cover. She could see Jan's shadowy shape, half-sitting, her head bent.

Susan pulled her damp shoes out of the sleeping bag where she'd stuffed them to keep them safe and slipped her toes into them, just enough to plod over to Jan's sleeping bag. She squatted down and put her hand on her friend's shoulder, not saying anything, just offering silent comfort.

The worst of it was over for a moment, and Jan lay back, shaking.

"Did this just start?" Susan asked.

Jan nodded. "I feel awful. My head and my stomach."

Susan put her hand on her friend's forehead. "You're a little warm. It's probably just a bug of some kind. I'm sure it won't last long." She tried to sound confident. These things usually ran their course, but it took at least twelve hours. And twelve hours meant they wouldn't be at the takeout point on time. Nor would Jan feel up to paddling them downstream when whatever it was was over. Navigating the rest of the way would lie on Susan's shoulders, which at the moment were feeling pretty broad since she was essentially doing what she did best: mothering.

"I'll go get a piece of ice out of the cooler for you to suck on. Keep your fluids up." She knew the routine; she'd been through it enough with the kids. Susan gently pulled Jan's hair away from her face, then finished putting on her shoes. "Be right back."

She picked her way cautiously back to the gravel bar, relieved to be up and moving, silencing the self-deprecating voice inside her head. Her footsteps crackled on the rocks as she walked, the only close-at-hand sound.

It was radiantly beautiful by the river. The moon hung jewellike overhead in a star dazzled sky. It far surpassed her view of the sky at home, where the city lights almost obliterated the stars.

Once, when she was about ten, she'd been invited to spend the night outside at a neighbor's house. It had sounded like a wonderful adventure. She and Belinda told riddles and giggled till late. The lights in the house were out by then; only one house a few backyards away had a light in its window. Everybody else was asleep. Suddenly, she was petrified, afraid to move but unwilling to admit her fear to her friend. A dog barked far off somewhere. "Belinda," she whispered, "are you still awake?" No answer. The lump in her throat seemed enormous. She wanted to move her cot nearer to Belinda's, but she was afraid to get out of it. At last, by what felt like some miracle, she fell asleep. In the middle of the night, she awoke, and the fear had mysteriously evaporated. A sense of peace came over her as she lay under the stars in the darkened neighborhood. Everything seemed crystal clear, and she felt content and unafraid.

The same feeling flooded over her now, awakened by the

splendor of the sky overhead and the memory of that night at Belinda's.

She chided herself. She was supposed to be getting some ice for poor Jan and here she was being introspective.

A pocket of moonlit mist hovered over the water's edge. She was almost to the canoe, still marveling at the beauty around her, when she saw the man facing her. One of those men, she thought, the blank-faced one, had come back. His features were indistinct in the moonlight.

Her stomach lurched, the sense of peace dissolving like a bitter pill. The gun, safely under Jan's pillow back in the woods, fleetingly crossed her mind, but the man's weapon was already trained on her. It was no frogging gig.

"Move right over here," he said quietly but firmly, gesturing with his gun.

She crunched across the rocks toward him, the adrenaline pumping through her, her heart in her throat. "What are you going to do?"

"Get in the canoe."

"No, please. Leave me here. Take the canoe, take the things. But please leave me." Her words tumbled out in a desperate hiss. She could see, now that he was closer, that it wasn't the blank faced man from the night before.

Ignoring her plea, he wrenched her arm and forced her to walk to the canoe. The boat rocked uncertainly as he pushed her into the bow. Her shin scraped against a rough edge on the gunwale as she fell forward into the bottom, and she cried out.

"Shut up," he growled.

Susan bit her lip against the pain in her leg and arm and cowered there as he prodded her with his gun, an ugly reminder that she had no choice but to comply with his every wish.

He put the last of their plastic bags of supplies in the canoe, keeping the gun pointed at Susan, then edged the boat out, wading into the water with a quiet sloshing.

She lifted her eyes to watch him. He was scanning the trees, probably to see if someone was going to come out to help her. Satisfied that no one was observing, he swung the canoe around and turned his back on the gravel bar. The canoe dipped low as he climbed in, then he took up the paddle and started them downstream with a powerful stroke. Susan clung to the gunwales, dazed.

Jan wasn't asleep, nor was she fully awake. She felt locked in a netherworld, the blood beating behind her eyes, blurring the dawn that was stealing in. Her mouth tasted so bad. She let the saliva collect for a moment, then spit it out. It didn't help much.

Her mind drifted down near sleep, then back. *Susan. Where was she? Didn't she go to get ice? Ice. I'd kill for ice,* she thought. Jan pressed her hand against her eyes. Maybe Susan had been back and gone again. Gone where? She raised her head slightly, sending a sharp pain through her temple. "Oh, Lord," she said, grasping it. After a moment, the feeling subsided, and she looked around. Her friend's sleeping bag was empty.

"Susan?" her voice didn't come out with much strength, and she knew it wouldn't carry through the trees to the gravel bar. She dropped her head and waited.

The sour smell of her vomit drove her to struggle weakly out of the sleeping bag. She rose too quickly, and everything went black. She managed to stay on her feet and in a moment, when her vision cleared, she took hold of the foot end of the nylon bag and pulled it a few feet. The effort exhausted her, and she dropped back on top of it, her legs shaking.

She'd slept naked and now she lay there, chilled by the morning, but too weak to crawl inside her bag. She drew one long side up over her, but the minute she let it go, it fell flat again, and she was too weak to repeat the effort.

Her stomach began to churn again. She took a deep breath, fighting back the queasiness. Nausea swept over her and she threw up again.

Afterward she lay there, the cramps receding, and gathered her strength to head for the gravel bar. She needed that thermos of water. The thought of it was tantalizing, giving her the incentive she needed to move.

Once she'd gotten there, she thought perhaps she'd become disoriented. There was no sign of Susan or the canoe. Where was her friend? More importantly where was the thermos?

Despair engulfed her. Her thoughts began to run together. Susan must have gone for help. That was it: she had taken the canoe to get help. Jan's already frowning face fell. Feeling abandoned, she allowed herself a low moan as she sank down on the deflated air mattress and sleeping bag she'd dragged behind her, covering her aching head with her arms. Why hadn't Susan told her she was leaving?

Oh, dear God, I feel terrible. I think I'm going to die. Where is Susan? Her eyes filled with tears. *How long will I have to wait to be rescued? If Susan doesn't come back, could I manage to walk—and where would I go?*

Her stomach had begun to throb again, and she knew the awful retching was about to begin once more. A few moments later she lay back, exhausted, but feeling slightly better.

Out of the protection of the forest, her nakedness increased her feeling of vulnerability, so she slowly took her clothes out of the sleeping bag and pulled them on. One leg into the canvas shorts, then she rested. The other foot dug for the other leg hole. Then Jan rested again. After a few moments she pulled the shorts up. Finally she pulled her T-shirt over her head and lay back down.

I'll take a look around, she thought. But her body wouldn't respond, so she added: *in a few minutes.* She couldn't get up yet. Her legs felt too weak.

Her fingers touched the cold steel of the gun, still hidden under the life jacket, reminding her of the men they'd confronted last night. *What if,* she thought, *what if they came back and stole our canoe? And Susan happened upon them when she went for ice, and they grabbed her?*

She clapped her hand against her head, blaming herself for challenging the men the night before, for pulling the gun. Maybe if she'd been patient—maybe they were all bluff, just trying to frighten them. But no, she didn't believe it. No telling what they'd have done if she hadn't had the gun. That brought her unpleasantly up against the next thought. If they had Susan, what would they do to her?

The light blow she'd given her temple intensified the dull ache lingering in her head, and she became aware of the cramps still gnawing at her stomach.

Jan moaned again. There was no one to hear, so she didn't have to be brave.

The sun still hadn't broken over the bluffs, and rising eddies of mist gave the valley an otherwordliness as a canoe slipped along with the current. Stillness, broken intermittently by an early bird and the stroke of the paddle, signaled the beginning of the new day. Nearly everything was resting.

The bearded man lifted his head from the floor of the johnboat, which was tied to a dead tree that had fallen into the water. The boat was almost totally concealed by a bower of leaves. He'd just been getting settled again after relieving himself over the side of the boat when he heard the dip of a paddle and peered over the side, parting the leaves, to see a man and woman slide by in a canoe. His eyes narrowed as he watched.

"Newton, you scumbag," he muttered to himself. "What are you doin' overnight on the river with another woman?" He was thinking of his sister, Ruthie, who was living with Newton in that Compound like like some latter-day hippie, and who was now carrying the guy's whelp.

He scratched his head, then yawned. Right now, he needed more sleep. Later he and Three-fingers would figure out what they could do about that two-timin' Bible thumper. He smiled at the prospect. He'd never liked the guy, with his holier-than-thou ways.

Susan's insides felt like mush, but at least her heart had settled down to a more normal rate. She could no longer feel the exaggerated pounding.

The situation was surreal: sitting in a canoe with a stranger—a stranger who had a gun. He was in the stern, paddling at a steady speed, and hadn't said more than a couple of sentences since he'd taken the canoe.

Susan remembered the man at the basket store had said something about a state patrolman being killed up north. Could this be the fugitive? Oh, no, surely not; this was too far away. The trooper had been killed over the state line in Presley County. She didn't even want to entertain the thought, so she pushed it away.

How deceptive appearances could be. There were probably hundreds of life-and-death dramas all around her in the water and in the woods, enemies locked in combat over territory, but on the surface the scene was peaceful. And to an observer no drama would appear to be taking place in this canoe. Just a couple on a weekend outing.

She felt suddenly separated from reality and was surprised to look down and see her fingers gripping the gunwales so tightly that her knuckles were white. Her teeth were clenched. She tried to relax with a few deep breaths, but they didn't stop the queasy feeling in her stomach.

The canoe was moving quietly through the water. A dense stand of water willow began to push the current into a narrow channel, and the canoe rode swiftly but uneventfully down a chute, slapping its aluminum bottom against the water with regular thuds as the boat rose and fell with the rough surface. A lazy pool, crystal clear, awaited them. Susan's attention was riveted to a flash of movement as a great blue heron took off.

Sunlight began to edge the rim of the bluff, touching the world with realism, making her predicament all the more incredible to her. But here she was, in this idyllic setting, with an armed stranger.

She turned slightly, catching a glimpse of him in her peripheral vision, almost as if she were trying to prove to herself he was really there, that it wasn't Jan back there. He was. A nice-looking young man with short blond hair. Very Scandinavian looking. Was he a killer?

And what about poor Jan? How sick was she? She was stuck back there on the gravel bar with no water, no food, and no canoe. Only a gun. What would she think? How long would she wait there before realizing her friend wasn't coming back? *Not coming back.* That sobering thought made Susan's skin turn cold so suddenly that she shivered.

The morning sun was streaming in the sliding door at the Kendrys'. Diane Kendry, in a long white terry cloth robe, was standing beside the glass-topped breakfast table, pouring coffee from an insulated carafe into her husband's cup.

"You know, I can't understand it," she said.

Tom looked up from the morning paper. "What's that?"

"There was a bag of food by Mitzi's dish, and now it's not there."

"Maybe the cleaning lady moved it."

Diane sighed. "She never has before. She just leaves it by the dish."

"You're not suggesting Mitzi took it with her, are you?" he asked with a grin.

"Maybe someone stole her."

"And left the TV, the CD player, the computer—"

She waved him quiet and sank down in a chair. "Well, what else could it be? She's never not come home before."

Tom folded the paper and put it down. "I know. I miss her. I half expected her to be at the door when we got up this morning."

They'd driven back and forth on the nearest county roads calling for the dog after they'd gotten home from work Friday and realized she was really missing.

"What else can we do?" Diane asked, selecting a Danish from a plate on the table.

"I'll put an ad in the paper on Monday, and we'll hope she shows up before then."

A hostage hadn't been part of Lee Newton's plan, but he figured God had presented this opportunity, so what choice had he but to take it? He'd seen this woman from the bluff. He was glad it was her and not the other one. This one was—what would he call it?—more timid. She hadn't wantonly thrown her clothes off to go swimming like the other one. She hadn't been the one who'd pulled a gun.

Perhaps this woman was not completely spoiled by the temptations of the world.

The morning was slipping away, and so far they hadn't encountered anyone. Unfortunately they were approaching the confluence of the Upper Fork and the Big Pine, and it was a popular spot on weekends. He calculated for a moment what day of the week it was; he'd lost track. Saturday. Bad news. He should've holed up until nightfall. With the moon, traveling by night would be no problem. But now he was committed because there was no secluded place to pull out before the other river joined this one. They'd just have to get through the popular stretch quickly. Maybe this early in the day, there wouldn't be many people out.

They were approaching white water, a short but tricky stretch coming in the middle of a meander. They had to avoid being swept against the wall of rock and also miss several elephant-sized boulders which had dropped ages ago from the bluff.

"Do you know anything about canoeing?" he asked.

"Not much," she answered, picking up her paddle. "Just a few basic strokes."

She glanced around at him, their eyes meeting. He could read her silent question: *could I bash you with a paddle and make a getaway?* He smiled slightly because he knew what she was thinking. It gave him a sense of control. The increasingly swift water must have taken her mind off of escape, though, because she turned away without trying anything.

Thinking she might be more handicap than help, he decided to go through the rapids at an angle, a little trick he used when he canoed with beginners. This way he could see what was coming up. He pried the stern to the left.

"Don't try to keep us straight," he hollered at her. "Just let the canoe drift, until I tell you what to do."

The sound of the water surrounded them now, a symphony of white noise. A spray of water rooster-tailed off the bow of the canoe as it fell forward over a submerged shelf of rock.

"Draw now," he shouted. They shot past a boulder, and the boat went cascading through the standing waves as the power of the river came out in the open.

Lee felt high. If life were only a white-water canoe ride! He licked a spray of water from his lips and suppressed a smile. He gave her another order and the canoe moved to the right, still angled and following the channel. They were moving at the speed of the current now; he wasn't holding the canoe back. It shot down through the last of the foaming haystacks and rounded a bend into a slow-moving pool, and the excitement of a moment before disappeared abruptly. His mouth gaped. There were throngs of people. He stared in disbelief. An acid taste came up in his throat.

Police! That was his first thought. They knew his route; they'd blocked off the river and were waiting for him. He grabbed at the gun on the floor of the canoe, then stopped himself. The throngs of people were dressed in casual clothes—cutoffs, shorts, halters, swimsuits.

"It's a raft race," the woman said, her eyes fixed on the bluff which had red-white-and-blue bunting draped over a huge sign:

THE GREAT INTERNATIONAL RAFT RACE

A beer company's logo on a canvas banner flapped against the rocks in the light breeze.

They were in the midst of the crowd now, where any one of them could glance into the canoe and see the gun. Lee shoved it partly under one of the plastic bags. He was breathing hard, still feeling the physical effects of his momentary fear.

He couldn't help staring, wide-eyed, as they passed a floating coffin, being held back by a man in a top hat and black swimming trunks. An old-fashioned bathtub was threatening to topple over, and two men tried to steady it as a third crawled in.

There were people milling all around them. Several Huckleberry Finn–type rafts were being shoved out from the bank, and one man was paddling a surfboard across the current. Lee blocked it out, returning his gaze to the river. He wanted to be out of this jam of people. Dip and pull, dip and pull. He kept at it, trying to get beyond them.

A radio-deejay type voice came over a loudspeaker, interrupting the music. "Will all contestants in the novelty craft race please make sure you've signed in. You need a number." Pause. "That event will begin in approximately five minutes."

The woman looked toward the voice, her chin tilting up in an expectant way. "Just keep your mind on me," Lee told her. He had to raise his voice louder than he wanted to be heard above the rock music and the general hubbub. "No funny business."

Susan felt an instant sense of relief amid all the people, as if their mere presence would somehow save her. The feeling was illusory: if she tried something, jumped out or caused a commotion, someone would probably get hurt. Her heart began to pound as she tried to make a decision, and her eyes darted from one person to another in the crowd. For now, she had only to keep quiet and she would be safe. But what might happen later, when she was alone with him again? Did she dare take the risk and jump from the canoe?

The participants in the race were stretched wide across the river, which was thigh deep here, perfect for launching their makeshift boats. It was impossible to avoid them. Susan stared at the shore. Were there any security people? And if there were, would it do any good?

There was a girl about Jennifer's age, near the water's edge. Susan allowed herself the fantasy for a moment that it *was* Jennifer and that somehow she'd rescue her mother. And there were boys Jeffrey's age. A few middle-aged people, no old ones. And little children playing in the shallow water under adults' watchful eyes. *Notice me, too,* she willed them, *help me!* She concentrated on the words, hoping to send them by telepathy, which she really didn't believe in. One freckle-faced boy of perhaps seventeen met her eye momentarily, then looked through her as if she were invisible. It happened all the time. Teenagers never saw her.

She had faded into middle age. *See me!* If only someone would remember them—the blond man and the older woman.

Two young men were pushing a surfboard out to the middle of the river and almost ran into the side of the canoe, the anomaly in this collection of novelty craft.

"Watch it," her captor—she wondered what his name was—growled. One of the two grinned inanely at him: the other scowled. Maybe one of them would remember.

The canoe slipped past the line of contestants, the man pulling solidly on his paddle. They were leaving the people behind. She felt frantic, knowing she would be alone with him again. She half turned to look at him; he stared straight at her, his eyes too wide and bright, but not with the glaze of fear. Craziness, she decided, would be a better term for his look.

And this whole thing was crazy. Those last rapids they'd been through—they didn't even have life jackets. What kind of a maniac would attempt that run without a life jacket? If they'd capsized, what chance would they have had in that kind of current?

"Paddle," he told her. She'd been sitting idle, entranced by the activity around her.

She lifted the paddle and pulled, lifted and pulled, lifted and pulled, taking herself farther away. Tears moistened her eyes, and she blinked them back.

I should have jumped out, she thought. *He probably wouldn't have shot me.* Probably *was an iffy sort of word. And what if he'd panicked and shot into the crowd?* She sighed quietly. Could she live with that sort of guilt? But what was the use of thinking about it now? Her chance was gone. She hadn't done anything—no, she'd just sat there like a lump, passively taking what was dished out to her. Well, she wasn't going to take it. She didn't have a plan yet, but she wasn't going to just take it like a good little girl.

Oh, dear God, I know I'm indecisive, but did I have to learn independence like this?

They rounded another bend and civilization was gone. They were once again in the wilderness—alone.

* * *

*A highway patrol spokesman said today that fugitive Lee
Newton is being contained within a five-square mile area in
the southern part of Presley County. Law officers have been
called in for a massive manhunt in the area and are asking
residents to keep their homes and cars locked. Newton is
wanted in connection . . .*

Saturday Afternoon

6

NEAL LASSITER FOUND himself anticipating the pickup at the Blue Creek takeout. He was looking forward to seeing Jan Spencer again, even though he knew she'd just drive out of his life once he'd deposited the two women back at their car. Unless he *said* something, got her to agree to running the Narrows with him. Thinking of her cool response the day before, he wondered if he'd have the nerve to show he was interested in her. He wasn't used to situations like this anymore.

He sped down the highway, breaking the speed limit, one eye out for the sheriff or one of his deputies. At the turnoff, he whipped around the curve too fast, and Brandy, riding with her head out the passenger window, did a quick two-step to keep her balance.

"Sorry, girl." He reached over and rubbed her behind the ears, then glanced at the stick-up clock on the dashboard. He was early. He slowed down, completing the trip at a more reasonable speed.

Two large cottonwoods marked the two-track lane down to the river. The van bounced over a ridge of soil left by a road grader and eased to a stop. After killing the engine, Neal got out and wandered over to the water, but there was no sign of anyone, so he went back to the van and sat down, one leg hanging out the door.

Down near the shoreline, Brandy was nosing along,

looking for anything that might prove interesting. Every once in a while she'd stop, face pressed into a clump of weeds, her tail frozen momentarily, then as if the scent had worn out, she'd move on. Always looking for something better.

Neal reflected, watching Brandy on her search, that he used to be like that, but now he felt he'd found the something better: his place on the river. All it lacked was the right woman, but he'd probably have a devil of a time finding someone who wanted to share a life in the boondocks.

An hour passed, and the women hadn't appeared. He'd give them another thirty minutes, then go home for a while. He got out of the van, went back and kicked the tire on the trailer, then walked around it and kicked the other one for good measure.

Had they had trouble? It was a long trip for two women, but Jan seemed to know anything she'd need to know for that stretch. My gosh! She'd been on the Chattooga after all. There was nothing difficult here compared to that, even excluding Bull Sluice.

How long to wait? He drew his hands through his hair, resisting making a decision. He felt the anger rise in him. To hell with them, putting him in this position. The flare-up subsided, and he realized his teeth were clenched tight. He rubbed his hand down over one side of his face. It was a forty-five-minute trip back to his place; he was going to spend the whole day running back and forth. Thirty more minutes, then—then what? Should he come back this evening? Or tomorrow? When should he start searching the river itself? He could call the sheriff, but he himself was better at search-and-rescue than Billy Jay Ambler.

He called Brandy, who promptly came loping over. Apparently she was ready to give up looking for ultimate happiness.

The sun beat down on the gravel bar with midsummer fury, driving a sweltering Jan to drag herself upright. The world went black again. After a moment, her vision cleared, and she seized her life jacket, buckling it on as she walked, and headed for the water.

Dehydration was taking its toll. Her mouth was dry and her lips were cracked, but she was afraid of the river water. Some foreign bacteria in her system would just cause more problems. She needed to find a clean spring.

She waded into the cold water, the intrusion of her feet scattering a school of minnows. The rocks were small here where she entered the water, but she soon encountered some the size of grapefruits, which were coated with slimy moss. She slipped dizzily and almost caught herself, then one foot slithered out from under her, and she went down into the water on her knees. The current made it difficult to stand up again. Finally, she just relaxed and got her feet in front of her and let the buoyancy of her life jacket float her downstream. *Give in,* she told herself, *let it take you.* There was such an urge to fight.

She floated into a pool and was able to stand up again. The water was getting deeper, so she moved toward the side of the stream, but there the water was freckled with stagnant-looking beige foam, and she hated to walk in it. She skirted it and walked along the rocky shore till it merged into a bluff.

The rock ledges hemmed the river in, and on one of these stone faces she saw a welcome sight: the bluff bellied out and where the belly met the flat of the cliff again, half-hidden, there was a tumble of ferns and mosses growing down a crevice dripping with spring water. Well, she *hoped* it was spring water and not the septic-tank runoff from a backwoods house high on the clifftop. The water had spread out over the wall surface by the time it reached the bottom of the bluff, but she could see where it started, about fifteen feet up. And there she could get a drink.

She waded over to the wall and got one foot up on a narrow shelf of rock just above the water level and reached up for a higher ledge. Every movement seemed to sap her remaining energy but there was still an urge to fight. She dragged herself up slowly, face against the cliff, to a higher ledge. She repeated her effort again and again, working her way into the crevice, which was full of footrests and handholds where chunks of rock had broken off. She was almost there. Her hand groped upward and touched something alive. It jumped, startling her for a moment, but it was just a toad. She rested a moment, then pulled herself up.

The exertion made the water all the better when she reached it. She laid her mouth against the drip, catching the clear liquid with her tongue, funneling it in. She hovered there a long time, but finally pulled away, wishing there were some way to take some of the water with her.

She started down, which proved more difficult than going up. The water below wasn't deep enough to jump into safely, so she slowly descended.

Once off the ledge, she surveyed the river both up and down. She'd left her stuff on the gravel bar. Should she go back? What had she left behind? She pictured the camp. Her sleeping bag and the deflated air mattress. The flashlight. What about in the woods? The second sleeping bag and air mattress were still there, she was sure. She squinted her eyes, trying to recall. What about the life jacket? Susan wouldn't have left it behind, unless . . . Jan shook her head to dispel the dark thoughts settling there. *Think about now,* she commanded herself. *Was there anything else at the campsite?*

Yes, Jan thought, *there was the gun.* She looked up at the sky. It had to be past noon. Could she walk to civilization before dark? No way to tell, but she did know she didn't want to be out here alone without that gun tonight.

Going upstream was difficult. Why hadn't she brought the gun with her? *Stupid,* she chided herself. At one place, she ventured to the edge because she saw some blackberries. Most were dried out, but a few were still succulent. Her grandmother had used blackberry juice to cure diarrhea; she hoped the fruit would be as good for what ailed her. She gobbled the berries down greedily. They did little to ease her hunger, but they were better than nothing. Overhead there were clusters of wild grapes, but it was too early in the summer and they were still green. An aluminum can gleamed beneath the blackberry brambles. The litter she'd condemned the day before was now a sight for sore eyes. Her hand snaked in, carefully missing the thorns, and pulled the can out. This would hold water. So what if it was an old used can. She was beyond squeamishness. She needed more water or she wasn't going to get out of here.

She moved back downstream and started up the bluff to the spring, climbing with the can awkwardly clasped in one hand. Nearly there, her grip tightened and the can shot out, bouncing off the wall. A grab for it tipped her balance, and she followed the can's descent, bumping and grating against the rock. She hit the water hard and awkwardly, legs and arms askew. The can landed a short distance away, bobbing in the water.

Jan tired to haul herself upright to retrieve the can before the current took it, but her whole body rebelled with pain, and she watched as the can drifted away.

Downstream Susan numbly watched the overgrown banks slide by.

"Where were you going?" the man asked her.

"Just canoeing," she said after a moment, surprised to hear him ask her a question. He'd hardly said a word all day.

"I mean where was your takeout?"

"I think we passed it." She *knew* they'd passed it. Even before they'd gotten to the site of the raft race; she'd recognized the old bridge pilings Neal Lassiter had mentioned as a landmark. The takeout had been just beyond them. There'd been no sign of him. It was way too early.

"I'm going to pull in here. We can eat. And wait." He maneuvered the canoe under a canopy of low-hanging branches. She hadn't even noticed the creek outlet up which he was now forging his way. It was apparent that he knew the river, or at least knew what to be looking for. Their progress against the current was slow, so he slid out of the canoe into the calf-deep water and pushed the boat along until he saw a spot where he could push it onto the bar. "Get out," he ordered.

She didn't move very fast, a little act of defiance at his tone, but it was wasted on him.

"What's in here?" he asked, indicating a plastic bag he'd unloaded.

She shrugged. "Why don't you look?"

He narrowed his eyes and clenched his mouth into a tight line. One finger went up as if he were going to make a point, but he held it back.

He opened one of the bags and looked in.

"We were traveling light," Susan said.

He pulled an apple from the bag, rubbed it on his pant leg, then crunched loudly into it.

"Why are you doing this?" she asked, trying to keep her voice even.

"Better to travel after dark."

"No, I mean why did you kidnap me? I'll just slow you down."

The finger raised again, while he swallowed. "You were a gift from Providence."

She gave a little snort. "I could hardly be that."

"God presented you to me for protection."

"I'm not a very good bodyguard."

"Not that kind of protection."

"What do you mean then?"

He didn't answer, but she didn't really need a picture drawn. A hostage was a special kind of protection, tying the hands of the law-enforcement people.

After a moment she asked, "How about some cheese? There's some in the cooler."

He nodded.

She took the cheese out and fished out a paring knife. She felt the cool steel in her hand, wondering. But how could she kill someone with a paring knife? It would take multiple stabs, and by then he'd have disarmed her. She thought about hiding it on her person somewhere, but she had no pockets. She sighed inwardly and handed him a chunk of cheese, then cut one for herself. The first bite made her realize she was hungry.

"What's your name?"

"Susan." She hesitated a moment, weighing whether she wanted to know his name, wondering if somehow that would make their relationship different. But she asked.

"Lee." He bit noisily into the apple again. "We're going to stay here a while. Until evening."

It was that raft race. It had scared him. Somewhere downstream there were throngs of people at the finish line, and he wanted to avoid them. He was definitely on the run from someone.

He stood up and tossed his apple core far into the woods, then walked over to where she was squatting on the gravel. "C'mon," he said.

"Where?"

He reached down and grabbed her arm, yanking her upward. "Don't question me." She gasped involuntarily and looked down at her arm. The imprint of his fingers still showed as a pale impression on her sunburned skin.

"I said c'mon." He pushed her.

"What are you going to do?" Her voice had become slightly shrill.

He didn't answer, just continued to prod her along toward the shade of the woods, where he ordered her to sit down with her back to a tree, facing into the woods, then proceeded to tie her wrists behind it.

Susan protested. "You don't have to do this. Where can I go?"

He worked silently until he had her firmly secured. She strained against the rope and twisted her neck around to see what he was going to do.

He walked down to the shoreline and began to strip off his clothes: first the boots, then he grasped his T-shirt at the neckband and pulled it up and over his head, the muscles in his back tightening as he did so. His blondness, spotlighted by a narrow shaft of sun on the gravel bar, was how she'd always imagined some god from Norse mythology. This Lee person, if he'd had the right kind of costume, looked straight out of a picturebook. He was going swimming; she didn't watch any further, but tried to get comfortable against the tree.

She rested her head and closed her eyes, conscious of the weeds which sprouted up beneath her at the base of the tree. Her arm began to tickle where one of the grassy strands brushed against it. *Agony,* she thought, unable to reach the itch. It was hot, even here in the shade. Perspiration dappled her face and she began to think about it and immediately her forehead began to itch. She drew her knee up and rubbed it. *Think of something else,* she thought. *Distract yourself, think of the forest.*

High overhead the *tic, tic, tic* of a cicada chorus began in unison, then ended in a strident buzz, while nearby another similar refrain began. Some dry leaves rustled, catching her attention.

A snake was slithering toward her.

Reason fled, and she screamed, "A snake!" With her legs she began thrashing at it, beating at the ground to scare it away.

Behind her, she heard Lee splashing out of the water, and in a moment he was beside her, naked and dripping, his knife in hand.

"There," she gasped, gesturing with her head and shrinking against the tree trunk with her back.

The snake was slinking away by this time, but Lee seized it and held the writhing thing up in front of her, bringing it near her face. His eyes glistened as Susan twisted away, and he followed her movements with his hand. She could see the snake's forked tongue flicking toward her. The tail end of the snake dragged against her body, back and forth as Lee tracked her head's movements with the ugly creature. *Flick, flick.* The tongue came close.

"Behold the serpent, woman, Satan incarnate," Lee said, his voice modulated to a hiss.

Finally he stopped tormenting her and with a bare foot on the snake, drew his knife slowly across the shiny patterned body, severing the head. He then put the point of his knife in the head right behind the eyes and shoved it in her face.

He's crazy, she thought. Her mouth twisted in disgust, and a shiver ran down her spine. Then suddenly, in spite of her fear, or perhaps because of it, she felt a chuckle start to bubble up in her. The situation was ludicrous: a naked man hovering in front of her, waving a snake head in her face. She bit her cheeks to suppress the giggle, knowing instinctively that Lee Newton wasn't a man to laugh at.

She closed her eyes and took a deep breath to get control over herself, and was aware that he had moved closer. When she looked up again, any thought of humor in the situation vanished. Her captor knelt down, straddling her legs at the knees. His face was red. The knife point lifted her T-shirt while he undid the front fastener on her shorts with his other hand.

"Don't," she said. "Please don't."

It wasn't Susan's words that stopped Lee Newton. It was an internal struggle. As he undid her shorts, a vision began to form in his mind of the evil snake. Had he killed it? Or was it taking over his body? He felt himself become tumescent as he knelt there. It was the serpent, a fiery devil raging within him, tempting him to indulge his weakness. Satan was tempting him as surely as he had tempted Adam at the beginning of time.

The fire of the demon singed his loins, and Lee fought to quench the flame before he gave in to his unholy desire. He rose, naked before the Jezebel, and behind his eyelids he saw her stroke her milky thighs, inviting him to plant his seed in her.

No! he silently screamed at the cloven-hooved demon dancing in his head. His seed already resided in the belly of Ruthie and, if God so willed, soon in Joanna as well. They were worthy of his seed, and their children would be blessed.

Still the vile images flashed across his mind. His head lolled back as he struggled to fight off the demon lust. His knife hand flew up, and he jammed the weapon blindly into the unholy figure that now taunted him from the tree. He would kill the mocker of God!

He pulled the knife back and the impaled snake head dropped to the ground, but the fiery devil still writhed wantonly before him, beckoning. Lee stabbed at the tree again, twisting the knife to pull it out.

His erection began to disappear as he repeatedly thrust his knife in a frenzy. He was winning! The vision was beginning to pale, then it was gone. He sank against the tree, then without a look back, left the woman behind.

Was she a trial God had sent him rather than a blessing? He sank down to pray. God would tell him what to do about her.

"Morning, Ted."

It was Jason Sims, the next-door neighbor. Ted was getting ready to mow the lawn, pouring gasoline in the mower.

"Do you have a file I could borrow?"

Ted stood up and went over to his toolbox on the utility shelves. "There should be one around here somewhere," he said, with a vagueness that was less than honest. He knew precisely where the file was: on the second tray of the toolbox. "Here you go," he said, handing it to the young man, who seemed still to have peach fuzz on his face instead of whiskers. Youngsters, he'd called them the other day. Susan had chided him, saying he sounded like an old man. Sometimes Melissa, Jason's wife, would go outside in a bikini to sunbathe. How long had it been since Susan had sunbathed? Years. She'd long since decided that the sun was probably less friend, more enemy, just waiting to encircle her neck with wrinkles, dry her face to parchment, and patch her skin with age spots. She was probably down there in that canoe right now, her creamy skin gleaming with sunscreen.

It was the first time he'd actually pictured Susan and Jan on the river, in the canoe, and he wondered if they were enjoying themselves roughing it. In their place, he thought, he'd be miserable. His idea of roughing it was having to watch a black-and-white television.

"—oughta hang that guy when they catch him," Jason was saying.

Ted nodded, only then tuning in from his reverie, but unwilling to admit he hadn't been listening.

"And they better bring out all the reinforcements they can to track him down. If those guys think they can kill a cop and get away with it, hey man, we're in big trouble."

Ted rocked back on his heels and frowned, continuing to nod.

"Well, guess I'd better quit talking," Jason said. "I gotta sharpen the blades on my lawn mower. It won't cut diddlysquat. See you later. And thanks," he added, saluting with the file.

Lunch provided the next milestone of Ted's day, an automatic time filler. He stacked bologna, cheese, lettuce, onion, and tomato on whole wheat bread, got a beer and a bag of chips, and wandered first out into the backyard to admire the freshly cut grass, then into the house after deciding it was too hot outdoors.

He had nothing to do, he realized, as he looked for the television remote control. Giving up, he stooped in front of the set, holding his glasses so the bifocal lens was higher, and finally located the power spot. Whatever happened to dials and knobs? he wondered. Something a guy could get his hand on. He settled back in his chair with his sandwich and beer.

Outside of the office, Susan planned his life—their lives. Other than watching television, he had no hobbies. How had it come to this sorry pass? That his whole life revolved around the office?

He thought of George Self, a guy he'd known at work. Died the week after he got his gold watch. What was it he'd heard? They give a guy a watch when he no longer needed one. George really hadn't needed one. Was he himself one of those guys who would die soon after retirement? Ted wondered. Or maybe sooner.

As if the thought were prophetic, a pain hit him in the middle of his chest. He broke out in a sweat at its intensity. It gripped his insides and tore at them.

He clumsily put his beer down, wiped his forehead, and gasped. *Oh, Lord,* he thought, *it must be a heart attack.*

And I'm alone. I'm going to die here alone, and they won't find me until Susan gets home. He pressed on his chest, got up carefully, and began to search for his keys. Where in God's name were they? He pawed through the things on the desk in the den, shoving papers on the floor as he looked.

The pain remained steady as he went to the kitchen. He suddenly remembered where they were. Upstairs on the dresser, along with his wallet. *Can't go up the stairs,* he thought. His breath was coming in short gasps. There was an extra car key on a keyholder in the utility room. He plucked it off its peg with a trembling hand and went to the garage. *Hang my driver's license,* he thought.

Once he was behind the wheel, he lifted his glasses to wipe his eyes, then backed the car out. *The pain!* he thought. *I've never felt anything like it.* It was excruciating.

The doors to the emergency room swung open automatically as he approached, letting out a burst of frigid air. His shirt was wet with perspiration and he shivered at the cold. Stiff-legged, clasping his chest, he approached the desk.

"May I help you?" a man at the reception desk asked.

"I think I'm having a heart attack," he muttered through tight lips, almost afraid to talk.

"Right in here, sir." He hurried Ted into a curtain-enclosed cubicle, calling for reinforcements.

A doctor appeared. "Do a CBC and hook him up to a monitor," she ordered, then disappeared into another cubicle, where a child was wailing over a mother's attempts at soothing.

The man hooked Ted up to a monitor, then a woman appeared with a tray of tubes, apparently from the lab. She stuck him and drew blood, thanked him, and left. Meanwhile, another young woman had appeared and began to take down information about him: who he was, whether he had insurance, next of kin.

A short time later, the doctor reappeared, checked the chart, looked at the cardiac strip. Ted was lying on a gurney, and she palpated under his ribs, not saying anything. Ted flinched at the pressure.

The doctor looked at the chart again, then pulled up a

chair and sat down. "I don't think it's your heart, Mr. Morrow. Could be acute gastritis, but it's possibly chole-cystitis."

"What's that?"

"Inflamed gallbladder."

"Does that mean I need to have my gallbladder out?"

The doctor evaded the question. "I'd like to admit you to the hospital and run some more tests and keep an eye on you."

Ted frowned. He didn't like the idea of going into the hospital on a Saturday. More than likely they wouldn't run any tests till Monday morning. Still, he hated to think of being home alone if he had another—whatever it was. The thought settled it. A clerk did the rest of the paperwork, then a nurse wheeled him to a room. After she left and he'd changed to a hospital gown, he made a phone call.

"Jennifer?"

"Hi, Daddy. How are you?"

"Well, not too good maybe. I just checked into the hospital."

"Oh, no. Daddy, what's the matter?"

"Nothing to be alarmed about. I was having some pains and I thought since I was alone—"

"Alone? Where's Mom?"

"This is the weekend she went canoeing."

"Oh that's right. Poor Daddy. I can be up there in—"

"Now that's not necessary, honey. You've got things to do and I'm in good hands."

"Are you sure, Dad?"

"Yes, I'm sure. I just thought someone ought to know where I was. I didn't want you to worry in case you called."

"I appreciate that. I actually was thinking of calling later. So, um, what have the doctors said?"

"She doesn't think it's my heart. Maybe my gallbladder. They want to run some more tests."

"I'm glad it wasn't a heart attack."

"Me too. Well, honey, how're you doin'? How's the job?"

"Just fine. It was really tiring this week because the

senator has been getting things organized here, moving things to storage to make more room for campaign stuff, and I've been buying media."

"Buying media?"

"Purchasing time for radio and television spots."

"I'm impressed. You're beginning to speak jargon," he said with a laugh.

They talked a few minutes longer, with Ted again assuring his daughter she needn't come up, then he hung up and lay back on the starchy sheets. He raised the head of the bed and pulled the little television over in front of him. Cute idea. He could hear it without disturbing the man in the other bed, who was making weird sleeping noises inside his curtained-off area nearest the window.

Just then a woman in a blue smock came in with a tray. "You're late getting in here, but I managed to get you some supper." Her tone was confidential, as if it were a special favor, but he imagined he'd pay royally for it. He almost expected the woman to chuck him under the chin, the way his Aunt Mabel used to.

She lifted a cover from the plate. Smothered minute steak, mashed potatoes, and carrots, butterscotch pudding for dessert.

He pressed the control for the television with his left hand, while he ate with his right. Saturday television was for the birds. He finally settled on an old Randolph Scott movie on an independent channel.

Susan sat frozen, almost afraid to breathe after Lee walked away. She didn't know what had caused him to leave, but relief washed over her. He could have been stabbing her as easily as the tree. Whatever had come over him, and whatever had saved her, one thing was certain: he was a madman. She was sure he'd been having hallucinations because of his muttering. After a long while, she strained around to see what he was doing now.

Lee, fully clothed again, had made a pad out of clothes he'd found in a plastic bag in the canoe and was now asleep on the gravel. She too could use some sleep, but she didn't think she could doze off sitting bolt upright, tied to a tree with a madman nearby and snakes lurking in the grass. She ached with tiredness, but at the same time her muscles felt wired. She squirmed first to one side, then the other, trying to still the nervousness screaming through her body.

Behind her, she twisted her hands together, flexing the fingers to pop the joints. As she did so, she felt the knot slip a little. She drew her fingers together, trying to make her hand as small as possible, cupping it first this way, then moving it that. Was the rope loosening? At least fifteen minutes passed; her wrists ached from her efforts, but the rope was as tight as before. She sighed and stopped moving.

Glints of filtered sunlight painted the forest floor with dabs of light. Nearby something glittered. Her eyes narrowed, attempting to bring it into focus. She edged her foot out to its limit and scuffed around the shiny spot, dragging whatever it was toward her. As she pulled it closer, she saw it was a jagged shard of glass from a bottle. Like a contortionist, she used her leg to pull it almost under her, then she began to edge her body around the tree. She was facing the sleeping Lee now, and her hands were on the forest side of the tree. Awkwardly, without the benefit of her vision, her fingers searched the ground till they found the glass. She grasped the shard but it slipped from her hand. Locating it again, she began to saw at the rope. With each movement, the glass pressed sharply into her hand as well. She wondered if she was bleeding.

After a few moments she could tell with her index finger that she wasn't making any progress, so she tried a new tack: she began to scrape at the rope. Maybe the glass would abrade the fibers gradually. Her wrists and fingers cramped, and she dropped the glass again. Her hands searched the ground within reach, but it wasn't there. She scooted around the tree on her buttocks again and saw the fragment. It had bounced away from the base of the tree, just barely out of reach. Once again she used her foot to pull it over, then she scooted back around, praying that Lee would remain asleep.

The shard was in hand again, wet and sticky from her blood. Slowly the fibers began to part, until, with a sharp jerk, the rope broke. Quietly she stood up, rubbing her wrists, aware that it would be hard to get across the gravel without making a sound. And was the canoe her best bet for escape? Perhaps she should just go through the woods.

No, the canoe would put the greatest distance between them. She took a tentative step onto the rocks, then another, shifting her weight carefully, her heart pounding.

It seemed to take forever to get to the canoe, but finally she reached it. She glanced at Lee; he still hadn't moved. This was it. One big push would have to do because of the sound the boat would make on the gravel; no one could sleep through it.

She threw all her weight against the prow and the canoe surged backward with a horrible screech, setting her nerves afire like fingernails on a blackboard. Lee was up instantly, looking fully awake.

The boat was in the water now, and she shoved it in deeper, hurling herself into it as the current caught it. Her breath was coming in gasps. Lee was to the shore, and Susan was in trouble. The water was too shallow to float the boat with her weight in it, and she heard the scrape of aluminum against the gravel creek bottom. She grabbed the paddle and tried to pole the craft into deeper water, but just then Lee put his hand on the gunwale to pull the canoe back. Susan stood up, the boat rocking precariously under her, and swung the paddle at his head.

His right hand shot up and caught it easily, and he yanked her forward across one of the struts. She fell into the bottom of the boat, letting go of the paddle, then scrambled up and jumped out of the canoe, which without her weight, began to float downstream again.

Lee grabbed it and tried to get her, too, but she jerked away and took off like a shot toward the woods. She heard him beach the canoe and knew he would be coming after her.

Her chances were slim. She knew that. His more muscular body was well adapted for the chase. When she got back home she was going to begin the exercise program she'd been putting off. The thought was fleeting, a pinprick of regret that she was out of shape; her main thought was searching for a direction to take or a place to hide.

The dense undergrowth hindered her speed. She tripped over a grapevine, which snaked across the path at ground level, and fell flat, the wind knocked out of her. She sucked in air, then clambered up and kept going. She tired to ignore the pain in her right knee, but each step sent a shock wave through her leg. Gasping for air, she scrambled over a rotten log, ducking through a welter of leaves. Her heart felt as if it were going to explode.

Lee caught up with her, as she had been certain he would. The hand seized her by the arm with bone-wrenching strength and yanked her around toward him. Tired but galvanized by her fear, she struggled against his grip, kicking and hitting, but he was too strong, and she realized she might as well give up—for now.

Saturday Night

7

THE MOON WASHED over them as Lee and Susan drifted through the night. The river was a black ribbon serpentining through the textured landscape. Occasional ripples shimmered with sequins of moonlight. They hadn't come to any heavy water in hours.

Susan was sitting in the wet bottom of the boat, leaning on the bow seat with her arms clasped around her drawn-up legs, trying to keep warm. Her chin rested on her knees, and she intermittently closed her eyes, trying unsuccessfully to doze off. The earlier incident was far behind them, but the escape attempt, though foiled, had left her feeling charged up, making it hard to relax.

"You're the one who shot that highway patrolman, aren't you?" she asked him against the sound of the bullfrogs along the banks. Occasionally the canoe would come too close to one, and the croaking would cease as the frog slid with a plop into the water.

"Yes," he said.

"Why? You must know that no one ever gets away with that."

"God is with me."

The answer angered her. "How can you kill a man, and then use God as an excuse?"

"You're uninitiated. The Cataclysm is at hand, and some choose blindness. So shall they go down."

"If God will protect you, why did you bring me along as protection?" she asked.

He hesitated. "You are somehow part of His plan. The Lord presented you to me. I merely had to be open to His suggestion."

"And the death of the highway patrolman? Was that part of His plan?"

"Yes. He thrust a nigger in my face to remind me that we must cleanse our country of the mud people and the Jews. They're all the enemies of white Christian Americans."

She had a hard time keeping her mouth shut. It was the nature of humans to feel self-centered. Everyone was looking for something that set him apart, made him a little special in an overwhelming world. She could understand that—the temptation to believe in one's own superiority, the need to belong to the right group. *If everyone were all one color or one religion, people would find other ways to differentiate themselves,* she reflected. *Elongated necks, right-handedness—whatever it might be*. Most people contented themselves with the occasional smug, prejudicial remark, but Lee had taken his hatred to the limit. He was insane . . . how could he believe his own words?

These thoughts were raging in her, wanting to be spit out, but if ever she needed to squelch her words, it was now. She couldn't argue with a crazy person, let alone one with a gun.

The peaceful sound of the water dripping off his paddle as he raised and lowered it offered a sharp contrast to his next words, uttered in an offhand way: "We are to cleanse the earth of the enemies to prepare for the New Order. One hundred and forty-four thousand of us will live through the coming Tribulation, and by our acts will we be known to the Almighty."

Anger flushed through her again. She couldn't resist a question. "And just why do you think you've been chosen?" Her voice sounded bitter.

"White Christian Americans are descendants of Abel, not of the serpent seed of Cain. When the Jews repudiated Jesus they were proving that they were descendants of the serpent. We Caucasians are descended from one of the lost tribes. Some of them escaped and went to the British Isles and Western Europe. God gave them grace to come to a new land, the Chosen Land, the U.S. of A." His voice had risen, a stark contrast to the quiet of the river. "And at precisely nine A.M. Wednesday we will begin the process."

Process? She waited a moment, letting it sink in, then asked. "What are you going to do on Wednesday?"

"We're making a strike on ZOG."

"What's ZOG?"

He snorted at her ignorance. "It's the Jews; they've taken over the government. The Zionist Occupational Government. The ones who aren't Jews are lackeys to them." His words were filled with venom.

She could hear the hatred and frustration in his voice, and it was frightening. He proceeded to tell her about his rise to leadership and how he'd been chosen to lead the mission Wednesday—it was part of his testimony to God. His voice mirrored his excitement, and he became wound up in his diatribe.

They came to a shoal, the water slipping restlessly downstream into the night, and he quit talking to maneuver the canoe.

She blinked hard, feeling as if she were awakening from a dream, and was surprised to find herself still on the river. She had a sudden, desperate longing for Ted, a need to talk to him about this crazy man sitting behind her, to share with him her fear and disgust. Ted. He wouldn't even realize anything was wrong yet.

Wednesday. And this was Saturday, or perhaps it was past midnight and they'd slipped quietly into Sunday. Wednesday. It would all be over by then. One way or the other. "When will we get where we're going?"

"I'm rendezvousing at River's Bend on Tuesday. We'll stay off the river tomorrow, then canoe through the morning on Monday. That'll get us through the Narrows—I want to do that in the daylight."

"The Narrows?" That was the stretch Neal Lassiter had mentioned. "Aren't those rapids pretty bad?"

"No problem. I've never capsized there."

"But we don't have life jackets."

"Don't worry. You'll have the ride of your life."

I'm already having that, she thought glumly.

Jan had struggled to another gravel bar similar to the one where she and Susan had spent last night—a hundred years ago it seemed now.

Well, she was surviving. That was the bottom line for just about everything.

A flash of anger toward the absent Susan struck her, but Jan quickly quashed the feeling, knowing it to be irrational. *She might be in worse circumstances than I am,* Jan thought, unwilling to dwell on what those circumstances might be. She crossed her arms and hugged herself close.

To go back upstream to the sleeping bags and the gun was beyond her strength, but her skin was chilled in the night air. She stood up and felt as if she were going to be sick again. Quickly she squatted down and put her head between her knees. *Please dear God, not that again.* The wave of nausea passed, and she stood up again, hesitating before she retreated, shivering, into the woods, where she cleared a small area of rocks and sticks, then raked leaves into a huge nest with her feet, removed her wet clothes, and climbed in. She had to get warm.

The rocks crunched under the tires as Neal drove down near the water. His headlamps spotlighted two men loading a johnboat into the bed of a parked truck. He remembered it from that afternoon.

Just then his friend Randy Darch pulled up behind him, killed the engine on his Chevy truck, and climbed out. Neal was going to leave his van there, and Randy would transport him back home. In the morning he'd begin his search, and this way his truck would be waiting for him at journey's end. The two walked toward the men with the boat.

"Howdy," Neal said. He vaguely knew them, had seen them around.

"Howdy yourself. Lassiter, ain't it?" the redheaded one said.

He nodded. "You out froggin'?" he asked, noticing a gig in the back of the truck.

"Yep. Gigged us a bellyful."

"You seen one of my canoes?"

"Nope. Ain't seen nary." He glanced at his companion. "River's as quiet as death, ain't it, Three-Fingers?"

Three-Fingers nodded.

"You been up there all day?"

"Two. But we spent some time up on Tunnell Creek. They probably passed us right by."

Neal grunted, running his hand along the rim of the truck bed. Randy asked the men a couple of questions, then he and Neal went back to Randy's truck.

"Those guys are real scuzzballs," Randy said as he started the engine. "The sheriff thinks they're pirating along the river, but he can't catch 'em at it." He snorted. "And no wonder. Eugene Rice's re—"

"He's the redhead?"

"Yeah. He's related to Connie Fisher."

"Who's she?" Neal asked.

"Man, you're out of touch. She's the cute little clerk down at the sheriff's office."

"I think I know who you mean."

"Well, somehow or other she's a cousin of Eugene's. Maybe one of those by-marriage-once-removed sorts of things. Emory Todd told me they were related though."

"So she could just tip Eugene off if the sheriff was planning to move in on him and Three-Fingers."

"Yep."

"Would she do that?"

"Man, blood is thicker than water every time, especially around here. Believe it." Randy, who was in his early thirties, had migrated to the area from Chicago for many of the same reasons Neal had. He was a carpenter, self-employed.

"Seems like everybody out here but us is kin."

Randy laughed. "If I could find me a woman"—he did a fair imitation of the local accent—"I'd be happy to get integrated into the clan."

"Well, the clerk—uh, Connie—is too young for you, you ol' reprobate."

They'd reached the highway, and Randy gunned the truck as it hit the pavement.

Forty-five minutes later, back at Neal's place, Randy let him out. Brandy came trotting over to greet him.

"I owe you one, buddy," Neal said to Randy. "Why don't you come on in for a brew?"

"Sure thing." He hopped out of the truck. "Hope you find those two women okay."

"Probably just some misunderstanding about the takeout. Jeez! Will they be mad if they've been waiting somewhere else for me." He grimaced. He hoped that's all it was: a misunderstanding.

Sunday Morning

8

TED'S HOSPITAL ROOMMATE died in the night. The morning nurse discovered it when she came in to take vital signs. Ted hadn't heard anything over there behind the curtain, no struggle as he tried to hold on to life, no death rattles. The man had simply slipped into a deeper sleep.

A hushed flurry of activity woke Ted, then they wheeled the bed out. And that was that. It was a while before the nurse was able to finish her rounds. Death had interrupted the routine.

After breakfast the housekeeper came to disinfect the room. She efficiently began wiping down every surface.

"Do you suppose you could get hold of a Sunday paper for me?" Ted asked.

"You just press that button there, and the nurse can probably help you." She kept wiping.

He pushed the call button and asked for a paper.

Thirty minutes later, the nurse bustled in, her uniform rustling, and handed him a paper. Another one followed on her heels. "It's time for our bath, Mr. Morrow." He must have looked startled because she laughed heartily as she opened his nightstand and pulled out a bar of soap. "I think you can manage all by yourself. Towels are on the rack." She pointed at the bathroom.

He took the bar of soap and acted as if he were going to

comply until she walked out of the room, then he settled back in bed with the paper.

The cleaning lady, who was gathering up her supplies, chuckled. "Ol' Mrs. Frazier'll get you if you don't follow orders."

Ted grinned at her, pushed his glasses up on his nose, and started thumbing through the paper, looking for the sports section. He pulled it out. The lead piece was about yesterday's baseball game. Down at the bottom of the page a photo caught his attention. There was a bikini-clad girl with a captain's hat standing on a raft, saluting. Ted looked her over with interest, then read the caption: CONTESTANTS LINE UP SATURDAY FOR THE GREAT INTERNATIONAL RAFT RACE NOVELTY EVENT HELD ANNUALLLY ON THE BIG PINE RIVER. He returned to the picture and picked out a bathtub and a floating coffin. A smile turned up one corner of his mouth. People were nuts! His eyes drifted to a spot of bold red-and-white in the picture. It was a striped shirt like Susan's. He looked closer, taking hold of his glasses. It *was* Susan's. Susan and Jan had gotten mixed up in a crazy raft race. His gaze moved to the other end of the canoe, and his mouth went slack. That sure as hell wasn't Jan! He looked back at Susan, just to make sure it was indeed his wife. The quality of the picture wasn't good, but he knew that shirt, the shape of her head, her posture. No doubt about it. His wife was at the Great International Raft Race with another man.

Neal didn't sleep well, but it wasn't nightmares that disturbed him. He was worried about what had happened to those two women.

He wasn't a pessimist, but he felt bad vibes as he tied a cooler into the canoe early Sunday morning. Meeting Three-Fingers and Eugene at the takeout hadn't helped; instead, it made him especially uneasy.

When he had asked whether they'd seen the canoe, Eugene said no. Neal hadn't mentioned how many people were in it, yet Eugene had said, "*They* passed us right by"—plural. Had he seen the two women? If so, why had he lied? Or was it just an accident of speech?

Brandy waded in after Neal as he pushed off. "Go home, Brandy," he ordered. Her expression changed from one of happy anticipation to a woebegone look, and she turned, with only a glance back over her shoulder to see if he'd changed his mind, and headed for the house. Normally he might take her along, but he didn't know what he might find. He might need the space in the canoe.

The river almost made him forget his task. It was an instant balm for whatever might be bothering him. He'd done a lot of dope in 'Nam; it had taken the edge off the fear and made some of the things he did bearable. It had also helped him survive emotionally, so he had no regrets. Once back, he'd continued to dabble in drugs, had tried the usual things, plus a lot of weird stuff his friends in California had manufactured. It was a wonder they hadn't all croaked.

When he'd moved to the Midwest, he quit the heavy stuff. Then teaching school put him on the wagon almost permanently. He figured he wasn't a good example to the kids; even though they wouldn't know what he was doing in his spare time, it was the principle of the thing.

Now if he found a patch of wild marijuana, he sometimes picked enough for a smoke or two, but for the most part he didn't need it. The river was his high.

He made good time and within three hours he saw the remains of the women's campfire. A sleeping bag lay nearby.

He grounded the canoe and disembarked to have a look around, frowning when he saw the gun. He picked it up to examine it and was relieved that it hadn't been fired.

He scouted the area and found the second sleeping bag in the woods. He rolled it up and carried it, along with the rest of the gear, to his canoe, wondering where the rest of the women's things were. And what about the women themselves? Why had they abandoned this equipment? Consternation showed on his face as he shoved the boat off the gravel, climbed aboard, and started downstream again, looking for any signs that they had traveled that way.

Neal saw her before she saw him. She was lying on the
rocks in the morning sun, warming herself like a lazy
alligator, he thought, but of course much prettier. The
canoe, he noticed, was nowhere to be seen. He started to
paddle right up to the bar, then thought better of it and
called to her.

As he drew closer, the lovely image he'd seen from a
distance melted into a more disturbing picture. Her skin was
blistered from the sun, and her lips were cracked.

She lifted her head at his call, then sat up. Her face
crinkled up like an old lady's at the sight of him, and she
began to cry. "I thought no one was every going to come
along here." He'd grounded the canoe, jumped out, and
moved over beside her, kneeling down.

"What happened?" he asked, his brow furrowed with
concern.

His question only made her cry harder. "Two men . . . I
think they've taken Susan."

"What do you mean 'think'?"

Jan's mouth quivered. "She disappeared early yesterday.
The canoe, too. I was throwing up all night, and when I
could finally get up, she was gone. They probably took her
and—" She started crying again, and Neal put his arms
around her gently and pulled her to him. He stroked her
back with one hand until finally she began to relax in his
arms. "It's okay," he kept repeating, rocking her slightly.

"Do you have some water?" she asked.

"You bet." He hated to leave her, but he pulled back and
put a hand on her shoulders in a steadying gesture, then
stood up and went to the canoe.

She grabbed the water bottle greedily when he returned.

"Take it slow now," he said. He reached out and picked
a tick off her arm and squashed it with his fingernail on a
rock.

She nodded, wiping her mouth with her forefinger. "It's
just so good." After a moment, a pinched expression
crossed her face, and she put her hand on her stomach. "I
think I'm going to be sick again."

It was a false alarm, though, and when her features

relaxed, Neal asked why she thought the two men had something to do with Susan's disappearance.

She briefly described the encounter on the gravel bar, then said, "The one guy was really mad."

"Redheaded guy?"

She nodded. "You know who he is?"

"Yes. I saw him last night at the takeout, but Susan wasn't with him."

"I'm so worried about her."

"Let's get you into the canoe and we'll go into town and report this to the sheriff." He helped steady her as she stood. "Wait. There's another tick."

Her mouth drew down, and she lifted her shirt, exposing her midriff to reveal a spatter of red insect bites. "I spent the night in a pile of leaves in the woods."

Neal clucked his tongue. "We'd better check you over. Don't want you to get tick fever on top of everything else. Wait here." He went to the canoe and got a first-aid kit he'd brought along.

Jan sat quietly while he removed several ticks.

"That's all I can see. You want to look yourself over better?" he asked. "I'll turn my back."

After a few minutes she said, "Okay. I think I've got them all off."

He dabbed calamine lotion on her other bites. She flinched when he touched one of her ribs.

"Sorry," he said.

"That's where I hit the rocks when that man threw me down. There, and here." She extended her scraped arm, and he examined it, again clucking in sympathy.

Neal snapped the first-aid kit shut, then helped her stand again and supported her as she made her way to the canoe.

"I'm sorry I started blubbering like an idiot when I saw you, but it was such a relief to see someone. And you, especially."

Her words made something in his heart jump. "You just lie down—here, take my hat," he said once Jan was in the canoe. He settled his baseball cap on her head with both hands, pulling the bill low over her eyes, then urged the canoe into the water, wading in after it. The boat dipped as he climbed in and took his place.

He could see her relaxing as his paddle began to shoot them forward with powerful strokes. They'd report the incident, then he might go looking for Eugene and Three-Fingers himself. A kernel of rage was beginning to heat up in the pit of his belly.

Lee had found a campsite shortly after dawn.

It had been over twenty-four hours since Susan had slept, but she was so keyed up sleep seemed impossible.

The food from the plastic bags was all gone. Last night in the dark, he'd handed her something to eat. She'd smelled it. Unmistakably dog food. He was already chewing on it.

"I can't eat this," she told him.

"Won't hurt you," he said, shoving some more in his mouth.

"But it's dog food."

"Won't hurt you."

She'd thought it over for a moment. She needed her strength if she was to get away from him, so she'd put one piece in her mouth. Her cheeks seemed to shrivel up as she tried to chew it. She'd managed to get down a few morsels, thinking back to her comment to Jan—an eternity ago—about being svelte. She was well on her way.

Jan. Where was she now? Had she gotten over her illness and made it back to civilization? Or was the canoe-rental man—she could no longer remember his name—was he wondering about their absence by now? Did Ted know she was missing?

Jan surely couldn't be in worse circumstances than she was—tied to a tree while her captor went foraging. He soon appeared carrying some blackberries. He fed them to her, then went to a pool of water that had gathered behind the gravel bar they were on. There he dug with a stick and unearthed a tiny freshwater clam, pried it open with the blade of his knife, and popped it in his mouth. Susan was glad he'd given her the blackberries.

A kingfisher landed on a piece of driftwood nearby,

watching the activity in the water for a moment, then taking off again.

Lee continued to dig clams. "You want some of these?" he asked.

"No." She wasn't that hungry yet. Maybe years of intermittent dieting had prepared her to tolerate this gnawing in her stomach.

"Squeamish?"

"Yes."

"I'll catch a fish and cook it for you."

He dug around in the water until he managed to get some kind of a larva and put it on the hook and line he took from the handle of his knife. He waded off downstream out of sight.

They were on a creek again, not the main river, so there wasn't much hope of someone coming by, but she couldn't help wishing. After fifteen minutes the only person who appeared was Lee, wading back, triumphantly dangling a fish from the line. For just a moment, he seemed like a little boy.

He built a small fire, stuck the fish on a stick, and roasted it, head and all. Then he laid it on a rock, deboned it, cut it up, and served a chunk of it to her on the point of his knife, the same knife that had held the snake's severed head.

Her throat tightened at the thought, but she put it out of her mind and seized the food with her teeth. The juicy morsel was hot, and she moved it around with her tongue for a moment so it wouldn't burn the inside of her mouth. It tasted good, and she was glad when he offered her another bite, this one cooler. It didn't take long to eat the whole fish, with him thrusting chunks of it into her mouth.

Lee wiped his knife back and forth on his pants to clean it before he shoved it into its sheath. Next he rolled the canoe over and lifted it, jockeying it around to get it balanced over his head, and then set off into the woods. She heard the sound of the underbrush being flattened when he put the boat down, and after a few moments she saw him coming back toward her.

"We're going to sleep in there," he said, tipping his head toward the woods as he untied her.

She stood up and rubbed her wrists to restore the circulation. He took hold of her upper arm and led her. In the filtered forest light, he tied her feet to one small tree, then her hands to another.

"Get some sleep," he said.

He wandered out of sight. She'd thought that sleeping on the ground Friday night was uncomfortable. Now it seemed like heaven. Trying to sleep like this, or sitting up as she'd been yesterday, was infinitely worse. Her stomach growled, unsatisfied with the small amount of food it had been given, but she wasn't uncomfortably hungry. Her body was sore almost everywhere. She tried to think of a place where it didn't hurt or ache. *My little fingers are fine,* she thought drily. She tested them, but even they seemed to ache when bent.

She shifted her weight, then wriggled her body to try to get settled in. Over twenty-four hours without sleep had taken its toll, though, and she finally drifted off into a slumber troubled with nightmares not too far from reality.

Law-enforcement officers have cordoned off a five-square-mile area north of Haverstown after two reported sightings of the man wanted in connection with the slaying death of Highway Patrolman Delano Smith and the wounding of Patrolman Clarence Ray Thursday night. The fugitive is armed and dangerous.

Sunday Afternoon

9

"MUST BE LOOKIN'" for that guy who shot the highway patrolman," Norm Burke said to his wife Marge. He was leaning forward over the steering wheel, his chin resting on it, peering at a helicopter swooping along above them. It had passed so close that the beat of the rotor could be heard above their car's engine noise. Norm glanced at the highway, then returned his attention to the helicopter which was making a wide graceful sweep toward the tree line.

"Watch out," Marge screamed. "You're over the center line."

Norm jerked the wheel and got back in his own lane just in time to see the driver of an approaching car shoot him a dirty look.

"Maybe we shouldn't be poking around in this neck of the woods with that killer loose," Marge said after a moment. "Do you think it's safe, Norm?"

"Now, listen, Marge. You talked me into this." For the moment he was keeping both eyes on the road.

They were on their way to a resort to look at a lot. Marge had been keeping him busy since he retired two months earlier. There'd been a trip to see their daughter in Ohio; then a weekend at a crafts festival, which he could have lived without. They'd even gone to Kansas City once. He'd really thought retirement would be easier than this, but Marge wasn't planning to let any grass grow under his feet.

"Well, you don't have anything better to do," Marge said. She gazed down the highway. "And besides, we'll get a prize."

Marge was always big on prizes, Norm reflected. She entered every sweepstakes that came her way and fully expected Ed McMahon to show up with a grand prize any day. *Ah well,* he thought, *at least she's optimistic*. His attention wandered from the highway again until his wife's voice brought him up short.

"Watch out! That car is putting on its brakes."

Norm jammed on the brakes at her exclamation, not focused yet on what her yelling was about. Their sedan fishtailed slightly before he realized the danger wasn't quite as imminent as she'd made it sound and released his foot from the pedal slightly, bringing them to a manageable speed. His forehead was prickly from the surge of adrenaline. "You don't have to yell at me like that. I saw it!" he said, which wasn't strictly true, but she didn't need to scare him. By now the traffic ahead had come to a complete standstill, Norm with it. He wondered what the holdup was. Maybe a wreck.

"I wonder if there's some construction," Marge said. "Did you see any signs, Norm?" She opened her window and craned her neck out.

"I'll get out and see what I can see," Norm said, shoving the gear lever into Park. Traffic in the oncoming lane was moving, so he got out very carefully and darted across to the shoulder, glad to be out of the car for a moment. Up ahead he could see at least one patrol car, its cherry top flashing. He returned to the car.

"Well?" Marge asked.

"Looks like a roadblock to me."

"You mean they're going to search the car?"

"I don't know. Just be patient, Marge. We'll see." The car ahead of him moved up, so he started the engine and followed.

Ten minutes later they'd reached the front of the line, where an officer politely told them they were searching vehicles in an effort to contain a fugitive in the county. With that, Norm popped the lid on the trunk and the officer looked in, then closed it. He thanked them, warned them not to pick up any hitchhikers, then waved their car on.

Once they were underway again, Marge said, "That was kind of exciting, wasn't it?"

"It would have been more exciting if that guy had been in the trunk." His eyes twinkled.

"Oh, you, go on," Marge said, and gave her husband a playful slap on the knee. She scanned the tree line of the hills where earlier the helicopter had disappeared. "Just think, he's out there somewhere."

Norm's gaze followed hers. It was a beautiful day. Tufts of clouds skirted along the horizon, not threatening anything. It was hard to believe that those peaceful-looking woods harbored a desperate fugitive. Norm was glad he wasn't in that guy's shoes—out there with the chiggers and the ticks, every law-enforcement person in the state looking for him. Even having to listen to a resort sales pitch would beat that.

Neal Lassiter drove Jan to Breedlove, the county seat, a community of just over six hundred people. It was tiny, but nevertheless the largest in the area, so it acted as a trade center and consequently had more services than a typical town of its size. There was even a motel on the highway that skirted the north edge of town, the only motel in the county, although there were some rental cabins scattered here and there, up on the river.

Neal took a left turn onto the main street. A grocery store, closed on Sunday, stood to their left, and on the right was a Texaco station. A block farther on they entered the town square, which was dominated by a two-story limestone courthouse.

The square wasn't large, and consequently the lawn flanking the county building was narrow, just wide enough to accommodate a park bench on either side of the walk to the main entrance. Two old men sat on one. There was a café on the west side with several cars in front, and the loud hum of its air conditioner indicated it was open. There was also a pizza parlor on the square, open for business.

Neal pulled in vertically on the north side of the court-house. Jan got out and waited for him to come around. He took her by the elbow and propelled her gently toward the side entrance, which led directly into the sheriff's office, holding the heavy door as she went into the cool interior.

A skinny young woman sat behind a desk, which held a typewriter and radio equipment. She was filing cards in a metal drawer. Her unkempt hair was cropped short and her face was devoid of makeup, giving her a pale, listless look. *I must look just as lifeless,* Jan thought.

"May I help you, sir?" the clerk asked Neal in a tentative voice.

"I need to see Billy Jay."

"What's this about?" she asked.

Jan started to speak up. "My friend has disappeared and . . ."

Neal held his hand up to stop her. "We need to see the sheriff."

"He isn't in." She kept filing.

Neal leaned down over the desk. "Who is in?"

"Chief Deputy Todd."

"Well, then I'd like to see Deputy Todd."

"Just a moment."

Jan looked questioningly at Neal, wondering what all that was about.

"She's related to one of those guys on the river," he murmured.

"Oh," Jan said. She leaned heavily on the desk, won-dering how much longer she could stand there. Her legs felt as if they were about to buckle.

Neal seemed to sense her thoughts and reached out to put his arm around her, and she leaned against him.

The woman came back just then and said, "It's lucky I caught him; he was on his way out the back." She motioned for them to go into an office.

A beefy man of about sixty was taking his straw cowboy-style hat off. "Just barely caught me," he said to

Neal. "How you doin', Lassiter?" He extended his hand, then he nodded at Jan.

"Fine, Emory."

"What's the problem?"

"Mind if I close the door?" Neal asked as he got Jan seated.

The deputy frowned slightly and said, "Just Connie out there"—he shrugged—"but go ahead."

"This is—" Neal hesitated a moment, and Jan could almost see him searching through his mind for her name.

"Jan Spencer," she said.

The deputy acknowledged the introduction, then Neal continued. "She and a friend rented canoes at my place on Friday. Jan here got sick that night, and when she got up the next morning her friend had disappeared with the canoe."

"That was Saturday?" the deputy asked, looking at Jan.

She nodded. "I don't know exactly what time, except it was before the sun had come up over the bluffs."

"Whereabouts?"

Jan looked at Neal, who told Emory the approximate location where he'd seen their campsite on the river.

"Did you and your friend have a disagreement, a little spat? Maybe he was upset about something?" Emory rubbed his double chin

"She was with a woman friend, Emory."

"Two women out there alone?" The deputy shook his head in disapproval, then said to Neal, "Are you lookin' to file a complaint against her friend for stealing your canoe? I think if you just wait—"

Jan closed her eyes and interrupted in a voice laced with impatience. "My friend did not steal the canoe. Someone kidnapped her and *they* stole the canoe."

"Hmmm. Well, I guess I'd better get a report." He started to open one of the desk drawers, but Neal interrupted him.

"She's pretty sure who, Emory."

"Oh?"

Jan started to describe the two men, but Neal broke in: "It was Eugene Rice and his buddy, Three-Fingers Purcell. I saw them down on the river Saturday at the place I was supposed to pick Jan and Susan up." His eyes narrowed. "If I'd known then—"

Emory waved him quiet. "Your word isn't what we need here, Lassiter. I'm talking to this lady. You want to describe them for me?" Jan did, and the deputy nodded. "Does sound like Three-Fingers and Eugene. Now why is it you suspect those fellas of kidnapping your friend?" His desk chair squeaked as he leaned forward toward Jan.

Jan began to explain about their confrontation on the gravel bar, then interrupted herself. "I don't feel so good." Her hand went up to her forehead, and she closed her eyes for a moment.

Neal rose and said to Emory, "She's sick. Maybe you can get the rest of this over at the hospital."

Jan started to get up, too, but everything in the room seemed to blur, and she crumpled to the floor.

Neal was relieved to see her eyes open. "You're going to be all right, Jan. You fainted." He was kneeling beside her, holding her hand.

"She's got a nasty bump on her head where she hit the chair," the deputy said. He was down on his knees, too. "You gonna be okay till he gets you to the hospital?"

"I—I think so." She touched the tender spot on her head.

"I could call the ambulance."

"No, I'll take her," Neal said.

"I'll follow you over and get her statement there," the officer said, as if it were his own idea.

Neal helped Jan up and wrapped his arm around her for support.

The little blonde clerk was watching them closely as they went through her office. Earlier Neal had noticed the nameplate on her desk; it read CONNIE FISHER. He wondered how he and Randy had remembered the girl as cute. She was plain as a rabbit. Maybe she was having a bad day. Maybe everyone was having a bad day.

Jan leaned against him as they walked to the car. He considered picking her up, but thought she might feel silly, so he just assisted her as well as he could. He settled her in the passenger seat of the car. "You okay for a moment?" he asked.

She smiled wanly, and he left her to walk around to the other side. His gut was tense; he was worried about her, and it was more emotion than he'd felt in a long time.

He revved the engine more than necessary, backed out into the quiet square, and drove a block south of the square to the rambling one-story brick building that was Memorial Hospital. He kept glancing over at Jan to see how she was doing and finally reached over and put his hand reassuringly on her shoulder.

She looked at him and gave a weak smile.

"Hang in there," he said. "You've had a rough time, but you'll be fine. They'll probably want to give you some fluids to get you rehydrated, then you'll feel a lot better." They were in the parking lot now with the engine off, and with those words, he got out of the car and came around and helped her into the emergency entrance at the hospital. There was a nurse's assistant on duty who took Jan's vital signs and did some paperwork, then made a phone call to a doctor.

"He'll be over directly," the man told them. Just then Emory came in.

"Sorry," Emory said. "Got delayed." He put his hat on a chair, then proceeded to take her statement, using a pocket-sized tape recorder. When they'd finished, he said, "I have to tell you, I'd be surprised if those two are involved in your friend's disappearance. Granted, you may have an assault case against them—I mean those boys've always had a lot of spirit—"

As weak as she was, Jan didn't let that remark get by her. "Spirit! Is that what you call preying on women? That's the most—"

Neal put his hand on her arm to try to keep her calm.

"Don't get excited," the deputy interrupted. "I didn't mean it like that. You women today are always on edge, lookin' for us men to make one little misstep with our talkin'. What I meant to say is that Eugene and Three-

Fingers may do some things outside the law, like gettin' drunk and disorderly." The idea seemed to appeal to him. "Yeah, maybe they were drunk when they came up on you. But I just don't believe they're involved in this other thing . . . you know, with your friend." He picked up his hat and fingered the brim.

"Well, let's just speculate, Emory," Neal said, "that maybe they were taking my canoe—a little spite for the incident the night before perhaps—and Jan's friend came down and caught them at it. Maybe they got a little rough, too rough."

The sheriff shook his head. "I hate to think it."

Neal started to say something about the deputy's attitude, but bit his lip. It wouldn't help to antagonize Emory. He jammed his hands into his pockets and turned toward the door.

"Are you going to start a search for her?" Jan asked.

He glanced at his watch. "Gettin' kind of late for that today. But I betchya I can find Eugene and Three-Fingers."

"What's to keep your dispatcher or secretary—whatever you call her—from warning them?" Neal asked, turning back toward Emory again. "She's kin of theirs."

"Hmmm," Emory said, pondering Neal's words for a moment. "Well, shoot, you're right. Connie is Eugene's mother's sister's granddaughter. What's that make 'em? Some kinda cousins, I guess. Yessiree, I'd forgotten that." He frowned and rubbed his chin.

"She already knows," Neal said.

"Yep."

Neal sighed. "She'd do that, wouldn't she? Call him and warn him?" It was like Randy had said: the ethical code around here lent more weight to kinship than law.

"Oh, Connie might try to warn him. You're right about that. Tell you what, soon as we finish here, I'll run on out to his place." To Neal he said: "You wanna go along for the ride?"

Neal nodded. "You bet." His voice was grim, but it softened when he turned to Jan and said, "Do you mind? The doctor will get some fluids in you, fix you right up. I'll see you later." His hand drifted to hers as he talked, and she didn't seem to mind. "Unless you want me to stay?"

"No, go on. And thank you so much for coming along when you did," Jan said. "I don't think I could have stood it much longer." She squeezed his hand lightly.

He brushed her hair back from her forehead. "You're strong, you could have managed. But I'm glad I came along, too." Their eyes held for a moment.

A nurse appeared just then.

"Good afternoon, Maudie," Emory said, touching the brim of his hat.

"What do we have here?"

"Uh, well, uh . . . the lady here was out on the river and, uh . . . got sick. Fainted in my office." Emory had become very tentative.

"What was she doin' in your office if she was sick?" the woman asked.

Now the deputy flushed. "Now, uh, Maudie, you just do the nursin', I'll do the law enforcement."

"She's dehydrated," Neal said. "She's had some sort of bug for a couple of days."

She narrowed her eyes at him. "Doctor will do the diagnosing. He's on his way over." With that she swished out of the area.

Emory turned to Jan. "I'll get the girl to type this up." He waved the tape recorder at her.

Emory walked into the office shaking his head, while Neal waited for him in the car.

The clerk, Connie, looked up at him as he entered, but didn't say anything. She was real quiet lately, he'd noticed, making him wonder if he'd said something to hurt the little gal's feelings. But no, she was quiet with everyone in the office. Not just him.

"I tell you, Connie, women oughtn't to be out like that alone." He handed her the tape recorder. "It just tempts men like Eugene and Three-Fingers. Shoot!" He slapped his hand on the desk. "I sure hope Mr. Lassiter is way off base—I mean about how those ol' boys might be involved in this woman's disappearance. I hope to goodness when I run 'em to ground they've got a good story." He caught Connie's eye, hoping maybe the girl would take a notion to call Eugene, tell him to get his ducks in a row, but she averted her gaze almost instantly.

He went into his office still talking. "Type that up, hon, but we won't get in too big a hurry to have it signed. Maybe if we find out Eugene and Three-Fingers didn't have anything to do with her friend being missing, she'll decide not to press charges. After all, she's the one who went for her gun. Why, I doubt Eugene and Three-Fingers even had a gun. Yep," he mused, "don't want to get in too big a hurry." He started to sit down, then remembered Lassister was in the car waiting for him. "Shoot!" he said, "where's my mind." He went out of his office, talked to Connie a moment more, telling her he'd be back in an hour or so.

Jan had just lain back on the examining table when the nurse reappeared.

"Doctor wants to examine you, so you'll need to undress and put this on." She thrust a hospital gown at her. "Can you manage?"

Jan nodded and the nurse swept the curtain shut, returning a few minutes later.

"Doctor is in the building, so it'll just be a moment," the nurse said, then she disappeared again.

Jan waited at least five minutes. Goose bumps covered her arms as she lay there. She hugged her arms around herself, and tears slipped out of her eyes and ran down into her ears. They had dried before the nurse reappeared with the doctor.

"Well, now, what's the trouble?"

She told him about the last two days as he began to write on a chart. The nurse bustled around behind the doctor and didn't appear to be listening.

"What a story," the doctor said. "You shouldn't have been out there without some men."

Jan flared. "Would a man have kept me from getting sick?"

The doctor jabbed at her rib, and she flinched. "That hurt? Sorry. We'll get an X ray of that." The nurse nodded. "You've got lots of contusions. In another day you'll be a beautiful patchwork of black and blue."

He asked her some questions about the illness she'd had and about the bump on her head. She was now sitting up, and he examined her pupils and reflexes. He wrote some things on the chart and handed it to the nurse. "We're going to keep you under observation a while and get you rehydrated, then you can go." He left her with the nurse, who had orders to administer an antibiotic and get an IV going.

The nurse was a woman of perhaps fifty-five, her graying hair cut short. "That's quite an experience you had," she said as she prepared a syringe. "What do you think happened to your friend?"

"There were these two men on the river. One was named Three-Fingers and the other"—it took her a moment—"his name was Eugene. I think they may have been stealing the canoe, and she confronted them." Before the words were out, she saw the nurse stiffen slightly and Jan realized it would be best to keep her mouth shut. Everyone out here probably knew everyone else.

"That's quite a lot of thinking you're doing. Probably not what happened at all. Now just get in this wheelchair, and I'll take you to X ray."

"I can walk," Jan said, pulling her gown around her.

"I'm sorry, Mrs. Spencer, but regulations say I have to wheel you."

After the X ray, Jan was wheeled to room 113. Alone at last, she placed a phone call to Ted. He didn't answer. She slammed the receiver down, angry because he wasn't home.

She tried to calm herself with a few deep breaths. Fifteen minutes later she dialed Ted's number again. Still no answer. *Why couldn't he be home?* she thought. *Does this have to be any more frustrating than it already is? What did I do to deserve this?*

Good question. Did I ask for it somehow? Should Susan and I have stayed home? She realized she had already convicted Eugene and Three-Fingers of kidnapping Susan. But what else could have happened?

She tried Ted's number again, her exasperation renewed. Finally, she had another idea. She called information in Marshallville and got Jennifer Morrow's number. Maybe Jen had talked to Ted. Her finger trembled as she dialed. This wasn't going to be easy: telling the girl her mother had disappeared.

"Jennifer."

"Yes?"

"This is Jan Spencer, your mom's friend." She hadn't seen Susan's daughter in a long time, not since she'd been away at college, and now she'd graduated.

"What's the matter?" Jennifer sounded puzzled. "Dad said you and mom were canoeing this weekend."

"You've talked to him? I haven't been able to reach him."

"He's in the hospital," Jennifer said.

"Oh, no. What happened?" Jan felt a stab of guilt over her anger at Ted.

"He thought he was having a heart attack, but fortunately they don't think that's what it was. I'm worried though." She gave a short laugh. "I've nearly made myself sick over it since I talked to him. I mean, what if they're wrong?"

Jan found herself shifted into the role of comforter. It would please Susan to have her daughter's fears quieted. "They're probably not wrong. There are lots of things that could make him think he was having a heart attack."

"Like what?"

"My ex-husband had acute gastritis, and he thought he was having a coronary. Another thing is a gallbladder attack."

"Well, I hope you're right."

"I understand why you're worried, but it won't do him any good if you make yourself sick."

"I know, but . . ." She sighed and shifted gears. "Uh, why are you calling?" Her voice had taken on a tinge of dread.

"I feel horrible dropping this on you now, but"—Jan

hesitated and took a deep breath—"your mom has disappeared."

"What?"

"She disappeared. I was sick night before last, and while I was out of it she vanished."

"What do you mean? People don't just vanish." Her voice was incredulous.

"Susan and the canoe were missing in the morning. The last I knew she was going to get ice for me." Jan had thought about it a lot. Had Susan returned with ice? She didn't think so.

Alarmed, Jennifer asked, "What could have happened? Where could she have gone?"

"What I'm wondering is whether she went of her own free will."

"I don't think my mom would have left you stranded there unless she went for help. But you know her—she doesn't do things on her own. I mean, I was surprised you got her to go on a trip without Dad."

Susan broke out of the mold enough to take this trip, Jan thought, *and as a result who knows what's happened.* Jan's posture drooped with added guilt. "She might have gone for help, but there were some local men hanging around the river, and they—" She didn't want to say it. "I'm worried that they—"

"Oh, no! Where are you?"

"In Breedlove."

"I'd better come over there."

"There's nothing you can do, Jennifer. I've reported it to the sheriff's office, so why don't you sit tight till I can tell you more."

"Well . . ."

"I do need to call your dad, though."

Jennifer gave her the number.

The talk with Ted was basically a repetition of the one with Jennifer, except he had an interesting sidelight. He told her about the picture in the paper. "They must have accidentally gotten mixed up in the crowd," he said.

"What does the man look like? Does he have a beard?" Jan asked.

"The picture isn't real clear. He's blond, but no features I can make out. Just kind of indistinctly . . . featureless. No beard."

It sounded just like the one called Three-Fingers. Just the evidence they needed.

Ted insisted that he was coming down.

"But you're in the hospital!"

"Waiting for tests. You know how that is. Tell me where to find you."

She told him.

He let out a low curse. "Why didn't you tell me you were in the hospital in the first place?"

"Because the story was bad enough as it was."

"Well, I'll be down as soon as I can spring myself."

Her estimation of Ted went up considerably at his words, and she found herself looking forward to the arrival of someone she knew, someone as predictible as Ted.

Susan was missing! He was ashamed about his earlier assumption that Susan was having a tryst of some sort. He should have known better.

He was pulling his pants on as the nurse came in.

"What are you doing, Mr. Morrow?"

"There's been an emergency, I have to leave."

"Well, I'm sorry, but you'll have to wait till the doctor discharges you."

"Oh. Well, you go call him pronto, because I'm leaving."

"He won't be making rounds till about seven."

Ted stopped what he was doing and rubbed his chin, nodding.

The nurse left, and he started to dress again. *Like hell I have to wait*. He thrust the clipping he'd torn from the newspaper into his pocket.

He would zip home and pick up his wallet, then head south. Shouldn't take him more than a couple of hours.

When he got in the house—luckily he hadn't locked the

door to the kitchen because he didn't have a key—the phone was ringing. It was Jennifer.

"Daddy, I called the hospital, and they said you'd left without medical approval."

"Honey, I'm fine, really. All that means is the doctor didn't discharge me. I wasn't going to wait around for him when your mother is missing. I've got to get down there."

"Then Jan got hold of you."

"Yes, she did. She told me she'd talked to you."

"Oh, Daddy, I'm so worried." Her voice broke as she said it, and he could tell she was crying.

"I know. But I'm sure everything will turn out all right. I'll go down and—"

"No!" Jennifer almost shouted. "You're sick. I don't want you to be out on the highway driving. What if you had another . . . another attack out on the highway alone? Call Jeffrey to take you."

"Sweetie, he's in Estes Park, remember?"

"I can't stand it, Daddy. Promise me you won't drive down there by yourself."

She was becoming more hysterical by degrees. Ted ran his fingers through his hair. "Settle down, honey." He didn't know what to tell her. This was the sort of thing Susan handled. "It's all going to be okay."

"Just please, please promise me." Jennifer was crying. "I'm just so worried. Are you sure you shouldn't be in the hospital."

"I'm sure."

They talked a few more minutes, and she finally extracted a desperate promise that he wouldn't leave home until he called Breedlove to see if he could really be of any help and made sure the trip wouldn't be pointless.

He hung up the phone with relief. Lord, that girl could work him. Was it always that way with fathers and daughters?

He picked up the receiver again and after a few moments was connected with the sheriff's department in Breedlove. The woman on the other end of the line told him that the sheriff was out, as was the chief deputy, but she'd take a message and have someone return the call. Ted left his name and number.

The road to Eugene Rice's house was winding and it took Emory and Neal a good half hour to get there, even though it wasn't far out of town.

They came upon it slowly, quietly, not wanting to alert Eugene. His truck wasn't there. There were lots of other vehicles around; most of them didn't appear to be in working order.

The hollow behind the house was filled with trash.

"This place looks like a dump," Neal said.

"It is. Eugene has him a trash-hauling business."

"Aren't there any regulations?" Neal asked, looking at all the piles of trash.

Emory snorted. "What the feds don't know don't hurt 'em. They got their fingers in too many pies already. No need to sic 'em on a man trying to make a living."

"You ever heard of hazardous wastes, Emory?"

Emory shrugged. "This is way out in the country, Lassiter. Besides, does that look like hazardous waste to you?" He cocked his head toward the rubble.

Neal climbed out of the car and promptly stepped in chicken droppings. "I think I just stepped in some," he mumbled.

"What?" Emory asked as he slid out.

"Nothing." He scraped his shoe on the grass. A flock of the perpetrators browsed across the dirt, pecking at anything that looked edible.

"Watch out for that rooster," Emory warned offhandedly as he stepped up on Eugene's porch. "He's stalkin' you."

Neal looked around and, sure enough, a white leghorn rooster, its feathers fluffed up grandly, had left the general area where the hens were and was nonchalantly examining the ground closer and closer to him.

Neal stepped back, but the rooster danced sideways toward him, then jumped, wings flapping, hackles up, claws extended. "Damn bird!"

"He's nailed you," Emory said, laughing.

Neal tried to shake the rooster off, but it was firmly attached to his pant leg. He stomped and cursed, hitting at the bird, till it finally dropped off. "Now, git!" The rooster wasn't sure. Neal kicked out at him, threatening, then stomped the ground. "Git, you stupid bird!"

Finally the leghorn rearranged his feathers and walked away, maintaining a proud demeanor all the while.

Emory was still laughing.

"I'm glad you enjoyed that so much."

"He thought you was after his girls. It's that cocky look you have."

Neal managed a smile.

"A rooster's always tryin' to show you he's in charge. Just like a lotta men spend their time puffin' theirselves up."

Eugene, who lived alone according to Emory, proved indeed not to be there, so next the two of them drove to Three-Fingers's house.

"Violet?" Emory said when he saw a pale young woman at the door. She stood behind the bulging and abused screen with a toddler on her hip. A little bare-chested girl with her thumb in her mouth clung to the woman's blue-jean-clad knees.

"Heard you drivin' up the road, Em'ry." Her voice was wary.

"I'm lookin' for Three-Fingers. He home?"

"Nah. He's out with Eu-gene. Left 'bout an hour ago." She pronounced the name with two equally emphasized syllables. "What you need 'em for?"

"Just want to talk to him, Vi. You know where they're at?"

She wrinkled her nose. "You know them. They're down at the river drinkin', most likely. Don't 'spect 'im home till time to go to work tomorrow."

"Where's he workin'?"

She grinned, exposing several spaces where teeth were missing. "He got his job back, over to the chicken plant."

"Violet, where do him and Eugene most often go down on the river?"

She stroked the baby's head. "They might be down at Blue Hole."

The deputy nodded. "Okay."

"But they got that old johnboat with 'em, so they may be anywhere."

"Yep, well we'll be on our way, I reckon." The deputy tipped his hat to her.

"If you see him, you tell 'im not to forget about work." Violet took the baby's hand in hers and waggled it up and down. "Say bye-bye to Em'ry, sugar."

"Bye-bye," Emory said, waving at the baby.

As they pulled away from the house, Neal asked, "Won't they just take off once they get wind that you're looking for them?"

"You got to understand, I doubt they think they've done anything wrong. 'Specially Three-Fingers. He's two bricks shy of a load, if you want my opinion."

"Does he have another name, other than Three-Fingers?"

"Yeah, it's Leroy. But no one hardly ever calls him that since the time his dog bit his fingers off."

"His dog?"

"Yup. He was raisin' fightin' dogs, and one of 'em bit two of his fingers off right down to the second knuckle." He released his right hand from the wheel and held it near his left to point out where he meant. "The dog musta ate 'em, 'cause they couldn't find 'em to sew 'em back on. Everyone started calling him Three-Fingers after that, and it stuck."

The deputy was heading for Blue Hole now, a favorite swimming spot among locals. They reached it about fifteen minutes later. Not many people were left this late in the day, but an earlier crowd was evident by its trash.

As Emory and Neal drove up, a boy about twelve was launching himself into the azure pool from a rope attached to an overhanging tree limb. Another one was paddling around in the water, and a third was waiting up on the rocks for his turn. A woman wearing a broad-brimmed straw hat sat watching from a lawn chair, half-submerged in the nearby shallows.

The deputy approached her and asked if she'd seen Eugene or Three-Fingers, but her answer was negative.

"Lord," Emory said, taking his hat off and wiping his head as he returned to the car, "that water do look good, boy. That Blue Hole is the finest." He hauled himself behind the wheel and started the engine. "This is a needle in the haystack proposition. I'd best line up some other deputies to start lookin'."

Neal nodded in agreement. He knew how many places two men could hole up for a drunk on the river. The question was: did they have Susan Morrow with them or had they abandoned her somewhere? If so, what kind of shape was she in? The Upper Fork and the Big Pine together flowed for about a hundred and fifty miles. One hundred and fifty miles of virtual wilderness.

Eugene and Three-Fingers followed the highway for fifteen or so miles, then took an overgrown road that went up at about a twenty-degree grade. The old truck had a hard time of it.

Eugene shoved it into first gear as the engine lugged down. The rear wheels spun, spewing rocks out behind, then the truck lurched forward. The transmission growled as the tires finally gripped the roadbed and began to pull them up to the crest of the hill.

The road was full of switchbacks, and its condition deteriorated as if got farther from the highway. There was one house about two miles back. After that it was just two ruts through the dense woods. The truck jounced over badly washed places, and finally Eugene pulled to a stop. "The end of the line," he said. It was only a short distance to the edge of the bluff.

They got out of the truck and Eugene took his compound bow, which was fixed up with a reel for bowfishing, out of the back of the truck and slung it over his shoulder. The two men walked to the top of the bluff. Below them the river poured through the gorge with restless fury.

This would be the place Lee Newton would get his comeuppance for two-timing Ruthie. Eugene Rice would

show Mr. Holier-Than-Thou that he wasn't such hot stuff—
that he could capsize just like anyone else. Eugene Rice was
gonna baptize the SOB.

Ruthie had introduced him to Lee and he'd run into him
a couple of times since, but the guy was standoffish. If
there's one thing Eugene didn't like it was someone who
acted like he thought he was better than everybody else. It
was the same with that woman on the river. He'd like to run
into her some time when she didn't have a gun.

"Whatchya grinnin' about, Eugene?"

"Nothin'," he said. His fantasy was his own.

This place was called the Devil's Staircase because of a
hidden crevice which offered a way down to the north side
of the river through its jagged ledges. The two men
scrambled down the narrow passageway like goats, familiar
with it from a lifetime of exploring the river. Once down,
Eugene lifted his bow over his head, took an arrow from the
quiver he wore, attached the line, then shot it across the
river.

"Looks good!" Three-Fingers yelled over the noise of the
turbulent water rushing through the Narrows. His blank face
lit up with a smile.

"Yeah," Eugene said. He broke off the line and began to
tie it to a rock.

"Whatchaya doin'?"

"I'm not leavin' my bow here, you idiot," Eugene
shouted back. "Somebody might steal it. Let's go."

Next they had to go up to the bridge and back down the
south side of the river. This face of the bluff wasn't going to
be so simple. There was no Devil's Staircase to give them
access to the water.

The plan was to drop Three-Fingers, carrying a coil of
wire, on a rope attached to the front bumper of the truck,
which was parked down the road. Eugene would drive
toward the bluff, lowering Three-Fingers as he went. They
figured it so Three-Fingers would have plenty of rope and
be down before Eugene, in the truck, was at the edge of the
bluff. It didn't work out quite as they expected. Later, when
Three-Fingers got over being mad, he told Eugene about it.

Three-Fingers had backed off the bluff, walking his way down as Eugene had slowly pulled forward. At the top there was a slope, but it ended abruptly. Three-Fingers slipped and found himself dangling as more and more of the rope played out, but there was no way to get Eugene's attention. Finally, Three-Fingers reached the bottom, and other than experiencing a few moments of intense fear, he hadn't suffered much.

He quickly found the arrow with the line attached. He cut it, then tied it to the wire he was carrying. Now all he had to do was firmly attach the other end to a boulder. So far so good. Now they were to return to the Devil's Staircase side and pull the wire on across, all before Lee Newton got to this part of the river.

Of course, it was just Eugene's speculation that Lee was coming down this far, but he was willing to bet all this energy he was expending on it. He figured the SOB was on his way to the Compound where he and Ruthie lived.

Three-Fingers got the wire attached, then pulled on the rope around his waist—his signal to Eugene at the top to jump in the truck and pull him up.

Three-Fingers started walking up the cliff, thinking he was going to be more careful going up. He didn't want another experience like he'd had coming down. Both of his arms were extended, hands clasping the rope tightly, pulling himself along. It seemed to be going without a hitch until Three-Fingers suddenly realized only his tiptoes could touch the wall. In a moment, he was dangling by the waist, and his body began to spin. Still the truck was pulling him upward.

"Whoa up there! Whoa, damn it!" he hollered, but Eugene didn't hear him. God Almighty! He was gonna get cut in half by the rope; it was up under his armpits now. He was still grasping it as it slid through a narrow crack in the overhang, dragging him along. He whacked into a rock that jutted out and clambered to push himself out. But it was impossible; he was being dragged too fast. "You stupid bastard! Slow down! You're killin' me." A steady barrage of curses echoed into the gorge, but Eugene, in the truck cab, had turned on the radio and was listening to Willie Nelson. He didn't hear a thing.

Three-Fingers was over the edge of the bluff now, on the slope. His fingers were wedged under the taut rope, and it felt like the skin was being burned off his knuckles. Finally the punishment stopped. Eugene came sauntering back and was surprised to see the venom in Three-Fingers' face as he struggled to get up and get the damn rope off. He went after Eugene with a vengeance, as if it were his fault.

They wrestled and tumbled there in the dry, summer weeds, and once Eugene thought Three-Fingers was going to toss him over the edge into the Narrows, but finally they got all fought out and lay there exhausted, the two lifelong friends.

"How 'bout a beer, ol' buddy?" Eugene asked, reaching over and patting him.

"Sure thing," Three-Fingers answered.

Jennifer blew her nose and sighed. All this was awful. Mom was missing and Dad was sick. She paced through her little house, trying to decide what to do.

The house was tiny, a two-bedroom frame, built in the fifties, perfect for someone just starting out. She was renting it from her boss and that made it ideal. If he transferred her to the Washington office, which she hoped he would, there would be no problem getting out of the rental agreement.

She paced a few more minutes, then made a decision. She went to her purse and pulled out her wallet, extracting a piece of paper. She stared at it for a moment. He'd told her to feel free to call on his private line, but did he really welcome calls?

This was an emergency; surely he would understand. She picked up the phone and dialed.

"Senator," she said when she heard his voice, "it's Jennifer. I'm sorry to bother you, but I just have to get some advice." She proceeded to tell him about her mother. "I thought maybe you could call over there and see if they're doing everything possible to find her. I know you know people—"

"You bet I do, Jenny. That's the very neck of the woods I grew up in. I'll call the sheriff over there—ol' Billy Jay Ambler—and see what's goin' on. And don't you worry. If I have anything to do with it, they'll find your mother pronto."

Jennifer hung up, feeling much better. It was nice to know someone with power.

The senator dialed the sheriff's office in Breedlove. "This is Senator Grindstaff," he said when someone answered, "Is Billy Jay there?"

"No, sir. And Chief Deputy Todd is out right now," a woman's voice said.

"Well, I want one of them to call me when they come in."

"Yes sir."

The senator placed the receiver back on the cradle and sat back in his chair. He was glad to help Jennifer out.

Susan awoke from a light sleep to find a hand pressed over her mouth. It took a moment to figure out where she was and that the pressure against her temple was the barrel of a gun.

Lee Newton had stolen up silently and was crouched beside her. *What's going on?* she wondered.

Then she heard them. Voices drifting up from the river. Men's voices. Were they just people floating on the river? Or could they be searchers? It was Sunday. Surely by now Jan had somehow found help—either been rescued by the canoe outfitter or by someone canoeing by the gravel bar. She was resourceful; she wouldn't just stay in the woods. Unless she'd gotten sicker. But even if a search for the two women hadn't been started, soon Ted would be expecting her at home. He would do something.

She watched as Lee's tense jaw began to relax. Gradually, the pressure of his fingers on her cheekbones began to ease. To him, the danger had passed.

Sunday Night

10

NO ONE RETURNED Ted's call.

So that's the way the operation is being run, he thought. He was going on down there. That way he could make sure they were doing *something*.

He dragged a small suitcase off the top shelf in the bedroom closet and put in a change of underwear and socks, his electric shaver, a tube of toothpaste, and his toothbrush. He'd gone to the hospital in his Bermuda shorts. Now he changed to khakis and a sports shirt. As an afterthought, he folded his Bermudas and Izod shirt and put them in the case.

Daylight was fading as he backed the car out of the garage. A thought about his health skittered through his mind, but he pushed it aside since he hadn't had any pain since the day before, and being out on the road seemed to be the best antidote to the worry that had been besieging him.

Darkness embraced the car before it reached the state line, and Ted had to slow down to maneuver the switchbacks as he came into the foothills. His eyelids began to feel heavy, so he pulled over at a café for coffee.

"Coffee, black," he told the young waitress, who wore blue jeans and a plaid shirt.

Her southern accent was pronounced. It was as if the state line were more than a political border. "Would you like a piece of blackberry pie? They're fresh berries, picked up in the hills."

He smiled. "No thanks."

The coffee was strong and good, and he ordered a second cup to go.

It was eleven o'clock before his headlamps reflected off the road sign that read BREEDLOVE at the outskirts of town. Just beyond it there was a small, white stucco motel. It announced a VA ANCY in blue neon letters. A smaller unlighted sign had been attached to the post. It read: AMERICAN-OWNED.

Ted turned off the asphalt into a gravel parking lot and pulled up in front of the office. He stretched as he got out of the car, flexing his shoulders, then walked over and rang the after-hours bell. Through an open door at one side of the office he could see the eerie reflection of a TV show dancing on a wall. After a few moments, a middle-aged woman came through the doorway and let him in.

"Want a room?" she asked tersely.

"The sign says you have a vacancy."

"Yeah." She put a form on a clipboard and shoved it toward him across the counter.

"How much for a single?"

"Thirty-five dollars."

"For a single?"

"That's the price, mister."

"Well forget it. It's a little steep for my blood."

"You'll be back," the woman said with a note of smugness in her voice. She grabbed the clipboard and slammed it behind the counter. "This is the only motel in the county."

She didn't know Ted. He found out she was telling the truth about its being the only motel, but he wouldn't give that broad the satisfaction of reappearing at her doorstep. He drove around town until he found the hospital, where he pulled into the parking lot and stopped. He would sleep in the car.

First, though, he'd see if Janice happened to be awake.

He went to the door, half expecting it to be locked for security reasons, but it wasn't. These small towns were so trusting. There was no one in the front admissions area, so he went on into the main hall.

A nurse looked up from her work behind a desk. "I'm sorry, visiting hours are over."

"Perhaps you could make an exception. I've driven a long way to see Janice Spencer, and if she's awake—"

"Absolutely no exceptions."

"May I see your supervisor?"

She drew herself up. "I'm in charge. You may see her in the morning at nine. And that's final."

Oh it is, is it? he thought. *Lady, I've walked out of one hospital today, I suppose I can sneak in another.* He went back to the car and waited.

"Senator Grindstaff," Emory said. "This is Emory Todd over in Breedlove. I have a message here to call you."

"Yes, Emory. How are you?" Always the politician, the senator proceeded to ask about all of Emory's relatives.

"What can I help you with, Senator?"

"One of my staffers called me earlier and said that her mother has disappeared over there in your jurisdiction. Can you tell me anything about it?"

"That would be Susan Morrow's daughter, I guess, sir. She and another woman started downriver on an overnight canoe trip Friday, and yesterday morning Susan Morrow turned up missing from the campsite."

"What light can the other woman shed on it?"

"Well, sir, she was sick and didn't even know her friend was missing till late in the morning. But she says she and the Morrow woman had an encounter with Eugene and the Purcell boy the night before the woman disappeared. She's bound and determined that it was them that took her friend." He paused. "And she's filing assault charges."

"Oh, Lord God!" The senator exhaled into the phone. "That boy's just bound to get himself in trouble."

"It looks like it," Emory agreed.

"But no sign of Mrs. Morrow?"

"No sir. I had some boys out searching before dark. But you know that river."

"Where's Billy Jay?"

"You heard about Lee Newton being a fugitive up in Presley County?"

"Yes, I heard that. You sure they have him contained?"

"Yes sir. Looks that way. Anyhow, Billy Jay's up there helpin' out."

"I see. My sister must be fit to be tied. All of this happening."

"I s'pose she'd heard about Newton, but she hasn't heard about the other yet."

"Well, see what you can do. Seems like maybe Billy Jay ought to be tendin' to things in his own county."

"Well, you know him, Senator. He likes to be in the middle of the hubbub."

The senator gave a snort. "Yes, he does. Well, listen here, Emory. I want you to keep me posted on what's happening down there, so I can tell my little staffer. She's pretty worried."

"Yes sir, I'll do that, Senator."

Susan lay staring up through the branches at the darkening sky. Surely soon he would untie her and they could start downstream again. Her muscles ached from being in the same position too long, and she longed to stand up and move around. She turned her head, but could see no sign of Lee. Where was he? It was getting dark; they should be getting underway. She considered calling out for him, but thought better of it. It might make him mad.

The damp humus under her gave off a musty odor. A mosquito came and landed on her arm. Unable to do anything else, she blew on it, trying to frighten it away, but it just sat there and drank its fill of her blood.

She hadn't seen Lee since they'd heard the voices on the river. That in itself was a worry. What if he abandoned her? Left her to die slowly, tied up helplessly in the woods. She felt so helpless, so . . . dependent. There was that word again. Always she was dependent. Dependent on Ted, dependent on Lee. But being a hostage was different, wasn't it? Or was she also a hostage to Ted in a way? The idea tickled at her mind, distracting her momentarily from her present dilemma. A hostage begins to identify with the captor. How many of her beliefs had been forged in the shape of Ted's?

The thought yanked her back to the present. She wasn't going to allow herself to identify with Lee Newton. Maybe she was a dependent personality type, but she also had strong values—had always prided herself on them—and she wasn't going to give them up, not even now. Determination gave her a temporary sense of strength and she forgot where she was. Then she tried to move her arm and the crushing truth came back to her.

You fool, she thought, *you are totally disabled. Why pretend otherwise? You are completely dependent upon him in a way you never were on Ted.*

Where was Lee? She strained against her bonds. Nightfall was on them. The tree frogs and crickets were beginning their refrains. It was time to move on.

Connie, the clerk from the sheriff's office, opened the outer door at the hospital, then looked both ways before entering. There was no one in sight, so she quietly went on through, letting the door rest against her hip and slowly close. The admissions area was empty at this time on a Sunday; anyone who came in would come through emergency.

The young woman quickly proceeded to the main corridor. Maudie was here somewhere; Emory had mentioned seeing her, and Connie didn't want to run into her, of all people. At the moment there was no sign of the woman.

Connie moved silently over to the nurse's station and, with a furtive glance to each side, turned the visible file around to see in what room Jan Spencer was. Her finger slid down the names: Barlow, Brown, Clay, Creighton, Haskins, Jones, Morton, Russell. There it was: Spencer, Janice—room 113. She slid the file back to its former position, then with another furtive glance, she sidled down the hallway from doorway to doorway, keeping her eyes peeled for Maudie.

She'd almost made it to her destination when the nurse

came backing out of a door, carrying two glasses of juice. Quickly, Connie darted into a supply closet whose door stood open. Her heart was pounding madly. She wasn't used to sneaking around, but this was something she had to do, and she didn't want Maudie interfering.

Maudie passed by, and the girl emerged, throwing a sidelong glance down the hall, then continued her advance to room 113. The door stood ajar, the light from the hall illuminating the woman's torso. Her head was in the shadows, facing away from the door.

Connie crept in, taking one last glance over her shoulder, then swinging the door shut.

Maudie sighed and glanced at the clock over the desk as she sank into the swivel chair at the nurse's station. Her shift would be over soon, thank goodness. Although why she wanted to get home just to worry more was beyond her.

She sighed again. *Need to look in on everyone,* she thought. The ache in her bunion caused her to reconsider making the rounds, and she opened the switch on the intercom, starting at the last room down the east hall.

A voice penetrated the silence around her. Her curiosity was aroused because visiting hours were over. Was it just the television, or had that man sneaked by? Then she heard Eugene's name and bent closer, listening. . . .

Someone was in her room. Jan could sense their presence even with her eyes closed. The light had changed. She cautiously rolled over and saw a human form looming over her. It startled her and her arm jerked up, wrenching the IV needle painfully against its tape before the fear drained from her.

"What do you want?" she asked weakly, pressing her fingers against the needle to ease its sting. She recognized the woman now; she was the clerk from the sheriff's office. The one related to one of her assailants. She reached for the call button beside the bed.

The woman grabbed her wrist. "Don't. I didn't mean to scare you, but I have to talk to you."

"About what?" Her voice held a skeptical note. What was this woman here for?

"Emory said maybe you wouldn't file these charges"— she waved the statement she was carrying—"if I let 'em sit a few days, and we found out that Eugene and Three-Fingers didn't have nothin' to do with kidnapping your friend." Suddenly the girl began to cry. Deep sobs that sounded as if they were wrenched up from her soul.

Jan was bewildered. "I'm going to file charges no matter what," she said.

"Good. It's good enough for 'em."

"Why are you so concerned?"

"Eugene, he"—her voice fell—"he raped me three months ago. And I couldn't say nothin' to no one, or he said he'd kill me. Well, it's killin' me anyway, not saying nothin'." She snuffled loudly. "And now—now I found out I'm gonna have Eugene's baby, so then everyone'll know. And I don't know what he'll do to me."

Jan was appalled. "Give me that paper." She almost jerked the statement from the girl's hand, then looked around for a pen. "Why don't you file charges, too?"

"I can't. You can leave this place behind. I gotta live here." Her voice became tight. "You make that Eugene Rice pay for his rotten ways."

"You're the one who needs to make him pay. Don't you see? He's the father of your baby, and he's getting off scot-free. You're going to be stuck with providing a life for that child for the next eighteen years, and he should be paying!" Jan scrawled her signature on the sheet of paper and put it on her bed tray.

Connie's eyes looked more alive than Jan had seen them. Was she getting through to the girl?

"You can file some kind of charges, a paternity suit or something, I'm sure." Jan reached out and patted Connie's arm. "Don't you have someone you can talk to?"

The girl shook her head. "Only you. My family's gonna kill me when they find out I'm having a baby." She dropped her head into her hands, her posture wilting. "I don't know what I'm gonna do."

Jan reached over and lifted the girl's drooping chin. "Have some pride, first of all. Act like you're someone. File charges against him. Between that and my charges, we can make that creep come to attention. And we'll get some help for you. I'll make sure."

"I don't know—"

"Listen, you've got to stand up for yourself. No one else will."

The door behind her slid open noiselessly, and Jan's eyes widened as she looked over her visitor's shoulder.

The girl jerked away as Ted came into Jan's room. "I've got to go," she whispered to Jan, "but please help me." She went to the door and looked both ways, then darted out.

Ted went over to Jan's bedside as the young woman left, but didn't ask who she was. He probably assumed she worked there, and Jan was too surprised to think of explaining. He turned to her. "How are you, Janice?" he asked with a frown, pushing his glasses up.

"Oh, Ted, I'm so sorry. Susan and I should have never gone on this trip."

He reached out and patted her hand, but showed restraint, she thought, in not saying anything critical. Finally he said, "That's spilt milk. Now we've got to concentrate on finding Susan. Tell me again exactly what happened."

She had just told Ted about her ordeal on the river when the battle-ax of a nurse came trooping in like she had a radar homing device for illegal visitors. She flipped on the light, blinding Jan for a moment. "I thought I told you visiting hours were over," she said to Ted.

"It's okay," Jan said. "This is—"

The nurse looked at her defiantly. "It is *not* okay," she said, then turned to Ted. "Now get out, before I call the police."

Ted shrugged, then turned to Jan. "I'll see you in the morning, first thing." He shot a dirty look at the nurse as he left. She turned out the light and shut the door, leaving Jan alone in the dark to think about her earlier visitor's request.

* * *

Eugene was going to be arrested. That seemed clear to Maudie. Well, she wouldn't allow it.

Maudie pushed the door to room 113 open. The patient appeared to be sleeping. The nurse's crepe-soled shoes made little sound as she approached the bed and looked down at the woman for a moment. There on the bed tray was the statement the deputy had taken—the one Connie had brought over. Maudie picked it up.

Hmmmm. Signed. She ceremoniously folded it and stuck it in her left pocket, then took hold of the portal clamp on the IV. *You won't cause my Eugene any trouble, lady.* Her jaw tightened as she drew a syringe from her other pocket.

"Maudie?" a voice whispered behind her.

Maudie's heart almost stopped. It was the late-shift nurse coming to relieve her.

"What?" Maudie snapped in a hiss, shoving the syringe into her pocket again, then turning to face the woman who was peeking in the door.

"I was just wondering where you were."

"Well, you shouldn't sneak up on people. You almost scared me to death. Aren't you early?"

"Oh, I didn't have anything to do. What's this one in for?" They were both talking just above a whisper.

"Dehydrated. She's on dextrose."

They walked to the door. "Aren't you about pooped?" Corrine put her arm around the older woman, who shrugged it off. "This weather doesn't help. It's *so* humid."

"Yes, as a matter of fact I am tired." They walked to the nurses' station, where Maudie gave Corrine a report on the patients. As she talked, she fingered a key in her pocket. When she got through talking to Corrine, she pulled the key out and went over to the key box and replaced it on the appropriate hook. It might as well be there as anywhere. Since Carl Haney was named coroner and his mortuary was right across the street from the hospital, bodies were usually taken straight there. The morgue here wasn't used much anymore.

Monday Morning

11

A SIREN WOKE Maudie about 1 A.M.—it was Carl Haney's ambulance. She knew because it had a distinctive sound to it, not like the sheriff's car or the highway patrol. What if it was Eugene, she worried, out drinking with his friends? It was the same thought she'd had since the day he started driving. She rolled over, pulled the sheet up around her, and remembered her son's current predicament—her predicament as well, one she was going to take care of.

She rolled over again, mumbling, "Why do they do this to me? First Thomas, then Ruthie, now Eugene."

Maudie had gotten pregnant when she was fourteen, and her eldest brother, Evan, who was like a father to her, saw to it that the other party to it, Bubba Stokes, married her. Thomas, their son, was forty-one now; she could hardly believe it. They were almost contemporaries. He'd moved off to Arizona and never wrote or anything. He was pretty much off her list.

The marriage to Bubba didn't last long enough to remember anymore, but afterward Evan had made Maudie finish school, then sent her off to nurse's training. She didn't marry again until she was in her mid-twenties, and that marriage hadn't lasted either. Coxsen Rice just stayed with her long enough to sire two kids, Eugene and Ruthie, then he'd run off with the preacher's wife. It was no wonder Maudie felt soured on religion.

Ruthie had always been a disappointment; Eugene said
her train didn't have all its cars. Maudie hushed him when
he said it, but secretly she was inclined to agree. The girl
kind of reminded Maudie of her own mother, who'd always
seemed to be in a dreamworld. She'd first attributed it to the
confusion of a household with eight children and no
husband (he'd died when Maudie was two), but later, when
the kids were grown, the condition persisted, continuing
right up until the old woman died. A person could be talking
to her, and she'd wander off or interrupt with a totally
unrelated thought. She seemed almost otherworldly, and
when she died, Maudie was comforted by the feeling that
her mother would probably end up in a place where she'd fit
right in.

Ruthie was like that, only maybe not so pronounced. She
also had a particular susceptibility to religion, just like her
grandmother. Every time a tent meeting came to town when
Ruthie was growing up, the girl had been saved. She was
undoubtedly a member of every fly-by-night proselytizing
group in these parts. By the time she was eighteen, she was
wearing long dresses, no adornment, and no makeup. Her
hair hung below her waist. She looked like a Puritan in
modern America, and she carried her Bible everywhere.

No one would hire such an odd-looking girl for an
ordinary job, so Maudie turned to Evan. He got Ruthie
work as a teacher for some children who weren't in the
public schools because of their families' beliefs. They lived
in a compound southwest of Breedlove and were reputed to
be a bunch of survivalists. It was one of the few times
Maudie had gotten mad at her brother.

"If anything," she said, "those people are going to make
the girl odder than she already is." At the time she was still
trying to hang on to her daughter.

"Maudie, Maudie," he'd said, "it'll be all right. They're
good folks. You'll see."

She saw all right. One day Ruthie dropped by, wearing
what her mother called her sackcloth, to say she had
married a man named Lee Newton.

Maudie'd had the two of them to Sunday dinner once,

just once, along with Eugene, but the afternoon was a failure. Newton said virtually nothing except to utter a few religious homilies designed, Maudie thought, to put the Rices down, and Ruthie spent her time hanging on his every word. They hadn't been invited back, and since then, Maudie had written her daughter off, too, just like Thomas. And just as well, what with this thing in Presley County.

Now there was Eugene. She knew he didn't seem to hold much promise, with his drinking and carousing, but maybe it was just a boyish phase. A criminal record wouldn't help him make a fresh start. She wasn't ready to write him off yet.

If the worst came to pass, there was still Evan. He had always been the stable person in her life, more than any husband, more than the kids. One of these days, she might just go live with her brother and take care of him. It would be nice, she thought, just the two of them.

The hospital parking lot where Ted tried to sleep was bathed with a blue-white glow from the lamps overhead, and a few lights shown from the hospital, but it wasn't enough to keep the night monsters of depression and remorse away from him. They were aided by the lonely hours of solitude, during which Susan's faults disappeared and her assets grew. He chided himself for not appreciating her more and darkly wondered if he'd ever get the chance to make it up to her.

An ambulance drew up at the mortuary across the street and was divested of its burdens. Fear solidified in Ted's gut, and he got out of the car and walked over.

"What happened?"

One of the attendants answered, "Car wreck outside of town."

"Have they been identified?" His heart stopped while he awaited an answer.

"Yep. Can't say more than that—you know, next of kin and all that."

Ted gulped. "Well, my wife is missing—"

The man frowned and slammed the ambulance door. "This was three guys—drunk."

Ted returned weakly to his car. Of course it couldn't have been Susan. She wouldn't have a car. He lifted his glasses and wiped his eyes. It was just the uncertainty—it was easy to jump to conclusions.

He crawled in the backseat, put his glasses in the foot well, and tried to sleep again. At the first welcome grayness of dawn, he sat up and rubbed his face, settled his glasses on the bridge of his nose, then got out and stretched, wishing he could wipe away the events of the weekend. He climbed behind the wheel and started the car, feeling guilty about disturbing the peace of the morning with the engine noise, and pulled out of the lot to look for a café where he could get something to eat and use the rest room.

He had to wait ten minutes outside the Curly-Q Café till it opened. A bald-headed man, Curly himself, according to the tooling on the man's leather belt, let him in, then took his order.

Ted lingered over breakfast, then phoned his boss to tell him he wouldn't be in. Finally, he could wait there no longer, so he paid his bill and left. He was hoping that nurse he'd encountered at the hospital the night before had gone off duty by now. She had, and the morning nurse greeted him and nodded when he said he was there to visit Jan.

"Ted," Jan said as he entered, "hello again."

"How are you this morning?"

"Better, I think. But I'm sore everywhere. Ted, I want to thank you for not—well, for not saying 'I told you so.'"

He frowned. "What do you mean?"

"I know you didn't approve of this outing."

He shrugged.

"I feel really responsible. If something has happened—"

"Don't." He held his hand up. "Let's not jump to conclusions," he said. "I've done enough of that."

"What do you mean?"

"Yesterday when I turned to the sports page in the paper, and there was the picture I told you about, Susan with another man . . . when I saw it, my first thought—I'm ashamed now—was that you two were down here playing around, that Susan was stepping out on me. But I blamed you, not her. It was just what I expected to happen if she ran around with a divorced woman. I was afraid she'd think the grass was greener . . . you know. I've resented the friendship between you two ever since you first met, but I never analyzed why until now. It's your confounded independence. I find it threatening."

Jan tried to stop him, but he waved off her interruption.

"Let me finish. Anyway, then your phone call came. And I began thinking about Susan and me and our relationship. I had that drive down here and then all night long to think. And it was a *lonnng* night." He smiled, but it faded quickly and he continued. "I've been afraid to let Susan be self-sufficient; I need her to need me." His voice dropped so it was almost inaudible. "I'm such a stick-in-the-mud."

Ted walked to the window and looked out. "Our relationship felt so safe as long as she was dependent on me. And now I'm afraid she's ill-equipped to deal with whatever it is—" His voice broke.

Jan was looking at him intently. "Don't jump to conclusions, remember? She's probably a lot tougher than either of us realize."

"I hope so." He hesitated, embarrassed by his confessions, then changed the subject to something safer. "I meant to bring that newspaper clipping in so you could see it. I'll go——" He was heading for the door and almost collided with a man coming in. "Sorry."

Jan said, "Hi, Neal. This is Susan's husband, Ted Morrow. Ted, this is Neal Lassiter. We rented the canoe from him." She realized her heart had started thumping wildly when she saw Neal. He did look good to her. Faded blue jeans, pale blue T-shirt.

"Glad to meet you," Ted said, and stuck out his hand, his errand to the car temporarily forgotten.

The two men shook hands, then Neal said, "I just wanted to dash over and see how you're doing, Jan."

"Better," she said. "I'm actually feeling halfway

normal." *Except my heart,* she thought. *It's going crazy right now. Good thing it's not being monitored.*

"You're looking better."

She smiled. "You're being kind."

Neal turned to Ted. "You'll be interested in this. I stopped by the sheriff's office on the way in, and the deputy has gotten some men together to start a search party. He said to get my tail right back over there, so I can go out with him to look for the guys who assaulted Jan. You want to go, too?"

"You're damn right I do."

"Jan," Neal said. "I'd like to visit a while, but—"

"No, go on. It's important."

"I'll see you later, okay?" he said.

Ted patted her on the arm. "Take care, Janice—Jan." He smiled at her.

She returned the smile and wished them good luck.

Ted followed Neal out to his truck, and they drove to the courthouse.

The deputy was sitting behind the desk, the phone to his ear, when the two men entered the outer office. He raised one hand in salute, continuing to listen, then said, "Okay, Fayette, you come in as soon as you can. I'd appreciate it. Bye."

He placed the phone in its cradle and stood up with a sigh. "The girl didn't show up for work this morning. Called her mama's, and she said Connie didn't come home last night." He rubbed his chin. "Just one thing after another."

"Another missing person?" Neal said.

"Maybe she's just got a boyfriend." The deputy frowned. "She's a quiet one though. Don't know her to have a fella."

Ted stuck out his hand. "I'm Ted Morrow. It's my wife that's missing."

"Chief Deputy Emory Todd." They shook hands and then the deputy said, "C'mon into my office." He sat down at his desk, and continued, "Senator Grindstaff called over here. It must be your daughter who works for him."

"Yes," Ted said. "She must have talked to him."

Emory nodded.

"What are you doing to find my wife? She's apparently been missing since Saturday morning."

"I just sent out five search parties." He unfolded a topographical map, put it on the desk, and pointed out where each group was going. "I have to tell you, though, that findin' someone out in that wilderness is like findin' a needle in a haystack. There's a million places to hide."

Eugene and Three-Fingers had finished setting their ambush across the river the day before, then they'd gone on down to the place where they figured all the booty would wash up. There they'd drunk beer and slept away Sunday night and Monday morning.

The place was a shady bank where they had a good view of the river as it bent around about a quarter of a mile below the Narrows. The water was nice and calm, making up for what it had just put a man through up above.

Three-Fingers and Eugene had picked up lots of good stuff along here. Boats mainly, and coolers, life vests. The stuff that would float would get backed up here and if a fellow was here at just the right time, no telling what he might pull out. They'd even found a body once, which they'd left alone. Usually they just took what floated their way. This was the first time they'd actually sabotaged someone.

Susan heard the roar of the white water as they rounded a bend in the river. It started softly, just a steady muted sound—an almost imperceptible background noise. Gradually it began a crescendo culminating in a roar. Susan's eyes widened as she saw the narrowing river racing downward in a leaping tumult through the gorge. Fear constricted her throat, making it hard to breathe.

Lee had already lashed his gun to one of the thwarts. "Move back in front of this crosspiece," he said. He back paddled while she obeyed, then he moved forward till they were close together in the center of the canoe.

"What are we doing?"

"I can override your mistakes here," he said loudly, a smug smile on his face. "Face the front and do what I tell you."

She swiveled around and grabbed the gunwales. Her body jolted as the canoe rose and fell over the churning water. She turned and shouted over the chaos, "Can't we walk it around? I'd help carry the boat."

He smiled, his eyes bright. "Too late." It was true. They were already between the high walls of the cliffs, and the canoe's speed was increasing rapidly. "Stay as low as you can," he shouted, "but don't forget to paddle." His voice was shrill.

Ahead the water looked like foam as it channeled through the narrow gorge.

Lee headed the canoe for the V that showed the main current. The first chute was easy, but after that the entire surface of the water buckled in confusion, and the main avenue disappeared. The force of the water began to shove the back of the boat harder than the front, and they began to slip to one side.

She pulled harder, paddling as he'd told her, eyes wide with fright. Water sprayed up over her as a wave swept into the boat, sending it downward only to be hurled up again like a piece of driftwood. They shot past a submerged boulder, then another one appeared out of nowhere, and the canoe banged against it, the force of the water pressing them there, wedged between it and another smaller rock.

"Push us away," he shouted at her over the deafening roar.

She halfheartedly shoved with her paddle, but there was no way to get any leverage on the slick surface. Water dashed her face.

"Push," he shouted again. "Harder."

"I can't," she screamed, "Damn you!"

The force of the water was releasing, then slamming the boat relentlessly against the rock. She felt sure that any moment the canoe was going to fold up on itself.

"Push us off with your leg or you're gonna die here," he yelled.

She glanced back at him for a moment, an incredulous look on her face. The veins stood out in his neck as he laid into the paddle, working against the water.

Susan struggled up onto her knees and got one leg over the side to jam her foot against the rock. The water sprayed against her, turbulent waves bashing the boat, threatening to push it out from under her at any moment. She pushed with one hand and one leg, hanging onto the gunwale precariously with the other hand. Her strength wasn't sufficient, but her fury was. She released her grip on the boat and left the canoe, except for one leg. With what felt like superhuman strength, she pushed against the rock; the boat began to slide off of it, stretching her away from the canoe's safety. She was hanging over the hungry water. With a silent plea to God, she separated from the rock, terror propelling her sideways into the canoe. The force of the boat's forward movement as they jolted across a submerged rock and came free pitched her into the bottom of the canoe. She righted herself and grabbed her paddle. The river, as if in an act of momentary compassion, let them slide around the rock and go tumbling down over a line of rapids, but in the next instant it spat its full fury in her face as they careened on through the narrow gorge. Susan wasn't paddling any longer, but was using the paddle as a pole. She stuck it out to keep them away from a rock that sprang out of the foam on their right, and the river sucked the paddle out of her hand, wrenching her wrist painfully as she fought to keep it. Empty-handed, she sank down as low as she could into the bottom of the boat, completely helpless now, with no control.

"Move back," she heard Lee shout.

Clutching the bow seat, she started to scoot backward just as the front of the canoe lifted as if it were going to take off. Just as suddenly, it dipped below the foam, blasting her face with water. She rose slightly to escape the wave. The boat dipped again, and something sharp struck her across the chest, flinging her sideways out of the canoe. She heard Lee cursing and caught a glimpse of him flailing the air as the canoe capsized. The river's rage swept it away before she could even attempt to grab hold. It seemed as if the water wanted its victim.

Without the canoe she figured she was a goner. Her body was under the water being tumbled along like a bit of driftwood, buffeted against the rocks. She fought to right herself. At last her head broke the surface, and she gasped for air, then the torrent submerged her again. She frantically fought the water's assault, and it fought back, slamming her against a boulder. Her arms and legs banged against underwater obstacles, hurling her in first one direction, then another. For a moment she clung to a rock and caught her breath, but her hands began to slip on the mossy surface, and she was pummeled back into the current by the water.

Time after time she surfaced only to be thrown under again, but she didn't seem to be going downstream. She was in some sort of eddy. Something clicked in her mind, and she struggled across the current for a brief moment and was released. A crash of water swept her upward and hurled her out of the mainstream, and her body stalled in a pile of rock. She lay there, drinking in the air, ignoring the pains in her arms and legs, grateful only to be in one piece and alive.

It was only then that she thought of Lee. She'd seen him thrown into the water. Where was he now? She lifted her head and looked around, but saw no sign of him or the canoe. This was her chance. He could be right on the other side of these rocks, she realized. She knew she had to get moving.

She sat up cautiously and gazed up at the bluff towering over her. Clouds moved swiftly above the cliff top, and their dizzying effect almost bowled her over backward. The bluff appeared to be falling forward. Quickly she averted her gaze and steadied herself, then looked back, concentrating on the rock face.

Stains left from organic material formed veils of black along the vertical surfaces, almost like paintings by some modern artist. Any other time she would have wished for her camera, but now she was concentrating on how to get out of this natural prison. Time had stacked the rock, while weather and cataclysmic events had shaped it, making natural ledges and handholds to use for climbing. She scanned the bluff as if she had many choices about where to start climbing out of the gorge. In reality, her perch made only one point accessible.

She cautiously began to scramble across the few remaining rocks in the area between the water and the base of the bluff. She still hadn't spotted Lee, but she had to take the chance; she couldn't just stay where she was. At least his gun was with the canoe.

She sized up each rock in her path, then leaped. One proved deceptive and her foot slipped sideways, down into the water. She fell forward on her hands and other foot, clutching at the rock, barely catching herself. She waited a moment, then pulled herself upright and hurled her body across the final distance to the narrow ledge at the base of the bluff.

Reaching the next ledge would be easy. It was as if there were stepping stones built into the wall right up to that first level. Once up there, she had a better view of the river. She wondered if Lee could be below the ledge somewhere. She flattened herself on the horizontal surface, crawled to the edge, and peeked over with cold dread, scanning the river again, then hanging farther over and looking below the bluff. There was no sign of him, just the tumble of rocks she'd been swept into earlier.

Fatigue overwhelmed her, and she was tempted to go to sleep. She closed her eyes. *Just rest here until someone rescues me. They always take care of me—someone does.* But no, not this time. She had to get out of there before he came to find her.

She stood up reluctantly, feeling like a target, and began to search for a place to climb up to the next level of the rock. Unfortunately nature had made no inviting path at this level. Cracks in the rock would have to do for hand- and footholds.

Her hand groped for a fissure and found one, and inch by inch she worked her way upward. About halfway to the next tier, her left leg began to shake so hard she thought she'd fall off the bluff. She laid her cheek against the cold rock

and closed her eyes, the physical and emotional exhaustion
tearing through her. Her fingers began trembling as they
pressed against the smooth, vertical surface above her head.
She worked her hand around, searching for a grip, while her
right foot sought a good foothold to help bear her weight.
Her breathing became shallow. Where could she put her
foot? Her fingers cramped. Her shoe moved up and down
and across the smooth stone until at last it found purchase.

She rested there, trying to stabilize her breathing, thinking of freedom and the trees and grass at the top of the
bluff. After a few minutes, she found a handhold and began
to inch her way up again. Flat against the rock, she couldn't
judge how much farther it was to the ledge, and when her
hands reached it she felt like rejoicing.

The feeling dissipated quickly when she looked above
her. She was beneath an overhang and there didn't seem to
be any way to scale it. To her left the ledge she was on
narrowed until it didn't exist, so she edged along in the
opposite direction. To her dismay it also ended, only to
begin again across a four-foot gap—not far, but all of a
sudden it looked like an insurmountable chasm. Below, if
she fell, there was nothing to receive her but the rocks at the
edge of the tumbling river.

She had only this one choice. There was no going down.
She steadied herself a moment, took a deep breath, then
leaped. She made it, plastering herself against the wall's
smooth surface to savor the comfort of its mass. At the same
moment her hand contacted something foreign feeling, and
she jerked it away, but almost simultaneously, a needlelike
pain stabbed her in the arm, then another in the hand.

At least a dozen wasps were circling her. Another one
stung her on the arm. She grimaced at the pain, but couldn't
stop to nurse it. She began to edge along, trying to get away
from the persistent and angry insects. Two more zeroed in
on their target. She flinched as they hit. Tears welled up in
her eyes at the deep ache. Finally, they gave up and left her
alone. Only then did she stop moving to examine the
punctures, now beginning to swell. She spit on the one on

her arm, rubbed it, gritted her teeth, and began to move again.

The overhang still cast its shadow below, but a way up presented itself: a deep fissure cleaving the bluff. She wedged her body in it and pushed up with her legs and buttocks, in a half-standing, half-sitting posture. Her position reminded her of a game Jeffrey and his friends played where they worked their way up doorjambs this way. She would keep that picture in her head as she tried to duplicate their movements.

Finding a new toehold, she turned and pushed herself a few feet farther. Just above her a tree limb lay wedged in the crevice, blocking her path upward. It appeared to be solidly jammed. She was going to have to climb on it to get by. Cautiously, she began to put her weight onto the pile of rubble accumulated on the branch. It was holding, then suddenly the whole thing gave way. Her hand grasped a rock overhead that was jutting out, but it came loose, and she went sliding down the crevice she'd just conquered. A jagged surface raked her leg as she jolted past it, and her fingers, grabbing at it as they slid past, managed to slow her fall. Finally she stopped, jammed in the crevice.

Gradually, laboriously, she began to work her way up again. Near the top, the fissure eased back and began to support life. Soil had collected, and there was a weedy tangle of mosses and woody vines. Only a few more feet, and she was there. Never had soil smelled so good. She drank in its scent greedily.

The incline was still precipitous, and she continued to crawl along on her hands and knees, pulling herself with vines and tufts of weeds. She grabbed the trunk of the first small tree she came to and clung to it, overjoyed at its sturdiness. She stayed there a few more minutes, clinging, then got up and started walking into the woods as the terrain flattened. Her legs were shaking and her gait was irregular.

A path became discernible, perhaps one animals used, and she followed it. *Paths lead somewhere,* she reasoned. This one did.

A house clothed in fake brick asphalt siding sat at the

edge of a clearing. Two propane tanks stood beside the house. A covered porch once painted white ran the distance of the front. A weather-beaten upholstered chair sat by the sagging screen door. She went up the two steps and knocked.

An old man appeared. He was wearing baggy overalls, no shirt, and a misshapen gray felt hat. A black-and-white mutt stood beside him. He greeted Susan heartily. "Come on in."

"I need your help. Do you have a phone?"

He chuckled and rubbed his whiskery chin. "No phone. You get a phone, and all them folks out there begins to want things. Nope. No phone." He frowned. "I could doctor those swole-up places on your face. You get into a wasp's nest? C'mon in here."

She went in and her heart sank. Sitting at the table gnawing on a piece of meat was Lee. A gun sat on the table in front of him. A half smile crept across his mouth. "Didn't expect to see me, did you? I told you, it's God's plan."

For a fleeting moment she wondered if he was right.

"How did you get out of there?" she asked. She meant the Narrows, and Lee understood.

"I came up the Devil's Staircase—it's a rock formation brings you right up out of the gorge. How'd you get out? I figured you drowned without a life jacket."

It wasn't worth answering. "You told me you were such a good canoer."

"We were ambushed," he said, almost defensively. "There was a wire strung across the river; that's what capsized us. And when I get time I'm gonna come back and cook the goose of whoever put it across there." He eyed the old man. "That wouldn't be your idea of fun, would it, Willy?"

The man let loose with a wild chuckle. "I cain't even get down there no more. No, it's some others what did that."

"Do you know who?" Lee asked.

"No, sir." He got some baking soda out of a cabinet, then made a paste. "Let me put some of this on those stings. It's what my mama used."

"Willy here is a survivor," Lee told Susan as she was getting doctored. "He used to live in town, then he left it all behind." Lee rose and walked around the table, then patted the old man on the shoulder. "But you better watch out, Willy, 'cause one of these days all those city folks are gonna come pouring out here, wantin' to take your place. You better be prepared to kill 'em, cause they'll try to take all your food. They'll be beggin' at the door, and ol' Willy'll be fendin' 'em off." He took the gun from the table and played it around the room. "Blam, blam, blam. You'll be a sight, Willy."

The old man had put the baking soda away and went over to sit down and listen to Lee's recital.

"Then the nigger police will come lookin' to make sure no white man has more than the niggers. And he'll sneak up on you in the night, Willy." Lee aimed the gun at the old man's head.

"Don't!" Susan shouted. "Leave him alone."

Willy was smiling inanely, both hands on his knees. He lifted his heels and let them down with a thump. "I don't want no trouble," he said.

"I'm going to the outhouse," Lee announced, his play over. He drew near Susan and told her privately, "You stay put, or I'll let him suffer the consequences. You understand?"

Susan nodded and Lee left.

She debated what to do. The old man still sat with his hands on his knees, grinning, his dog at his feet.

"Do you have another gun?" She looked around nervously.

"No, that was mine he was a-carryin'."

"How about that one?" She nodded toward a gun hanging on the wall.

"Nah, that one's no good. It was my pappy's squirrel-huntin' rifle, but it got rusty, and I ain't wanted to clean it. So I didn't."

She squatted down in front of his chair. "Willy, could you please get a message to the . . . to the sheriff's office that I'm being held hostage by—"

The old man's eyebrows slipped down in a frown. "I know who he is. He's one of them army fellas. They have exercises in these woods sometimes."

"He's not real army. He's—he's—" What could she say to explain? "Just please tell the sheriff. Tell him Susan Morrow has been kidnapped, and we're going to be at River's Bend Tuesday afternoon. Can you remember that?"

He just grinned at her. "He's borryin' my gun 'cause he lost his'n down in the river."

"Well, don't try to stop him, or he may kill you. He killed a highway patrolman."

"And him a army man. I don't mess around with those army men, no sir. They got important maneuvers."

"He's not an army man. Will you please get my message to the sheriff? Tell him we're headed to River's Bend. Susan Morrow. River's Bend."

She heard Lee's footsteps on the porch, so she touched her lips in warning and turned her back on the old man.

"Let's get out of here," Lee said to her. He grabbed up a sack of provisions which he'd apparently packed before she'd arrived.

The old man settled down in the easy chair on the porch, adjusting his felt hat back on his gray hair. His dog came over and lay down at his feet.

"Well, Georgie, this has been quite a day. Ain't had that much company in a long time." He drew his eyebrows together and gave it some thought. "Not since that army fella was here with his buddies, doin' their maneuvers."

When he'd lived at home with Mama and Papa, now that'd been different. There'd been visitors for sure, but that was a long time ago when they were alive. He couldn't remember exactly when they'd died, but it was a spell ago, because after that he'd lived with Cousin George. That's who he'd named his dog after. When George died there was enough money to buy this place, and his government money was enough to live on. He went to town once a month on the third to get his check and buy groceries.

"She said he wasn't a army man. Hmmm. What d'you

think of that, fella?" He reached down and scratched the dog behind the ears. "She was a nice lady. Like Aunt Carol. Kinda looked like her." His eyes misted. Aunt Carol had died before his mama. The old man wiped his eyes with his sleeve.

"So what d'you think, Georgie?" The old man shuffled his feet again and sighed deeply. The dog's head popped up. His tail began to thump on the porch, then he leaped to his feet to follow the old man down the steps. "Let's go to the highway and hitch us a ride to town, fella."

Monday Afternoon

12

THE DEPUTY SHERIFF crossed the center line and pulled off onto the shoulder of the highway. "You seen Three-Fingers Purcell and Eugene Rice today?" he hollered out his window at a man working in his garden.

The man stood up from his hunkered-over position, looped his thumb in his overalls strap, and started walking toward the car. Neal was riding shotgun, and Ted was in the backseat cracking his knuckles nervously. He felt as if they'd looked everywhere, been on the worst roads he'd ever seen, and still nothing. Susan was out there somewhere in who knew what kind of condition, and this old fellow, and even the deputy, were taking their own sweet time.

"Howdy, Em'ry," the old man said as he came up beside the car.

The deputy repeated his question.

The fellow spat a wad of tobacco, then said, "Seems like I saw them in Eugene's old truck hightailing it thataway this mornin'." He pointed down the highway the way the car was headed. "Leastwise I think that was this morning." He rubbed his chin and chuckled.

Emory laughed. "Know what you mean. Well, thanks. Sorry to interrupt your gardenin'."

"'S okay. See you." He watched as the deputy pulled back onto the highway.

"We'll stop at Henry's store and see if they've been by there. Chances are they have."

"Why's that?" Ted asked.

"Nearest place to get beer," Neal said over his shoulder.

"Everyone goes there to exchange gossip," Emory added.

"Maybe there'll be some gossip about where those two bastards have my wife."

Neither of the men in the front seat commented.

Ted had expected Henry's to be an old-time general store, but it turned out to be a blue metal building, four gas pumps in front, much like any other convenience store. Three soda-pop machines stood in front for after-hours traffic; next to them was an ice machine with a sign: ICE 99¢.

The windows had merchandise piled against them, and homemade notices about garage sales, auctions, and coming events in the area. There was a large placard announcing that the store had videos to rent.

Just as the deputy started to get out of the car, a black truck went barreling down the highway. "Shoot!" Emory said, slamming the door and throwing the car into reverse. "That's them now." He made a quick U-turn and started after the truck. He turned on his flashing lights, but Three-Fingers and Eugene were so far ahead, they probably didn't even see them.

Ted was holding onto his seat as Emory sped around the curves, finally getting the truck in sight on a straightaway.

"I bet that's my canoe," Neal said, seeing the one sticking out of the back of the black truck.

Emory turned on his siren, but it was still a mile before he got the two pulled over.

Neal was out of the deputy's car before it stopped rolling. He went to the door of the truck, jerked it open, and seized the bearded driver by the arm, dragging him out. He delivered a swift, sharp blow to the man's stomach, at which the surprised Eugene bent over double, gasping for air. Neal was a big man, but his opponent wasn't small. Nevertheless, Ted thought as he got over to the two of them, Neal made Eugene look like a wimp.

He looked around and saw the other man had jumped out. He was the one! Light haired, features which blended together indistinctly. He charged him. "You bastard, where's my wife?" he shouted.

Emory, last out of the car, pulled Ted off of the man and shoved him roughly back, leaving Three-Fingers free to go after Neal. Eugene was still gasping, so Neal turned his attention to Three-Fingers. Emory grabbed hold of him, but Neal shrugged him off. In exasperation, the deputy pulled his gun, waved it, and yelled, "That's enough. Back off. All of you." But no one was paying any attention.

Ted had Three-Fingers by the shirt and was demanding to know something about Susan. He could tell now why the man's reflexes were slow; he was drunk. Slow, but not gone. All at once, he pulled back his fist and punched Ted in the stomach. Ted saw it coming and almost saved himself from it. It landed, but not hard enough to knock the wind out of him. The force of his own blow almost bowled over the drunken man, and Emory took the opportunity to grab him by the collar.

"Purcell, down on your belly," he ordered.

The man sank down, almost gladly it seemed.

Neal had turned back to Eugene and landed a solid blow to his chin, making him stagger backward, and Emory stepped in between them. "Enough, Lassiter, or I'll arrest you for brawling." He looked around at Eugene. "You get down beside your buddy." He obeyed.

Three-Fingers lifted his head slightly. "Whas this about, Em'ry?"

"I'm haulin' you in for questioning about a little incident on the river Saturday. Get your hands behind you." He snapped cuffs on Eugene's wrists, then asked Ted to get another pair out of the car. "Also for drunk driving and resisting arrest."

"Don' know what you're talkin' 'bout," Eugene said. His voice was slurred. "What incident?"

"Assaulting a woman."

"She was askin' for it, Emory. She pulled a gun on us."

Emory snorted. "We want to know about the other woman, Eugene."

"There's nothin' to know."

"You saw them both on Friday evening at their camp-site."

Eugene had laid his head down again. "Maybe so, but we don't know nothing."

"She disappeared with one of my canoes," Neal said. He was looking at the boat in Eugene's truck. "And it appears you've got it here."

Emory frowned. "What do you have to say about that, boys?"

"We was returnin' it. It came floatin' down the river, and we jist fished 'er out. Right, Three-Fingers?"

"Thas right."

The deputy hauled first Eugene, then Three-Fingers up off the ground and marched them to the car. He told Neal to drive the black truck to the courthouse, so Ted climbed in front next to Emory.

"What next?" he asked.

"I'll tell you as soon as we deposit these two buzzards."

When they got to the courthouse, the deputy left Neal and Ted waiting near the clerk's desk. Fayette was on duty.

Something was bothering Ted. "I need to go to my car to get a picture," he told Neal. On the way to the hospital parking lot, he explained about the picture of the raft race.

The clipping was in the pocket of his bermuda shorts. He retrieved it from his suitcase, then climbed in beside Neal and laid the picture on the seat, smoothing it out.

"That's your wife, right? I remember the shirt."

"Yes. And when Jan described the one guy—it sounded like this man." He tapped the picture. "But—what do you think?"

Neal squinted at it. "I don't think so. That isn't Three-Fingers. This guy's more muscular. Shorter hair, too. Coloring's similar though."

They went back to the sheriff's office and put the clipping on the desk. They needed to show it to Emory. The clerk leaned over to look. "What's that?" she asked.

"This was in the paper yesterday. That's my wife." He pointed at Susan, then at the man in the canoe. "And I don't know who that is, but it's not one of the men we brought in."

"Let me see that," Fayette said. Ted handed the clipping to her. She looked for a moment, then pulled a picture of a blond-haired young man from some papers on the desk and help it up so they could see. "This came in the mail a while ago. Look similar?"

"Who is that?" Ted demanded.

"He's the guy they're lookin' for up in Presley County. One of those white supremacists who lives in that Compound"—she looked at Neal—"southwest of here. He's the one who shot that trooper."

Neal and Ted looked puzzled.

"Where have you two guys been?" Fayette asked. "Don't you listen to the news?" She told them about Lee Newton.

"I'd say it's the same guy, wouldn't you? I mean the picture is fuzzy, but . . ." Neal said.

Ted agreed.

"So Three-Fingers and Eugene were telling the truth," Neal said. "This white supremacist—what's his name?"

"Lee Newton," Fayette said.

"He was probably stealing the canoe, and your wife came along and caught him at it, so he took her hostage. They accidentally got their picture taken. But then how did Three-Fingers and Eugene get the canoe?"

"They know more than they're saying," Ted said. He fingered the clipping nervously. He wanted to be doing something, trying to find Susan.

Just then Emory reappeared. "They're so drunk they both conked out, so I stuck 'em in a cell to sober up."

"Look at this," Ted said, shoving the clipping toward him. He and Neal explained.

Emory slapped his thigh. "Hot damn! I didn't think those two boys were guilty."

Ted was surprised when Neal, who had been standing calmly beside him, exploded. "Damn it Emory! They're guilty as hell of assaulting Jan Spencer." He slammed his fist down on the counter. There was more going on here than Ted understood.

The deputy lifted his hands in a gesture of placation. "Okay, okay. Calm down. Just let me call up to Presley County and get hold of Billy Jay about this."

Minutes later the deputy was connected to the highway patrol substation in Presley County.

"No way he can be down there now," a sergeant told Emory. "He's been staying in a church up here. Broke in."

"Has someone actually seen him?"

The man hesitated. "Well, no, but he's contained."

"Any evidence of someone with him?"

"No."

Emory wondered if Lee Newton could have dumped Susan Morrow somewhere. It didn't make sense. If he was down here to get his picture taken Saturday morning on the river, why in hell would he run right back up there into the waiting hands of his pursuers?

He went back to Ted and Neal. "They say they have the fugitive surrounded up there."

Ted's hopeful expression fell, and he appeared near tears. "What about my wife?"

The deputy shook his head. "They don't think anyone's with him."

"That doesn't make sense," Neal said. "Why would Newton be up there when he was almost home free down here?"

"I wondered that myself. I think they got themselves the wrong boy cornered up there."

13

"IT'S NOT MY fault you didn't have a good time," Marge said. "And we did get a home spa out of it." The couple was driving along a curvy section of highway north of the Upper Fork River.

"Spa? That little thing they gave us? You call it a spa? Looks like the bathtub you used to bathe Tammy Sue in. And that eggbeater thing they call a whirlpool." He made a disgusted sound.

"Slow down on these curves, Norman." She always called him that when she disapproved of his driving.

What a distasteful experience the trip to the time-share resort had been. The salesman who'd delivered the spiel had been high pressure from the word go. A real horse's ass. But Norm had had the last laugh. He asked how long their mobile home had to be. The guy had pulled himself up pompously and informed them the area was restricted—no mobile homes. The sales pitch had ended forthwith.

"Norman Burke, you almost went off the road."

"Do you want to drive?" he yelled, glancing her way just as they entered a curve. As they came around it, the west sun hit Norm in the eyes. He reached for the visor and saw the old man in the road too late.

"Norm, look out," Marge shrieked.

Norm jammed on the brakes and the back ones locked, sending the car into a spin. Even so, they couldn't avoid the old man. The car hit him with a heavy thud, and his body was thrown to the side of the road. Norm fought the wheel and managed to get stopped. He was breathing hard, and he leaned his head momentarily on the wheel and asked, "You okay?"

Marge was already getting out of the car. She made a beeline toward the ditch. A black-and-white dog had gotten there first. It was licking the old man's face.

Norm got out, following his wife. "Is he alive?"

Marge was bending over to see if the man was breathing.

"Yes, he's alive. You're going to be okay," she whispered, close to the old man's ear. "You'll be okay."

Just then they heard an approaching car. Norm got out on the road and flagged it down. The car's occupants looked reluctant at first, but when they saw the old man in the ditch, they braked and agreed to go to the nearest phone and call an ambulance. The nearest town was Breedlove.

The dog had lain down at the old man's feet, waiting to see where they were going next.

When it became clear that there would be no questioning of Three-Fingers and Eugene anytime soon, Ted and Neal left the courthouse and drove to the hospital to look in on Jan.

She was just lying there, looking subdued, her hands resting palms-down on the sheet when they walked in.

"How are you?" Ted asked with a frown. "You don't look as if you feel too good."

Jan shrugged. "I thought I was ready to get out of here. I *feel* fine, but when the doctor looked at my chart a while ago, he said my temperature is up. He wants to do some more tests. And, of course, they won't do those till tomorrow."

"I'm sorry," Ted said.

"It's this atmosphere," Neal said. "Not exactly the Ritz, is it?" He pulled at the neck of his T-shirt and made a face. "Maybe you need some real food. We could smuggle in a hamburger or something." He jiggled the IV tube.

She shook her head and sighed. "They promised this is the last bottle. What have you found out about Susan?"

They told her about Three-Fingers and Eugene and about Lee Newton.

"So those two weren't involved in her disappearance. That surprises me."

"It surprised me, too," said Ted. "Especially after I launched into that one guy."

"Well, let's not forget they assaulted you," Neal said defensively. "They're not out of the woods guiltwise."

"Only the one with the beard."

"That's not the one I jumped on," Ted said. "Maybe he was so drunk he won't remember."

"You'll need to sign the papers," Neal told her.

Jan's eyebrows drew together. "I signed it. Last night when the clerk brought it over." She looked around, but there was no sign of the form.

"That's odd," Neal said. "Emory specifically said he didn't have a formal complaint, said he could only hold them for drunk driving and resisting arrest. Isn't that what he said, Ted?"

Ted nodded.

"You saw Connie, Ted. She hurried out when you came in," Jan said. "She must have taken the form with her."

"Well, then that's the problem," Neal said. "She didn't show up for work today."

"I bet she has the paper."

Neal reached over and smoothed Jan's brow. "There's time to worry about that later. Eugene and Three-Fingers are dead to the world right now, and Emory can keep them there a while. You concentrate on getting well."

Jan looked up at him. "You know, a man at a basket store where we stopped on the way down told us about this Lee Newton. But it seemed so far—" She began to fidget with the sheet. "If only I'd—"

"Neal's right. Don't burden yourself with thoughts of what could have been different, Jan."

"I was hoping to take you out to my place first thing tomorrow," Neal said. "It'd be a better place to recuperate than this." He looked around him. "So think good thoughts."

"You should have seen this guy tear into that redhead,"

Ted told Jan. "I thought he was going to beat him to death before I even got out of the car."

Jan looked pleased, as if she'd been complimented, but Neal didn't allow himself to bask in it. "You did some roughing up yourself," he said to Ted.

"Yeah. I kind of surprised myself. I think of myself as so civilized, but after a day of this awful waiting, it felt good to just let go on those two." Jan's attention appeared to wander, and she was gazing out the window.

"Well," Neal said reluctantly, "you're probably tired, Jan, so I guess we'd better go." He was perched on the edge of her bed.

"May I borrow your bathroom before we hit the road?" Ted asked.

"Sure, go ahead."

"Neal has asked me to spend the night at his place, and I've accepted," he told Jan as he retreated. "It'll sure as hell beat staying in my car."

Neal was glad to be alone a minute with Jan. "I really mean it about your getting out of here and coming out to my place. It's really peaceful out there."

She reached out and took a lock of his hair, twisting it into a curl between her thumb and index finger. "Are you sure you want a woman there, disturbing the peace?"

He took her wrist and pulled her finger down to his mouth and took hold of it with his lips. "The peace is already disturbed." His chest was full of butterflies, and he wondered if she was feeling the same way. He took a deep breath. "When you get all better, maybe we can do some canoeing."

"How long?" She seemed as breathless as he.

"How long what?" It was hard to get out a complete sentence. The air had left his lungs.

"To recuperate?"

"As long as it takes. Do you have a job you have to get back to?" He nibbled on her finger.

She shook her head. "Not this summer." Her lips were parted, and he could hear her breathing. "I'm . . . a teacher."

"Other commitments?"

"No, not a one." She gazed at him steadily and let out an audible sigh as Ted reappeared.

Neal pulled her hand away from his mouth and gave it a hard squeeze. "I'll see you in the morning," he said huskily.

After leaving the old man's house, Lee and Susan didn't return to the river. Instead he led her through the woods. The branches overhead made keeping a fix on the sun impossible except in the most general way, and Lee would stop occasionally and consult a compass in the handle of his knife. Susan could understand why. They might be going in circles for all she could tell. After perhaps an hour, the ground began to descend steadily, and soon a quiet leg of the river came into view before them. It was placid here, wider than upstream. Trees were being undercut by the water, but they clung tenaciously to the bank, their exposed roots providing sanctuary for the animal life of the river.

"Is this the Big Pine?"

He nodded his head as he took hold of her arm and urged her downstream until they found a good place to cross. He climbed up on some roots on the other side, and reached back toward her to give her a hand up.

So, she thought, *without our canoe, we're cutting across the throats of the meanders, but we're still following the river.* She'd assumed River's Bend was on the Big Pine, and now she felt sure she was right.

She'd been scratching for some time before she really became aware of it. She looked down at her sunburned skin and noticed a rash—poison ivy! *Damn!* she thought. She felt like screaming in frustration. It was just one more thing. How much was she going to have to take? She'd never been particularly susceptible but here she was, covered with it.

The cold bite of the river the next time they crossed was a balm to her body. In all, they crossed it three more times before they stopped for dinner, a welcome break for her weary legs. Lee pulled out some jerky and day-old corn-bread for them to eat. And two Snickers candy bars.

"The old man has a sweet tooth," Lee said.

She savored the sticky sweet candy. Thank goodness no dog food, she thought.

They went a few miles farther that evening, but darkness fell early in the woods, and the roof of branches overhead blocked out the moonlight to such an extent that going on was impossible. When Lee tripped over a grapevine, it spelled an end to the night's journey.

Susan slept fitfully, but couldn't be certain that Lee slept at all. It apparently wasn't in his plan to sleep, because he didn't bother to tie her. He sat up all night, a vague shape against a tree. Once when she stirred, he asked if she was awake. He didn't respond immediately to her affirmative answer, but then he began to talk, as if the loneliness of the forest at night overwhelmed him, driving him to fill the silence.

His voice droned on and on against the insistent buzz of the forest creatures as she drifted in and out of sleep. The words played at the edge of her mind: *ZOG . . . C-4 . . . detonator . . . Marshallville . . . feds . . .*

She wondered how Jennifer was. *Marshallville*. Her eyes popped open, wide awake in an instant. "What did you say?"

"What?" He sounded startled by the intensity of her question.

"Did you say something about Marshallville?"

"So?"

"Did you say it?"

"Yeah, I said it. Why?"

"And the federal building?"

He didn't respond.

She dredged up his words from the fringes of her mind. "You're going to blow up the federal building in Marshallville Wednesday."

"Yeah. It will be an explosive beginning."

Her stomach turned over. "That's where my daughter works."

She could hear the disinterest in his voice. "She a fed?"

"No." Her voice came down hard on the word. "She's

just a girl out of college who found a job there. It's her first real job. You can't mean you're going to kill a lot of innocent people. Tell me you don't mean to do that."

"Shut up."

"I can't shut up. You've involved me in your . . . in your *gospel*. Your gospel of hatred." She tried to blink back the tears that were welling up in her eyes.

"If she works there, she's one of the enemy."

"You can't believe such a stupid thing," she yelled at him. "Have you ever had a real job? Do you know what it's like? Or do you just play army all the time?"

"Shut up," he repeated.

"You are an ignorant . . . an ignorant *bastard*." The final word ripped through the forest, silencing the nearby creatures. Without warning she launched herself at Lee's shadowy form, grabbing him with no plan in mind, just in a primitive desire to attack. She could feel the skin of his face ripping under her nails.

He jumped up, dragging her up with him, then twisted her hands free and slammed her against the tree. "Don't ever do that again. You are scum. One of *them*. You can't even see the truth when it's all around you. Woman, the end is near and your daughter will die, if not Wednesday, then soon enough. And so will you and all your kind who refuse to face the truth."

The impact against the tree knocked her breath away, and she sagged to the ground and lay there aching in both body and spirit.

Where had his hatred begun? What seeds in ordinary life turned a person into a zealot? Some of her friends were bigots about race, politics, religion. She remembered being at a party recently where the guests had started telling ethnic jokes, one after another. Had she listened? Yes, she thought guiltily. Had she laughed? Yes. Otherwise they would have thought her a prig. She'd felt uncomfortable, but hadn't wanted to walk away.

And it had seemed harmless. After all, they were nice people, generally. Lee Newton was just those nice people a giant step farther from the mainstream.

* * *

Maudie closed the chart she'd been working on, stood up, and straightened her cap, glancing down the hallway at the same time. Most of the staff was gone, and she was practically alone. Only Bob remained down in emergency, and he was probably reading one of his science-fiction novels. The rooms for the most part were dark and quiet. The light in 117 was still on, but boredom or a sedative had worked like a charm on most of the others.

Maudie tiptoed into Jan's room and saw that she was sleeping. Jan's temperature had been normal all day, but Maudie had changed the figures on her chart when she first came on duty, before the doctor's rounds. A temperature of 100 would be enough to keep her in another day, giving Maudie another opportunity to finish this business about Eugene once and for all.

The nurse once again opened the portal on the IV, and this time, without being interrupted, injected a syringe full of air into the tube, then watched as the bubble slid down toward the patient's wrist.

Jan opened her eyes. She'd almost drifted off to sleep when she felt a slight movement of the IV tube.

"What are you doing?" she asked sluggishly.

The nurse jumped. "Just checking on the drip, dear."

The woman seemed nervous, but she was already leaving the room. Jan's eyes drooped as sleep overcame her.

Monday Night

14

"MILDRED, WHAT'S THAT dog abarkin' at? Get 'im in here," the old man said. He would have done something about it himself, but he used a walker and it was too much of a struggle to get out of bed.

His wife, who'd just gotten into bed, said, "Why, I hate to even open up the door, Jess, with that killer lurkin' around somewhere. What if he's standin' right there, waitin' for someone to come to the door, and when I open it, he grabs me and takes me hostage?" The news people had been advising all day to be careful. After all, this was the very area where they had him contained.

"You've been watching too many of them soaps."

"You know you like 'em, as well as I do."

"Only the one. I can't help it if I have to watch 'em all 'cause you have the TV on." He grimaced. "If you don't get that dog to shut up, I may become a killer myself."

"Okay, okay." She threw the covers back, put her slippers on, and went into the kitchen. "Scooter. C'mon, boy. Here Scooter." Scooter appeared from over by the barn. He moved a few feet across the yard, then changed his mind and faced the barn and continued to bark. Try as she might, Mildred couldn't get the dog to shut up.

She quickly shut the door and returned to the bedroom. "You know, Jess, I'm sure I closed that barn door earlier, and now it's open. And I can't get Scooter to shut up. There's someone out there, Jess."

He grumbled. "Scairt of your own shadow, you are." But she figured he wasn't quite so brave as he sounded when he said, "Call the sheriff. Tell him. Put your mind to rest."

Tuesday Morning

15

THE OFFICE STAFF hadn't arrived at the hospital when Neal and Ted arrived, so the two men went through the admissions area and to the nurse's station. It, however, was vacant, too. The whole sterile-looking place seemed like a mausoleum, with no signs of life anywhere. The soft pad of their shoes on the floor was the only sound as they proceeded down the white hall.

Jan's door was ajar, and Ted pushed it open. A nurse inside jerked her head up at the movement, frowned, and motioned them to stay out. A man in a white coat, presumably a doctor, was standing by Jan's bedside, his back to the door.

A knot of premonition formed in the pit of Ted's stomach as the nurse hurried over to them. Something bad had happened. "What's going on?" Ted asked her.

"Are you family?" the nurse asked, pulling the door partially shut behind her.

Ted shook his head. "A friend. But I'm sure as hell the closest person she's got down here."

The nurse gave him a disapproving look for the profanity, then said, "I'm afraid she's in a coma."

"Shit!" Neal muttered under his breath.

"My God," Ted said. "We saw her yesterday, and she seemed perfectly okay then." Depressed maybe, he thought, but nowhere near comatose. "What happened?"

The nurse shook her head slightly and sighed. "You need to stay out here. The doctor may want me." She went back in, leaving the door open far enough for them to see what was going on.

"I thought she was okay. What the hell . . ." Neal murmured.

Ted put his fingers to his lips. He wanted to catch what the doctor was saying.

". . . respiratory difficulty. Get me an E-tube. Let's get her to the unit."

"Intubate her first?" the nurse asked.

"Yes, yes," the doctor said impatiently. "Let's hurry it up."

"Yes sir." The nurse rushed past Ted and Neal and disappeared down the hallway.

"What do you think happened, Doctor?" Ted asked.

He turned toward them, the first indication he knew they were there. "We'll get her down to intensive care and run some tests, then maybe we can tell." He shook his head and peered more closely at Ted. "Who're you?"

"Ted Morrow. My wife and Mrs. Spencer were canoeing together down here. This is Neal Lassiter," he added, motioning toward Neal.

The doctor nodded, seeming satisfied. He put his stethoscope on Jan's chest again.

A nurse's assistant appeared with a gurney, accompanied by the nurse. Neal and Ted backed away from the door to let them by. After a few more minutes they transferred Jan to the cart. The nurse, carrying some sort of apparatus which was connected to a tube in Jan's mouth, walked briskly at the head of the gurney beside the nurse's assistant who was pushing it.

The doctor was giving the nurse instructions as they passed the men. "Monitor her and let's draw an ABG."

Ted and Neal followed at a short distance. A nurse Ted hadn't seen before was at the desk. She only looked up briefly when Neal stopped there.

Ted came to a halt beside him.

"Makes you feel helpless, doesn't it?" Neal said. He

looked slightly bewildered. "You know, I really like her"—
he rubbed his eyes—"and I'm counting on getting to know
her better. Damn!" He hit the desk with his fist, causing the
nurse to look up briefly and frown.

Ted sighed deeply and nodded. He was too overwhelmed
to speak.

Neal glanced at the clock. "Well, what now? I guess it's
late enough that we can go to the sheriff's office."

"Yeah. Just let me go down here first and see what
they're doing. I don't know, I, uh, I feel I need to make sure
they're taking good care of her." He shoved his glasses up
higher on his nose.

"Good, good," Neal said, nodding his head. He ran a
hand across his hair. "I guess I'll be in the waiting room."
He shrugged and turned away.

Ted continued down the antiseptic hallway. As he passed
a room on the right, he was surprised to hear someone call
his name. Automatically he turned toward the voice, then
wondered who would know him here. He stepped over to
the door, but the curtain was pulled around the nearest bed.
He couldn't see anyone, so he went in to investigate. There
was no one in the other bed.

Ted peeked behind the curtain and saw an old man there,
an IV dripping into his arm. His jaw appeared slack and his
eyes were closed. Stubby gray whiskers were bristling from
a flaccid chin, and the pillow framed a wild disarray of hair.

Must be hearing things, Ted thought. But just then the
man said it again, only much louder. "Morrow."

It was difficult for Ted not to respond to his name, so he
went closer.

"I'm Ted Morrow. What is it?"

The man's eyes flew open wildly, then shut again.

Just then the nurse from the desk swished in. "I thought
I saw you slip in here."

"I didn't see a No Visitors sign."

She tapped on the open door. Sure enough there was a
notice.

"It would help if the door were kept shut, so a person
could see that sign before coming in the room."

The nurse gave him an impatient look. "We're short-handed, and I have to be able to hear him."

"Well, I was passing by, and he called my name. Am I supposed to ignore that?"

"You must be mistaken. He's sedated."

"I'm not mistaken. He said 'Morrow' quite distinctly."

She made a derisive sound as if to imply Ted was rather stupid. "Oh, that. He was muttering that when I was in earlier to take his vital signs. He meant 'tomorrow.'"

Ted gave a little laugh. "Oh. That makes more sense, doesn't it. I'm a little on edge today . . ." He turned to go, but just then the old man muttered the word "kidnapped." Ted's eyes hardened. "What else has he said?"

The nurse checked the drip. "Let me think . . . it was the name of some place. Uh, River's Bend, I think."

At her words, the old man's eyes popped open again, and he said "River's Bend" quite coherently.

She patted his shoulder. "Just relax." She turned to Ted and whispered, "Just a lot of semiconscious nonsense."

Ted asked, "What happened to him?"

"Poor man. He was standing on the highway, and a car hit him." She was leaving and Ted followed her. "He's kind of well-known around these parts. Lives like a hermit up north of the river. When he comes to town, he hitchhikes. Comes in once a month to get a government check. I guess that's where he was headed. The truth is, though, he gets crazy notions in his head. All his muttering doesn't mean anything. Just some tangent he's off on."

They'd reached the nurse's station.

"When did they bring him in?"

"Sometime yesterday afternoon, after I went off duty at three-thirty."

Ted turned toward the old man's room again, telling the nurse, "I'm going down to intensive care, to see about Jan Spencer. I'll be back in a moment."

She nodded and became absorbed in a file at the desk.

Ted only went as far as the old man's room. After a furtive glance back at the nurse's station to make sure the woman wasn't watching, he quickly stepped in and closed the door, then went over to the man's bedside and picked up one weathered old hand.

"Did you see Susan Morrow?" he whispered into the old man's ear. "Who was she with?" He repeated his questions, hoping to draw the man up into a higher level of consciousness.

The old man closed his mouth and made a few smacking noises, but didn't say anything.

"Kidnapped? River's Bend?" Ted kept repeating the key words, trying to get a response, but nothing came.

I'll probably kill the old boy and get caught in here and blamed, Ted thought. He laid the old man's hand across his chest, then moved toward the door. He opened it, looked for the nurse, then darted out and continued down the hall toward where he'd seen the nurse's assistant take Jan.

The doctor was just coming out of the area, which was a single room with a glass window adjoining the emergency room.

"Is there anything I can do?"

The doctor shook his head.

"Will she have someone with her all the time?"

"The emergency room nurse will watch the monitors. And I'm on call."

"I want her to have her own nurse." Giving an order made Ted feel better.

The doctor nodded. "If that's what you want. I believe she has insurance."

"I'm sure she does."

The doctor frowned a moment, then said, "There's a nurse I have in mind who's off-duty today. I'll call her in."

"I just want Mrs. Spencer to have the best care you can find."

"Oh, this woman is well-qualified."

Ted nodded. "Good. Then I'll plan to check back later." He was eager to follow up on what the old man had said, especially now that he was feeling better about his responsibility to Jan.

"I thought you'd gotten lost," Neal said as Ted came into the waiting area by the admissions desk.

"You aren't going to believe this."

"What?"

"I thought I heard someone call my name down the hall, so I went in this room. There's an old man in there muttering about a kidnapping." He related to Neal what the nurse had said. "But this is the wrong time of the month for checks—they come in on the third—so chances are he was coming in for something else. Maybe to deliver a message . . . ?"

Neal looked at Ted skeptically. "That's presuming a lot."

"Not if you think about what he's mumbling."

"River's Bend? Well, we can check it out. I know where it is," Neal said.

"Well, what're we waiting for. Let's go."

Ted and Neal drove to the courthouse where Fayette, who was still filling in for the missing Connie, told them Emory had run up to Presley County to talk to the sheriff about the developments in Breedlove.

Neal sighed in exasperation. "Listen, you get Emory on the horn and tell him what's goin' on. We think that Newton guy and his wife"—he indicated Ted—"are going to be at River's Bend this morning—unless we're too late. We don't know why or when, but we're going up there, and you have him, or the sheriff—someone for God's sake—meet us at that old homesite on the North Creek road. Got that?"

She nodded.

"C'mon, let's get out of here," Neal said to Ted.

Neal backed out into the flow of traffic around the courthouse square, then took Oak Street toward the edge of town. Just north of the town limits, they crossed the river. It was spanned by a modern concrete-and-steel bridge, the only way across the river for forty miles.

Ted looked down over the railing as Neal sped across. Two tow-headed children were chucking rocks into the river while their mother watched from a lawn chair in the shallows. He remembered when he and Susan used to take the kids to a creek south of their house to cool off in the summer. That could have been Susan and their two kids down there, years ago.

His eyes glistened at the thought, and he rubbed his mouth. Where was she?

"We'll just stay here until we know that man's going to be okay." Marge Burke was sitting on the bed at the motel. "It's not like we have to be anywhere."

"Good idea." Norm was pretty shaken by the accident the day before. Thank God the man wasn't killed!

"The insurance should take care of all his bills." Marge frowned. "I wonder what an old man like that was doing out there so far from anywhere." She reached for one of her sports socks. "I hate to wear dirty socks."

"We can go shopping and buy you some more, you know," Norm told her, then added, "The doctor said that old man was a local character. Lives alone out there in the woods."

"Hmmm." She tied her shoe, then reached for the other one.

"This has turned into one hell of a trip," Norm said.

Marge finished tying her shoe and stood up. "I'm ready to take the doggie out for a walk now. You coming, Norm?"

Georgie stood up and wagged his tail.

The doctor stopped at the nurse's station. "Get hold of Maudie Rice, will you? See if she can work special duty tonight on the Spencer case."

"Yes, sir," the nurse responded. She picked up the phone and dialed.

Maudie was flustered. She'd fully expected Jan Spencer to be found dead this morning at rounds. So the call from the hospital asking her to work private duty with the woman tonight was totally unexpected. Apparently the air bubble she'd introduced into the IV tube hadn't caused a sufficiently large embolism to kill the woman. But Maudie prided herself, always had, on being able to handle the unexpected with composure. That was part of being a good nurse.

"Well," she said to Eugene, "that woman is still alive."

Her son was sitting in her kitchen eating powdered-sugar donuts, which he was dipping in a glass of milk. Maudie had bailed him out first thing this morning. Violet had also gotten Three-Fingers out.

"Why? What happened?"

Maudie didn't want to explain, so she just shook her head and waved his question off. "You really did it this time," she said scathingly.

"Awww, it woulda come out okay. All Emory has me for is drunk driving and resisting arrest. That woman never signed no complaint. Actually, it's you who kinda went off the deep end, Ma."

Maudie drew her lips tight. His words infuriated her. He didn't even appreciate that she was trying to help him. "You're not out of the woods yet, Eugene. How would you like to do time? Locked up for years? Would that make you happy? None of this going down to the river, spending days out there enjoying yourself. For your information, she did sign a complaint, Mr. Smarty Pants." Eugene's eyes widened. Let him stew a minute, she thought as she reached over and flicked some powdered sugar off of his beard.

"Well, what am I going to do?" he asked, alarmed.

She waved her hand at him impatiently. "I took care of it, destroyed it."

His confidence returned. "Well, how would *you* like to do time, Ma?"

"Don't get smart with me, Eugene Rice. *I* know what *I'm* doing. I don't let liquor dim my senses! Can you say as much? Do you think you can stay off your liquor long enough to help me? I'll need you to bring your truck to the hospital this evening. Just come like usual to pick up the trash, and if anyone says anything—no one will, but if anyone does—just say you missed your regular time. Which is true."

"Gotcha," he said, dusting his hands off on his overalls. "You heard from Ruthie lately?"

She threw up her hands in exasperation. "No, and I don't even want to think about that right now."

"Well, I think her ol' man's in deep shit of some kind."

That caught his mother's attention. "You haven't heard?"

"What?"

"He killed a highway patrolman up in Presley County. They've got everyone out looking for him. It's all over the papers. I talked to Evan, and he said it looks bad for him."

"Killed a cop? Damn!"

"Why did you think Ruthie's husband was in trouble?"

"Well, this woman that Three-Fingers and me are accused of attacking—which I didn't do, Ma, I promise you—anyhow, she and her friend were out on the river together, then the next morning I saw the friend going downriver with Lee. Me and Three-Fingers, we didn't know what he was up to, but it turns out the woman is missing. Emory asked me about seeing her, but I didn't tell him nothin' about seeing her with Lee. Can I have some coffee, now?"

His mother got up, poured a cup from the percolator, and brought it to him.

He continued to talk as he put two spoonfuls of sugar in the coffee and began to stir it. "He's Ruthie's husband, even if I do think he's kinda weird. I didn't wanna sic the cops on 'im."

"What do you mean by weird?"

"Well, this is a good example. He's such a goody two shoes, Mr. Holier-Than-Thou. Yet he don't think nothin' of killin' a cop. See what I mean? Weird."

"He and Evan just feel they have a higher purpose, that they're carrying out God's plan."

"Well, save me from God's plan."

Tuesday Afternoon

16

LEE PULLED A weary Susan through the dense thicket of oak and hickory trees. Skinny sassafras and chokecherries, starved for light, were tangled with Virginia creeper, grapevines, and poison ivy. A thick layer of decaying leaves compressed beneath each footfall, but Susan was past worrying about what might be lurking under them. Her mind seemed to be clicked into neutral.

A brittle stick snapped as she stepped down, and in a flash of movement Lee dropped her wrist, turned, and had his gun at the ready. His quick action reminded her why she was still following along docilely, why she hadn't tried to make another break for freedom. His reflexes were so well honed, ready for anything. It was the same kind of quick reaction that enabled him to field the canoe paddle she'd swung at him on Saturday. Saturday. It seemed so long ago. This was Tuesday. She had an appointment with the dentist today. Tuesday—four days of this, and she was still alive. If he decided to kill her there'd be no second chance, so she had to be careful.

"It was just a stick," she told him quickly.

He took the piece of rope he'd been wearing like a bandolier across his chest—the two-liter bottle of water had been discarded in favor of first the thermos, then a canteen from the old man—and began to unwind it.

"What are you doing?"

He didn't answer as he fashioned a loop at one end, then pulled her over toward him and dropped the noose over her head. When he had it just the way he wanted it against her neck, he said, "I'm tired of hanging onto you."

The rope bit into her neck as he tested the knot with a sharp jerk. She did a quick two-step to keep her balance as he tied the other end of it to his wide belt, then turned and started walking again.

She could sense the gradual deterioration of his stability. At first he'd been moderately polite to her; now he pushed through the woods with no regard for his hostage. Sleep deprivation and stress were beginning to reshape him.

He shoved through a welter of branches, and one of them snapped back, flailing her across the face. She cried out involuntarily.

Again he jerked around, his eyes too bright, the craziness threatening. His sudden movement pulled her off her feet. She fell to the ground, tightening the noose almost beyond her endurance. The bag of provisions she'd been carrying opened when it hit the ground, and the contents scattered. She squirmed on the ground, coughing and sputtering, trying to loosen the rope.

"Get up, woman," he muttered. "And pick up my food." He yanked on the rope and she struggled up, still pawing at the rope to give herself some slack.

She stumbled along, ducking under low branches, shoving aside brush. She was kidding herself to think she could escape. As long as he had that gun, nothing was possible. Up in the tree she heard a blue jay scolding, then the twittering of chickadees. Those were the sounds she heard at her window birdfeeder. Ordinary, everyday sounds in this haywire experience she was having. *Can this be happening to me?* she thought.

She was still working to loosen the noose. It was no longer with the thought of escape; simple survival took precedence. Her windpipe felt as if it were being crushed.

Lee turned and saw her struggling with it. He put the barrel of the gun under her chin, pushing it up, and said simply, "Don't."

"But . . . I can hardly . . . breathe."

His lip curled up at one corner in a sneer. "The weak will perish."

Her jaw tightened. *Not me, buster!* The thought came in an energizing surge. Hours ago, she'd felt she couldn't keep going, but here she was still trudging along. And just now, a sense of renewed purpose came over her. *Maybe,* she thought, *I'm beginning to flip out. How can I feel purposeful when I'm so obviously powerless?* But she did. She couldn't think in hopeless terms or she wouldn't be ready if an opportunity to get away presented itself.

"May I . . . have . . . a drink?" she gasped, her head bowed before him. Her finger worked at the rope.

"We'll stop and eat in a little while." He started walking again.

"You bastard," she muttered.

"What?" he asked, stopping abruptly.

"Nothing."

"What did you say?" he demanded, the gun pointing at her again.

She looked at him defiantly. "I just want a drink."

"And I said in a little while." Two pairs of eyes locked in a stare—a test of wills—but then he reasserted his dominance with a yank on the rope, which drew her toward him. The noose cut in sharply, and he put his finger up against her neck for a moment, then drew it away. The fingertip was red with her blood. He smiled slightly, then wiped his finger on her cheek. Then he touched her bloody neck again and drew his finger on her other cheek.

Fine, she thought, looking at him through narrowed eyes. *War paint.*

As he'd said, they stopped a short time later at an old homesite. A stone chimney stood as a lonely testament to what once was. He sat her down on the old foundation, and while he was occupied drinking from a canteen he'd gotten from the old man, she loosened the rope slightly.

Then it was her turn. She gulped the water greedily, small rivulets running down the sides of her mouth. She wiped her mouth and put the canteen down. God! she hurt. Her latest pain was a blister that had developed on her left heel. It had broken and was stinging like hell.

Lee took out the last hunk of cheese and some more of the jerky and gave her half. She sank her teeth into the cheese and looked around. She'd just noticed an overgrown road leading away from the site when she heard an engine.

Lee stopped and cocked his head to one side, listening, too. A van appeared. Her heart fell. She couldn't see the river, but this must be the rendezvous point. This must be River's Bend. Whoever they were meeting was in that van.

The cold reality hit her: once he met his cohorts and fell under their protection, his hostage would be expendable. Her eyes darted around, looking for an escape route. It might be her last chance.

Lee spotted the vehicle and jumped up like a shot, taking off for the woods. His movement propelled her upward and after him. The canteen clunked to the ground, and Susan was pulled after Lee, tripping over her own feet, the loop around her neck choking her again.

The van careened to a stop, and in a desperate glance back, she saw the door opening and Neal Lassiter flinging himself out of the driver's side.

"Susan!"

That was Ted's voice! She jerked her head around again to see if she could see him, but as she tried to spot him, her neck was wrenched around by the rope as Lee dashed for the cover of the woods margin. He rolled to the ground, pulling her down beside him. Concealed by the massive root ball of a long-dead tree, he leveled his gun.

"Watch out," she screamed just as Lee pulled the trigger. The blast was still resounding in her ears as he yanked her up and began crashing through the woods again.

It was hard to keep up with his headlong flight. She tripped and stumbled, the branches tearing at her as they thrashed through the trees. Her chest ached from the strain on her lungs, and the tether around her neck kept tightening. She gagged at the pressure and tried to get her fingers in the loop, but that only made it tighter. She was going to choke to death if she didn't keep up with him. She pushed herself harder.

Neal was hit.

Ted had jumped out of the van as it stopped rolling, but the shot had sent him back to it for cover. He had no weapon.

The shot had knocked Neal off his feet, and now he pulled himself over behind the van as well. "He nailed me," he said through clenched teeth.

"How bad?" Ted asked as he took a look at Neal's leg, pulling the fabric away from the wound.

"I don't think it's too bad. It went in here and came out back here. See?" He looked a little pale as he pointed at the wound. "There's a first-aid kit in the glove compartment. Will you get it?"

"Sure." Ted went to the van and found the kit, then returned to squat beside Neal.

"What do you think?" he asked him.

"It's not bleeding much. Must have missed the major blood vessels." He flinched as he poured antiseptic on it. "I think I'm going to live."

"If you think you'll be okay, I'm going after them."

"You better think twice about that."

"That was my wife he was pulling along like a dog. I've got to go after him. Where's this River's Bend?"

Neal pointed. "You go straight through there till you come to North Creek. You follow it downstream to where it goes underground, then cut over the ridge. Just on the other side it flows into the river. That's River's Bend."

"Okay. Will you be all right?"

"Yeah. At least till the sheriff or someone gets here."

"One more thing. I need the gun and some shells."

"You could wait for the sheriff."

"And lose them altogether?"

Reluctantly, he handed over the gun. "I'll send the sheriff or Emory after you, if either of 'em ever get here."

With a nod, Ted took the gun and darted into the woods

toward the place where he'd last seen Susan's red-and-white shirt.

Emory slowed to make the turn into the North Creek road. The road itself hadn't been graded in years. No one lived down it anymore, so there wasn't much need.

The car rode heavily over the bumps as the forest thickened up around him. He'd run up to Presley County to see the sheriff. He found him not out in the field stalking the prey, but hobnobbing with the brass at the command post. That was just like Billy Jay, Emory thought.

He'd pulled him away and tried to tell him what was going on down in his own territory, including the fact that Senator Grindstaff had called him about the missing woman.

"That old interferin' fart," Billy Jay said, then grinned. "Now, Emory, don't tell him I referred to him thataway." He put his hand on Emory's shoulder. "You know, there's no way in hell that guy could be down there. Look here." He waved his arms around.

"When'd you last spot him?"

"We thought we had 'im last night. Some people called in, said he was in their barn. So we all go out and surround the place. He slipped out before we got there, though."

"How do you know it was him?"

"'Cause Em'ry. These guys know what they're doin'." He emphasized each word by chopping one hand up and down, fingers extended.

Emory had to admit it *was* impressive. There were a lot of vehicles at the command post. And a helicopter had just flown overhead.

"The whole area is sealed off. This is *big,* Emory. They got state patrol, local law enforcement, and the FBI. That's their helicopter. I never seen anything to beat it."

"Well," Emory said, scratching his head, "these guys down in Breedlove, they got a picture of this missing woman in a canoe with some guy who looks a lot like Lee Newton. I figure he's headin' for that Compound down there."

"A picture?"

He explained the newspaper photo Ted Morrow had brought in.

"Did you bring the picture?"

"No."

"Do you know what they'd think if I went in there and told them they were all wet?"

"Yeah, but listen up, Billy Jay. Just imagine how they'd feel if we caught this guy, and they were all up here still waitin'?"

Billy Jay was greeting a highway patrol lieutenant who was passing by.

Emory had lost his attention. Just then the deputy was called to the phone. It was Fayette relaying Neal and Ted's message. Moments later he rejoined the sheriff, who was standing at the outer edge of a group which was poring over a map.

"That was Fayette," he told Billy Jay. "I've got to meet those fellas I was telling you about on the North Creek road. You want me to take care of this?"

"Yeah, Emory." He pursed his lips up tightly in a way Emory hated. "I'd just hate to miss it when they pull this guy outta here. You understand."

It'd been like talking to a wall. Emory sighed, thinking about it. That was Billy Jay. He could win elections all right, because he was a political animal, always glad-handing everybody. Emory remembered watching him at the VFW picnic last month, working the crowd, listening to someone's story, nodding and murmuring, but with his eyes always searching for the next person. Too bad he had so little interest in real police work. He never wanted to do anything that actually involved putting his life on the line.

He sends me, Emory thought. *He struts and I work. So let him just stay up there and act like he's doing something, being somebody. Meanwhile, I'll take care of whatever this is.* He smirked. *Kinda hope it is that ol' boy escaped out of their dragnet. Billy Jay'll miss out.*

He drove slowly down the road, trying to go easy on the

car, eyes darting left and right, alert for any movement that didn't belong to the woods.

Somewhere ahead of him a loud report split the air, sending the birds to wing. Rifle!

Emory sped up, hitting the bumps recklessly now. The seat belt strained against him. Caution had fled with the sound of the gun.

He spotted Lassiter's van and braked to an abrupt stop close behind it. Emory jumped out of the car, unsnapping the flap on his holster. He waited a moment behind the door, using it as a shield while he scanned ahead of him. A movement at the door of the van arrested his eye.

"Freeze!" he yelled.

"It's me, damn it . . . Lassiter." Neal pulled himself upright. "I've been shot."

Emory ran between the two vehicles and knelt down beside Neal. "Who did it?"

"We spotted that guy and Mrs. Morrow going off that way." He pointed. "He saw us, too, though, and let me have it."

"Where's Morrow?"

"He's following them. They're heading to River's Bend. I expect they'll follow the creek, then go up over the ridge, so I sent him that way too."

Emory frowned. "You shouldn't have sent him in there alone. He's a city boy."

"It's his wife, for God's sake. How was I going to stop him? Now go help him out. I can wait here."

"Let me radio in for some help." He was eyeing Neal's wounded leg.

"You'll lose him. Go on. I'm okay."

Lee was running now, crouched over. Susan tried to keep pace with him, but her chest felt white-hot from the exertion.

They emerged on a hillside above a creek, where he reconnoitered for only a moment, then began a controlled slide down the hill with her slipping along behind, not so controlled. She fell once and continued sliding on her buttocks until she could regain her footing.

Someone was following them. Susan could tell Lee knew it because he kept looking back warily. If only they'd catch up and shoot him! But she was the fly in the ointment. Most of the time, she'd be between Lee and any pursuer. It would take a good shot to pick him off. If only she could get free. Her hand went up to the noose around her neck once again.

They came to North Creek, a tumble of monstrous boulders with water swirling around them on its steep downhill course to the river. When they reached the creek's edge, Lee plunged right into the cold spring water, dragging her along. He was safer there, camouflaged by the rocks as he waded downstream.

She fell down once, dragging him back. He grabbed her up by the arm. "Stay on your feet," he ordered.

The water got deeper as it approached a bluff. Susan expected the current to swing around, but at the face of the cliff, the creek disappeared. She looked up briefly at the wall of rock. *I can't do it,* she thought. *I can't climb it by myself, let alone tethered by the neck.*

But Lee wasn't climbing. With one last glance over his shoulder, he yanked her down into the water. "Hold your breath," he said, and disappeared, pulling her along.

"No," she started to scream. Before the word was out of her mouth, the rope around her neck dragged her downward into the turbulent creek. Water shot up her nose, burning the back of her throat as she fought to grab hold of something. She surfaced briefly, gulping air, then went under again. Her arms flailed the water and grappled wildly around her, trying to resist being pulled under the ledge. Her head banged against it as the current swept her beneath the cliff.

She threw up her hands automatically to save herself, and they met rock and latched on as her legs and torso were pulled downstream by the flow of the water until she was fully extended under the rock. Her face scraped against the hard surface, and she gasped, sucking in air from a tiny space where rock met water.

The heavy weight of Lee's body at the other end of the

rope pulled mercilessly on her neck. His hand seized her ankle. He was trying to drag her farther under the ledge, under the water. Futilely she tried to dig her fingers into the ledge. He was working his way back toward her; she felt the pressure of his hand tugging at her shirt as he grabbed hold of it.

Her head slipped down, and water filled her mouth. She lifted her chin, desperately seeking the finger's breadth of air again. No sooner had she inhaled than Lee's hand seized her around the waist.

He was almost abreast of her. She wrapped her legs around him like an octopus, holding on. The rope was tangled between the two of them now, and her movements to restrain Lee caused the noose to tighten. She struggled for air, sucking it from against the rock again. He grappled with her legs, trying to loosen them, but she held on tighter. Her hands were giving way. The weight of two people was too much. One by one her fingers began to slip. The struggle was over. She could no longer hold on. She went limp as her hands came loose and her body plunged into the dark, swirling water under the ledge and into the unknown beneath the cliff.

Ted was breathing heavily as he made it over the first hill after leaving Neal behind. He peered through the trees and didn't see anything for a moment.

Damn, he thought, *I've lost them.* Then he saw a flash of red and white, and he set out again. "Got to keep sight of them," he mumbled, struggling for breath. He was carrying Neal's rifle, and he knew he wouldn't hesitate to use it if he could just get one clear shot.

Susan was drowning.

She'd had nightmares like this, and now it was reality. Panic overwhelmed her as the last whisper of breath in her lungs staled. Instinctively, she drove her body upward in the current, expecting to hit her head on the rock, but instead she surfaced and drank in the cool air. Her eyes shot open, but there was nothing to see, no way to orient herself in a world gone black.

The creek had plunged into a subterranean grotto under the bluff. There was no light; no way for her eyes to discern anything. She found her footing on a smooth rock bottom, but almost lost it again when Lee continued his relentless pull on the rope.

"Stop!" she demanded. "Let me get my footing." Her voice echoed eerily. Still he pulled. She groped for something to hold onto to get her balance, but she seemed to be in the middle of the place.

"Where are you?" she asked. He didn't answer. Her shoulders began to tremble. "Answer me." Echoes bounced back in the nightmare world, and she wanted human contact, even if it was with the enemy.

She began to shove through the water toward him, but he moved away at the same rate. "Please. Stop." She came to a halt, both hands grasping the rope in front of her. "You bastard!" She yanked it in desperation and was surprised when he came her way.

Reality dawned on her slowly; Lee hadn't made it through the passage. He had drowned, locked in the grip of her legs. There was a dead man on the other end of the rope.

She pulled the weight toward her, then released it, and felt the current take it away as far as the tether around her neck would allow. She repeated the motions, testing, dazed by the realization of his death.

She'd occasionally, over her lifetime, wondered what it would be like to be responsible, even indirectly, for another person's death, and now she was confronted with it. She had expected to feel *something,* but there was nothing. Her feelings seemed suspended. A mouse in a trap would elicit more sorrow. Lee's death was just a fact. Later perhaps there would be some feeling, but for now she was not burdened by emotion. Her only burden seemed to be his weight trying to pull her back into the current.

She hauled him in once more, but couldn't get enough slack to get the noose from around her neck before the current dragged the body away again, trying to suck it and her downstream into the unknown. She needed both hands to work the wet rope loose.

She pulled Lee to her again and grabbed his shirt. A shudder went up her back as her fingers groped for the knot where he'd tied the rope to his belt. The fibers were tight and waterlogged. As she felt it, her hand brushed his knife sheath. She grappled one-handed with the sheath, opening it awkwardly and pulling the knife from it. Grasping it tightly, she began to saw at the wet rope. It finally snapped, and the body was instantly drawn away from her.

She dropped the knife as if it were hot, then reached up in relief and loosened the noose, pulled the rope over her head, and hurled it into the water in the direction she supposed the body had gone. She put her hands in the water and rubbed them. Lee was dead. It was over.

Susan closed her eyes, a reflex only, because even with them open she couldn't see anything. Her senses were alert, and the clammy air convinced her that she was in a rather large cave. She moved away from the current and tripped over an underwater shelf. Regaining her footing, she stepped up and now was only thigh-deep in the water.

Her arms served as antennae, feeling ahead of her. A few steps more and her hands felt the cold wall of the cave. There was no bank, no place to climb out of the water on that side.

Slowly, with deliberate steps, she moved across the current to explore the other side. It was the same. There was no bank. It was simply a wormhole of water through the limestone bluff. She realized with a sinking heart that there was only one passage. There was no way she could fight the current and go back the way she'd come, although because she knew the way was relatively brief, she'd have preferred it. But even if she weren't fatigued from days of strain and deprivation, she couldn't have made it against the current.

No, the only way out was downstream, surrendering to the terrifying sweep of the water. She felt the current against her legs and went with it, walking, to see where it led, her arms in front of her. Within fifty feet she found the other end of the cave. She was in a tomb. The water swirled around her here as it channeled itself through the narrow tunnel. It tried to grab her and pull her along, but she wasn't quite ready. She stood there, trying to get some sort of grip on herself, trying to tell herself it was going to be okay. But she didn't really believe it. The cold water felt like death itself, and she wanted to give up. Through all of this, she'd felt a tenacious desire to hang on, but now, when perhaps the terror was almost over, she wanted to quit.

But what about Jennifer? What about the plan for Wednesday? Would it still be carried out with Lee Newton dead? The weakening of her will to survive suddenly made her ashamed. Tears sprang to her eyes.

She drew one last deep breath. There was no telling how long this passage was. She knew it might stretch her lungs beyond their limits, demanding more energy than she could give. But it was time to give it a try.

She plunged underwater and let the current take her. Her eyes were open, and she could see light. Relief filled her; the passage couldn't be too long if there was light. She would be there soon.

Suddenly, she bumped into something blocking the way. Her hands reached out and grasped the dark shape in front of her; it was Lee's body, hung up on a rock. She was trapped unless she could get it out of the way.

Frantically, holding her breath, she tugged and pushed, trying to free the cadaver. She tried to pull it toward her, but the current was working against her efforts, relentlessly pushing her against the body. Her lungs were beginning to burn. The clumsy limbs of the body kept hitting her as she wrestled with its dead weight. Her hands groped to find what was holding it. Finally something worked, and it came free.

Her time was about up; she was going to have to take a breath soon. Her eyes began to bulge. The body slipped away from her, moving in the current, and she followed it. Her mouth involuntarily opened, trying to suck in a breath, but got only water as she was thrown out of the hole. She

plunged over a short ledge, gasping for air, and landed in a
pool.

The water was not deep and she stood up, coughing and
sputtering. After she'd recovered she saw Lee's body
bobbing on the surface nearby. She took hold of the back of
his shirt and dragged him to the edge of the creek. The dead
man lay there rocking in the minor backwash current,
dismal in death. She sank down, staring at the body,
thinking that perhaps in the cold clarity of daylight she
would feel something, some sorrow at this wasted life.

His clear blue eyes gazed up at her, unrepentant, filled
with hate even in death.

So that's that, she thought.

A voice behind her caused her to jump. "Well, well,
well. What happened to our friend here?"

The man who spoke was about thirty-five, she judged,
with short-cropped blond hair which hugged his forehead
close like a knitted cap around his face. There was another
one, standing slightly behind the first. He was the bigger of
the two, well over six feet, a bear of a man with stooped
posture. His graying hair looked as if it had been cut with
clippers because it was the same short length all over his
head. Both men wore gray T-shirts and camouflage pants.
Like Lee.

"He *did* have a hostage," the big man said flatly.

The blond nodded.

Will it never end? she thought. She glanced around,
measuring her chances of escape.

The blond knelt and felt Lee's pulse. "He's dead. Larry,
can you carry his body back to the truck? I'll bring the lady
along."

"Sure thing, Coy."

The big man waded into the water and clumsily lifted
Lee's body. The arms flopped down limply, and Susan was
reminded of a child carelessly carrying a rag doll. He got
him over his shoulder as Susan was standing up. She took
a quick look at the men, then bolted. Larry dropped Lee
unceremoniously and started after her, but the blond was

quicker and grabbed her before she got far. Larry picked up his burden again.

"You go on, Larry, I got 'er," Coy said, holding her tightly by the arm. She glared at him.

He spoke quickly and softly into her ear as he urged her along. "You've got to trust me. I won't let anything happen to you, just do what I tell you." He paused and looked in her eyes. "I'll get you out of this."

"Who are you?"

"Sssh. Think of me as the Lone Ranger."

She managed a weak smile, the first since Friday. A wave of immense relief suffused her. This man was going to take care of things. Somehow she trusted him. Maybe it was the look in his eyes. They didn't have the crazy glint she'd seen in Lee's. "Are you—?"

He interrupted her. "We'd better get along, or Larry'll wonder what happened to us." It was obvious the conversation was closed.

They went along the creek, following the other man's path, and the still water soon gave way to a visible current again, the banks flattening into gravel bars where the creek met the river as it made a wide hairpin to the south. The bluff she'd tumbled through skirted the river on the north and east. So, Lee made it to River's Bend, she thought. But not how he expected.

The river was a wide but shallow ripple here, and they waded across. The sun hit them in midstream, and it felt good, warming her. She was reluctant to go ashore, into the shade, but Larry was waiting for them, still carrying Lee's body. She and Coy crunched their way across the gravel.

Ted looked up into the sunlight, shielding his eyes. He didn't know what had happened to them, but he figured from the top of the ridge he'd be able to spot that red-and-white shirt. Holding the gun carefully, he began to climb. The angle wasn't steep, but he was soon out of breath, and he vowed he was going to get in shape when he got home.

Once at the top, he could see the river below him. And

there was Susan with her captor. The man, thank God, had untied her, and right now he didn't even have hold of her; a clear shot would be possible. But Ted had to narrow the distance.

He scrambled down the other side of the ridge, trying to be quiet but unleashing a shower of small pebbles as he slid downward. Surely the rush of the river would mask any sound he made.

He came down behind some boulders and skirted them, then hurried along the creek leading to the river. Just at the side of the Big Pine, he figured his range was close enough. He had to hurry, or they'd reach the truck he could see waiting on the other side. He knelt and put the gun across a boulder to steady it.

Coy lurched, and an instant later the echo of a rifle shot pierced the air. Susan ran to the truck in an instinctive attempt to find cover. Larry was quick. He dropped Lee's body unceremoniously right where he was, then grabbed her and, in one fluid movement, had the door open and was shoving her in and climbing in after her. Keeping his head low, he started the truck and took off.

Her name came in a wave of sound across the river. She turned to look through the back window of the truck and saw Ted running across the water, a sight she was sure she'd always remember: water splashing up, the gun held out to one side.

Ted, she mouthed the words. *I am so stupid! Why did I run for cover?* She made a quick attempt to slide toward the passenger door, but Larry grabbed her by the neck, pressing his fingers into her flesh brutally. He picked up speed, hitting bumps and ruts with careless abandon, sending both of them jostling all over the seat. He dropped his hand, but now they were going too fast for her to leap to safety. The truck bounced hard over a rut. Susan tried to catch herself, but didn't anticipate the movement in time. A quick blow to the top of her head, then down to the seat again. One more assault on her already abused body.

* * *

Emory heard the rifle and began to run toward the water. He was too late—he didn't know for what, but he was too late. He felt it in his bones.

He made a slipping descent down the ridge, arms out to maintain his balance, and headed toward the gravel bar where he saw Ted. Ted wasn't standing still though. He was plunging through the river, and for Emory everything took on the look of a tableau: the truck roaring away, the body lying on the other side of the river. Two bodies!

Ted was examining the man he'd shot when Emory reached him. The other body lay nearby in a contorted position.

"Is he dead?" Emory asked.

"No," Ted said. "I didn't kill the bastard."

"What about that one? You get two with one shot?" Emory bent over to examine the wounded man, who was lying on his stomach.

Ted stood up. "Who's that other one?"

Emory stood up and walked over to the body. "That's Lee Newton—the one they're lookin' for up in Presley County." He couldn't help but feel a little surge of satisfaction, remembering ol' Billy Jay up there hotshottin' around.

"Well then who the hell is this that I've shot?" They returned to the unconscious man.

"I don't know. Looks like one of those survivalists though, by his clothes." They were both kneeling beside him when the man's eyes fluttered slightly, then opened. He moaned.

"I'm Deputy Sheriff Todd. We're gonna get you some help, fella," Emory told the man, who was struggling to roll over. "Just lie still there. Can you tell us who you are?"

The voice was weak, and his eyes weren't tracking. "F—FBI," he managed to sputter. Then his eyes shut, and he lost consciousness again.

"Shit," Ted said incredulously, his face going white. He had just wounded, maybe killed, a federal agent.

Tuesday Evening

17

IT ASTONISHED SUSAN to see such a civilized-looking gate in the middle of such a wild and overgrown place. The six-foot-high chain-link fence acted mainly as a trellis for the length of it Susan could see. It was overgrown with vines which she recognized as kudzu. It snaked up into the trees and hung in fluid sculptures, making a blanket of foliage that hid whatever lay under it.

"What is this place?" Susan asked as they jolted to a stop.

"Well," Larry said slowly, "seems like it used to be a rocket test site back in the early fifties. Then they didn't need it anymore, I guess."

A guard dressed in camouflage gear, even to his hat, stood in front of the gate, his legs apart, his gun held in both hands before him. He walked over to Larry, saluted him, then asked about Coy.

"They got 'im."

"Shit, they did."

"You don't see 'im here, do you? They blasted 'im."

"Where's Newton?"

Larry nodded his head toward Susan. "I think she drownded him. He's dead anyway."

"The Colonel's gonna be madder 'n hell."

"That's not how I see it. After he killed that nigger, it was like he was just bringin' trouble down on us."

"Well, if you ask me, she looks like trouble."

"I thought of that, but I couldn't just let her walk away. She probably knows too much."

The guard nodded. "Well, I'm glad I'm on duty out here tonight." He opened the gate and waved them through.

The trees with their monster drapes of vines encroached on the narrow track forming an eerie passage. The road bent to the left, then swung to the right, following the path of least resistance through the terrain, and after what she guessed must have been about a mile of such curves, they came to a place where the large trees had been cleared and the kudzu formed cushiony mounds on the ground as it grew over the natural contours of the earth. The skeletal remains of several concrete structures jutted up here and there.

Larry began to slow down as they came to a building which seemed intact. The south end of it, a blocky structure, was two stories tall, but the part they approached was more like an earth-bermed basement with concrete buttresses on the east and west sides of its flat roof, forming a bay rather than a second story. A metal track ran the length of the bay, ending abruptly at the north edge. This end wall wasn't bermed, but had no windows. In fact, the whole building seemed to be windowless.

Larry parked and pulled her out of the truck behind him. To the south was what looked like a barracks building, World War II vintage, although it had been well maintained. Three cars were parked beside it, but she saw no one. The only incongruous thing in view was an elaborate backyard swing set near the barracks.

They crossed an abandoned railroad spur, with tall grass sprouting up from between the ties, and went toward the heavy metal door into the building. Larry pulled it open and held it for her.

"Go on in," he said, shoving her. Inside it was dark, and once the door clanged shut behind them, echoing in the emptiness, it took a moment for her eyes to adjust. They were in a stairwell which only led down. Larry prodded her to start descending the metal staircase.

Clinging to the cold railing, she picked her way down to the next level, Larry at her heels. The dampness became palpable. Naked bulbs made pools of light on the floor, marking their progress as they proceeded along a six-foot-wide hallway.

"Take a right," Larry said when they came to a T-shaped intersection. Now they were under the bay she'd seen from outside. There were doors along this passage. A shaft of light shone from one open door halfway down the hall, and she could hear voices.

She halted abruptly just before reaching the open doorway. It seemed that to go any farther would seal her fate. Her mouth grew dry and she licked her lips. Larry pushed her into the room.

Three pair of eyes turned toward the door to look at the intruder. Susan scanned the scene. A desk with a gooseneck lamp in the center of the room gave a first impression of an office, but the rest of the room seemed incongruous. The walls were waiting for paint with the seams between the pieces of wallboard already spackled. The concrete floor was spotted with dry spots of joint compound that had fallen from the tools and hadn't been cleaned up. A wad of plastic dropcloth lay along one wall. Two men, both dressed like Lee had been, in camouflage pants and gray T-shirts, were leaning on the desk, while an older man sat there. He was dressed differently. He looked like an executive, in a light blue shirt and a striped navy tie which had been loosened at the collar. His bald pate gleamed under the fluorescent light.

Susan's mouth fell open. "Senator Grindstaff!"

When Emory went back to get the car, a nervous Ted stayed behind with the wounded agent and Lee Newton's body. He'd appeared relieved to find out that there wouldn't be any charges filed against him for shooting the agent. When a cop went undercover he did it knowing there were certain risks, including the possibility of getting shot by his own side. So there wouldn't be any repercussions. Nevertheless,

Ted was showing signs of strain. He was getting agitated and was talking about the two of them rushing the survivalist headquarters. Emory had calmed him down, stressing that the place was guarded and heavily armed; they had to get some help. He'd heard it was an arsenal.

It was a good hour before Emory made it to the clearing where Neal was waiting in the van, eager for news about what had happened. They left the van behind, and Emory filled Neal in as they drove toward the highway. Then the deputy radioed in and told the dispatcher to send Carl Haney and his ambulance out to the south side of River's Bend.

The dispatcher objected. "He can't get in from that side."

"Don't argue with me. A truck went out that way a little over an hour ago, so there's some way to get in. I'm gonna try it, so I'll let you know if I run up against any hitches." He signed off, sighing. "I wish Connie would show up. She doesn't give me any arguments." He'd filed a missing persons on her.

They went eighteen miles downstream to the Plummer crossing, a low-water bridge, and carefully negotiated it. The water was about a third of the way up the tires and Emory hugged the upper side of the concrete pad as he slowly moved to the south shore.

"You guys need four-wheel-drives," Neal said.

"Tell that to the taxpayers," Emory replied with a dry laugh.

The dispatcher was nearly right about the south entrance to River's Bend. The road was grown over, barely a track, although the truck that had gone through there earlier had broken back a path of sorts.

"I didn't even know there was a way in over here," Neal said.

"Used to be a farm back here."

"I'd have never seen that entrance."

"I grew up around here."

They jolted down through a dry creekbed, and the car

whined in protest as it climbed the other side. Rocks spewed out behind.

"She's a workhorse," Emory commented as they made it over the ridge.

"Will the ambulance be able to get through here?" Neal was thinking about how long and low Haney's old ambulance looked.

Emory picked up the radio mike and called in. "Is Haney on his way?"

"Nope. Couldn't find him right away, but he's standing right here."

"Put 'im on."

Haney's voice came over the speaker.

"Listen, Carl," Emory said, "I've got me a dead man and a wounded one needin' transport, but I think I can get the dead one into the trunk, once I rearrange all the crap in there. Anyhow, I'm gonna try it; save you a trip out here. I can sign the certificate."

"Sounds good to me. Or I can sign it. Whichever. Listen, though, boy, I got me a full house over to the mortuary from that car smashup, so maybe you could take him to the hospital. Put 'im in the old morgue. I'll arrange it with the doc."

"Ten-four, Carl."

Senator Grindstaff rose.

"Mrs. Morrow." He used his genial public-official voice. The woman looked a mess. Sunburned, her hair awry, nothing like the neat and tidy middle-class mother he'd seen earlier in the summer when Jennifer was showing her around the office. Lee had put this woman through a lot. It was a wonder she'd survived the ordeal. But then, he had a lot of respect for women; they were survivors. His eyes darted beyond her, looking for Newton.

Susan broke away from Larry and came to the desk, a look of urgency on her face, her eyes glistening with tears. "You've got to stop them. They're planning to blow up the federal—" She stopped and looked at the map and the lists in front of him on the desk, and then her eyes lifted and met

his. He noticed that her eyes were much like Jennifer's; they
looked intelligent.

Susan backed off several steps and gave a quick desperate
look over her shoulder as if she were planning to flee. But
escape was impossible.

"What about Jennifer?"

His mouth twisted slightly, and he waved her question
aside and addressed Larry. "Where is Newton?"

"He drownded, Colonel."

"What?" Senator Grindstaff said.

"Coy and I come on her and his body."

"Well, man, where's Coy?"

"They shot 'im."

"They?" the old man asked. "Who's 'they?' "

"I don't know." He gave a self-conscious laugh. "I didn't
stick around to find out. I grabbed her and got outta there."

"How much do you know about our operation?" he asked
Susan.

"Nothing."

"You've been out with Newton since—when was it,
Friday? Saturday?—and you want me to believe he told you
nothing?"

"How did you know I was with him? He certainly didn't
have a chance to tell you."

"Deduction, my dear. They've got quite a few people out
looking for you. They're in a real stew. But back to my
original question: What did he tell you?"

"We didn't talk much."

"But you knew about the federal building."

She didn't say anything.

"Why in hell would Newton tell her even that?" The
senator exploded up out of his seat and pounded his hand on
the desk. "He was a two-bit self-centered fanatic." He
picked up a set of keys and tossed them to Larry with no
warning. "Get her out of here," he said, waving his hand in
dismissal. "Put her in the room next door and lock it!"

After Carl Haney's call, the doctor alerted the nurse's
assistant that they were bringing a cadaver to the hospital
morgue.

"Will you open it"—he dangled a key—"and make sure we don't have a bunch of files stored in there or anything. Get it cooled down, too."

A few moments later, the nurse's assistant returned. His face was white.

"Doctor?"

"Yes, what is it?" the doctor said, looking up impatiently from some papers.

"Well, there weren't any files in the morgue. And it was already on."

"So what's the problem?"

"There's already a body in there. It's Connie Fisher."

The doctor's eyes widened, and he elbowed his way past the young man into the operating room, and over to the morgue's door. He pulled the heavy door open and cold air drifted out.

"My God," he murmured.

Jan was a child again, and the adults were talking as she lay half-asleep, their voices playing soporific melodies. Only something was different.

She tried to pull herself farther into wakefulness, but there was a cloud around her. She couldn't drag her eyes open. It was a dream within a dream.

". . . pregnant . . ."

The voices droning over her were unfamiliar. ". . . body's in the morgue."

The lights were so bright, they blinded her when she tried to open her eyes.

". . . can get it out . . . take it out to the place . . ."

"I'll watch the door while . . ."

Jan drifted off again for a moment, but the voices drew her toward consciousness again.

". . . won't have you going to prison."

A man's voice. "You're the one who should worry."

". . . the kind of gossip Evan doesn't need . . ."

She caught the next words clearly.

"How will he like 'his sister the murderer'?"

"Hush!"

Jan felt herself slipping pleasantly away again. *No, can't let go, can't let go*. Her mind pushed itself toward consciousness once more.

". . . this one. I'll be right there as soon as I take care of . . ."

Jan knew it was important to wake up, but, Oh dear God, she couldn't drag herself all the way up. There was a blanket of fog around her, insulating her from reality. Sleep was so comforting.

Neal hobbled in through the emergency entrance at the hospital, leaning on Ted Morrow and accompanied by the deputy. The FBI man lay unconscious in the backseat of the car.

"Looks like everyone's on vacation," Emory grumbled, gazing around the empty room. "I told 'em to be ready for us; I'll go see if I can scare up someone to get a stretcher out there and get that fella out of the car."

"Yeah, let's hurry this up," Ted said. "We have to get back out there and find Susan."

"I gotta call up north to the sheriff and tell 'im about Newton, too. Then they'll probably all come flockin' down here, and we'll go out and surround the place."

Ted nodded. "Sounds good, but we need to hurry." His glance toward the hall was impatient. "If we can get some help here . . . ," he called.

Neal was wondering how Jan was getting along, so he limped over to the intensive care unit—which was just a room really. A curtain was pulled shut behind the windows, but he went over to the door, which was not clicked shut, and pushed it open slightly. Jan's bed was just inside. Her breathing tube had been removed; that was good. She must be stabilizing, he thought. The nurse was getting ready to insert a syringe into the IV.

Down the hall, he heard a commotion.

Eugene had walked boldly down the hall, not worrying about whom he might run into. The nurses were used to seeing him since his mother worked there and also because he hauled away the hospital trash. He did, however, look both ways before he opened the operating room's double doors, then slipped through, resuming his air of nonchalance as he approached the door to the morgue. He wasn't too thrilled about this task. First of all, he didn't like the idea of touching a dead body, and secondly, he was a little upset that it was Connie. She was a sweet little gal.

Preoccupied, he stepped into the morgue doorway, then felt the blood drain from his face when he saw the doctor.

"Eugene? What in hell—"

The redhead didn't wait to hear the rest of the question. He swung around and bolted for the double doors. As they swung open, the right one clipped Emory Todd, who was walking by outside. The deputy fell back with a crash, then, on instinct, reached out and grabbed Eugene by the sleeve as he tried to get by.

The doctor came tearing out of the swinging doors just then, crashing into the two other men. Eugene fell against Emory, knocking him off balance. He went down, dragging Eugene with him.

"Emory," the doctor said, not even flustered by the two men floundering around awkwardly before him. "I've found Connie Fisher. She's dead. And keep hold of Eugene. I think he knows something about it."

. . . must wake up . . .

Jan could see the nurse's white uniform although nothing seemed focused. The woman had a needle and was coming toward her.

Move . . . , she willed herself. Nothing was working.

Clench your fist . . . She felt the fingers pull together, but her hand felt as if it had a sock over it.

Pull yourself together . . . you can do it. Her mind was working, but her body was so sluggish.

The fist was made, but it lay there like a lump.

She gathered her strength and launched a massive effort. She drew her fist back, it gathered momentum, and accompanied by a hoarse cry of "Murderer!" she let it go smashing into Maudie's face.

The syringe clattered to the floor as the woman moaned and clasped her nose.

Jan's arm dropped limply beside the bed, her strength gone. But she wasn't alone. Her eyelids drooped, but not before she saw Neal Lassiter grab hold of the nurse.

Larry hustled to comply with the senator's order to lock Susan up. He shoved her into a dark room next to the one where the men were doing their last-minute planning and quickly locked her in.

Her glimpse of the room had been brief before the door closed. There was no furniture. In the center of the room lay several sheets of gypsum wallboard. The powdery gypsum and the scent of new lumber gave the room a new-house smell. Apparently they'd been remodeling.

She found a light switch, but nothing happened when she threw it.

She sat down on the Sheetrock, despair washing over her. What could she do now? The silence in the room, she realized, wasn't quite complete. She could hear the men's murmurs from next door. Planning. Planning what to do about tomorrow morning with Lee Newton gone. Lee was to have led the charge of the New Order.

Susan jumped up and groped her way back to the door. She rattled it and fiddled blindly with the knob. But the door and its hardware were solid.

Her instincts raged. There had to be a way to save her daughter. If there'd been any light, she would have paced. She threw herself back down on the Sheetrock.

Perhaps half an hour later, she heard the lock being opened, and the senator's large form appeared in the doorway, silhouetted against the hall light.

"Believe me, I'm sorry you became involved in this, Mrs. Morrow. And I'm sorry about Jennifer, too. I believe you both to be decent people, but sometimes innocent people get caught up in destiny."

She couldn't believe what she was hearing, but she knew

what she needed to do. "Maybe I can help you—if you'll get Jennifer out of there."

"How can you help?"

"Let me take Jennifer's place. Anything."

"I understand how you feel, Mrs. Morrow, but it wouldn't work. If someone in my office were to mysteriously come through unscathed, it would cast a shadow of suspicion on me, and I'm running for reelection this year. I can't risk it. You see, the governor's going to be a hard man to beat. Surely Jennifer has told you that."

"But she's young. She has a lifetime ahead of her."

He gave a dry laugh. "You think I'm over the hill, do you? May be, may be. But I have an agenda I want to see carried out."

"You're insane, Senator. Why would you blow up your own office?"

"Long ago I learned that throwing a red herring to my opponents is an effective method of dealing with them. There've been rumors about my link with the white supremacist movement, and the Zionist hounds are starting to nip at my backside. Don't get me wrong. We have plenty of sympathizers. But the country, even down here, is not ready for someone like me, so I've kept a . . . low profile, shall we call it?

"Of course, this action is just one small skirmish in the war we have planned. Just a beginning, my dear. The country is on the brink—"

"But you aren't some young psycho like Lee Newton. You've been around . . . how could you get involved with such people?"

"I went to Washington with high hopes. I thought I could make a difference. But I couldn't . . . do you know why? Because nothing gets done there without deals and power-brokering. And it's the back-room players, the ones the common people don't even know about, who are running the show. The Jew bankers. You've never even heard their names. They run everything. And they're dragging the coloreds right up with them. They want to mongrelize the white people. They want to wipe us out, Mrs. Morrow. You included."

"You can't really believe there's a conspiracy like that."

"Oh, I firmly believe it, my dear. The Jews control television. They control government."

"Does that mean you? You're part of government—do they control you?"

"I'm an exception. A few of us have resisted. That's what I'm doing here. This place was abandoned by the government, and I was able to buy it . . . well, behind the scenes. It always helps to be in the right place at the right time. It was this place that helped my ideas begin to gel. I decided I was going to start working to counteract the conspirators right here at home. And we're declaring war starting tomorrow."

"Did it ever occur to you that maybe the Jews are hardworking, and that's why there seem to be so many of them who are successful? For God's sake . . . what about all the Jews who aren't rich or powerful? The whole idea is insane. Why do you and Lee Newton insist that it's us or them? We're all God's children, remember? You've conveniently forgotten some of the lessons of Jesus."

"Ah," he said, "you've been listening to Lee's religious prattle. To me this has nothing to do with religion. The religious right is useful—they've been very supportive of me—but my doctrine is not one of religion. It's survival."

Her voice became shrill. "Well, damn it, that's what I'm talking about, too! My daughter's survival." She launched herself toward him, but he quickly subdued her and shoved her back into the room, then slammed the door shut.

She stumbled backward and fell onto the Sheetrock.

As he was locking the door, she heard him say, "I'm sorry, Mrs. Morrow. I really do understand how you feel, but your daughter just got caught up in a leap forward in history."

Susan sat up and took several deep breaths. What now? she wondered. Would they just leave her in here? Well, why not? They weren't interested in humane treatment. If she were left here long enough she would die. What better way to get rid of her? There would be no muss and only the fuss of burying her out here beneath the grasping tentacles of the kudzu.

But what about Jennifer?

18

"EMORY!"

The deputy looked up. He'd just clamped handcuffs on Eugene, and now he saw Neal limping out of the intensive care unit, pulling a struggling Maudie behind him. Her face was red with rage.

"I need some help down here."

Just then, the nurse turned and jabbed Neal in his wounded leg. He cringed at the pain, and Maudie took full advantage of the moment, jerking away from his grasp and running down the hall toward the nurse's station.

The doctor and Emory, dragging Eugene by the arm, reached Neal, who had turned white and had broken into a sweat at the new assault of pain.

"You okay?" Emory asked.

The doctor knelt and looked at Neal's leg.

Neal shook his head and leaned against the wall. "Get—get her. She tried to kill Jan." Ted, who had joined them, took off down the hall after Maudie, followed by Emory, who was still encumbered by Eugene.

Maudie had ducked into a supply room and locked the door by the time the men reached her.

"I didn't know what to do," the nurse on duty said. Her eyes were large. "She came tearing by here and—"

"Do you have a key?"

"Uh, yes, let me find it," she said. "There should be one

here." She opened up a key box and began to fumble nervously through the contents. "That's funny. I don't see it. It must have been left in the door." She didn't look at Emory as she said it, and he surmised she'd been the one who'd left it in the door, probably against regulations. Maudie must have grabbed it as she'd gone into the closet.

"There's no other way out of that room, is there?" Emory asked.

"No sir."

"And is there another key?"

"The doctor has a master key."

The doctor had left Neal and was now in emergency, examining the FBI man they'd brought in. Emory sent Ted for the key.

But it was too late by the time they got the door unlocked. Maudie was slumped in the corner, a syringe on the floor near her.

An animal cry escaped from the back of Eugene's throat when he saw his mother's body. He broke away from Ted and dropped to his knees awkwardly in front of her. "Oh, sweet Jesus, Ma. You shouldn't 've. Oh, Ma, Ma. Jesus."

Emory let Eugene have a few moments to say good-bye, then he gently pulled him upward. "C'mon, son, we gotta go over to the courthouse. Carl Haney'll take care of things here." The nurse had disappeared, so Emory called Carl from the desk. Then he stopped at ICU.

Neal, whose color had come back, was there with Jan, stroking her forehead gently. The nurse's assistant stood nearby.

"I'm taking Eugene over to the courthouse," Emory said. He repeated the message to Ted, who was with the doctor and the unconscious agent in the emergency room.

"All hell's breakin' loose here, Emory," the doctor said. "And I was planning a quiet evening in front of the tube."

"That guy gonna make it?"

The doctor nodded.

"Then you wanna come with me?" Emory asked Ted.

"Absolutely," Ted answered.

Emory bustled Eugene into the backseat of the car, just as Carl Haney and two of his employees came across the street.

"Thanks for coming right over, Carl," Emory said, putting his hand on the other man's shoulder. "We've got us a houseful in both places."

After Lee Newton's body was removed from the trunk, Emory and Ted drove to the courthouse, where the deputy delighted in calling up the command post in Presley County.

"Got your man, Billy Jay. He's deader than a doornail down here in the hospital morgue."

"Like hell. We have him contained."

Emory snorted. "Then that body in the morgue must be his twin brother."

"Are you sure?" Billy Jay asked.

"Sure, I'm sure. I know Newton by sight."

"Well, if that purely ain't somethin'. All these high-powered folks up here and"—Emory could almost hear Billy Jay's mind humming, trying to turn his poor judgment call around—"our little hick department pulls out the plum. It'll look good for us, Em'ry. Yessiree."

"We have other complications. Maudie Rice killed herself."

"Well, I'll be damned. She was one of my best supporters." He paused. "Say, she was Lee Newton's mother-in-law. Is that why?"

"Don't think so. Best I can tell she was trying to kill the woman Eugene assaulted and got caught at it. Oh, yeah, and Connie turned up—"

"Good."

"Not so good. She was in the hospital morgue. Cold dead."

"My Lord, why didn't you—?"

"Now Billy Jay, we still got that woman missing down here. The woman Lee Newton had as a hostage. They apparently rendezvoused at River's Bend, and when Newton died—I think he drowned—some other guy grabbed the woman and took off. I guess he's taken her to that

Compound southwest of here. Maybe the thing to do is get some help down here, and we can go in there."

"I'll report the news about Newton. They'll want to come down and verify that it's him. I think the thing to do is to get some help down there, maybe storm that place and get her outta there."

Emory was nodding at the telephone receiver. So clever of Billy Jay to think of that. After he finished talking to the sheriff, Emory tried to reach Senator Grindstaff, but no one answered.

Susan rubbed her head and squeezed her eyes shut, trying to concentrate. *Don't give up,* she urged herself.

Obviously she had to investigate the room, see what was there.

She started along one wall, using her feet and hands to probe her surroundings. In the northwest corner she stumbled into something. A sawhorse. Not exactly a weapon.

She continued her search, feeling for the other sawhorse frame so she wouldn't trip over it. She found it a few minutes later. Other than some loose nails she found with her feet, there was nothing else.

There's got to be something I can do!

She sat back down on the stack of wallboard as a memory nagged at her. Ted had insisted that the family have a fire drill one time, and she remembered something he'd said: "If you're trapped in a room without a window, break through an interior wall to another room."

She'd scoffed at the idea. Only Jeffrey had immediately assumed he could do it. But he'd been into superheroes at the time and was always certain he had superhuman powers.

"No, I mean it," Ted had insisted. "Any of you could break through a wall. You think of a wall as extremely solid, but most of them are just half an inch thick." He'd knocked on the wall to emphasize his point. "Sheetrock— and what's that but a bunch of chalk between paper."

Not long after the fire drill, Jeffrey accidentally proved his father's point. He threw their heavy front door open with

boyish vigor, and the knob punctured a hole in the Sheetrock. Most walls only *looked* formidable.

Okay, Ted, I'm going to try it and I hope you're right.
Maybe she could get into the room next door. And just
maybe the door in that room would be open to the hall.

Most of the building was concrete. What if the Sheetrock
was just covering it? But why? Why not just paint the
concrete? More likely they had put up a wall to divide one
large room into two. And to do that, they used boards.
Sawhorses, nails, Sheetrock. It gave her a small glimmer of
confidence, but what did she really know about construction?

She stood up and groped for the sawhorse, then carried it
to the wall. How far apart were studs? She tried to
remember from hanging pictures. Twelve inches or sixteen?
She thought it was sixteen. She estimated the distance from
the corner so she could thrust one of the two-by-four legs
between the uprights. Picking a likely spot, she jammed the
sawhorse against the wall, but not hard enough. The
sawhorse didn't break through, but she'd felt some give in
the wall. It wasn't solid. Again she pulled back, and this
time struck with all her might. The leg penetrated.

She waited a few minutes to see if anyone came running,
but no one did. She rammed the wall again. A hole began
to crumble in the gypsum material. She gave several more
solid blows, then wedged the leg behind the Sheetrock and
used it like a lever. This proved to be more effective than
ramming because she wasn't working against the studs.

She worked steadily but slowly because of the dark—
everything was by feel—until only the paper covering was
holding a sizeable piece of the wallboard together, so she
tore it off. The opening was now large enough to get
through on this side and with her foot, she kicked the
Sheetrock on the other side of the wall into the adjacent
room. It came loose after several solid blows, and she eased
her way through.

The room where the men had been earlier was dark, too,
but she remembered approximately where the desk was.
She felt her way to it and turned on the desk lamp, then sat

down in the chair behind the desk and pulled open the drawers. Just the usual assortment of office supplies and files. There was nothing that could serve as a weapon.

She estimated the distance to the door, turned out the light, and made her way blindly across the room and turned the knob. Good! It was unlocked.

The hallway was pitch-dark. Hearing nothing, she stepped out and began to move carefully along it. At the next doorway, she tried the handle. It was locked. She repeated this as she proceeded the way Larry had brought her in, removing her hand from the security of the right wall only at the end of the hall, where she turned left to go back to the entrance.

The way seemed interminable. Then abruptly she slammed into the metal staircase. Wincing from the sharp pain where it caught her on the shin, she turned and started up, only to find the door at the top locked.

"Damn, damn, damn," she muttered. She paused there a moment trying to get hold of herself. Her hand searched the wall. A light switch. If she flipped it on, she could really search, quickly and efficiently. Her finger touched it. Just then the door opened. Fortunately, she was standing to one side. Her heart jumped to her throat.

"We really don't have time, Colonel," a deep voice said.

A sigh. Close enough to where she stood that she heard the expelling breath. Sweat broke out on Susan's hairline and her chest ached with adrenaline. "Well, okay." It was the senator's voice. "I don't suppose she could go anywhere." A dry laugh, and the door shut.

Susan sank down against the wall to the floor. Her knees wouldn't hold her. Her whole body trembled convulsively. How much more could she take?

She waited there, regaining control, then she retraced her steps to the T-shaped intersection, this time going straight instead of turning toward the office. This corridor was a mirror image of the other. The door at the top of this stairway was just as solidly locked as its counterpart. She slowly moved back toward the office, then beyond. There simply had to be a way out of this prison.

But it wasn't at the end of that hallway either. She fought to keep despair at bay.

She went back to the office, closed the door, and turned on the light, then rested against the door.

Think, she told herself. *You have to think.* Her eyes drifted around the room and came to rest on a vent in the ceiling. *No*, she thought. *Don't think that. I'm not going up there.*

The other voice started up—the reasonable one. *Of course you are. There's no choice.*

With a resigned sigh, she went over to the desk and heaved against it. With an earsplitting screech of metal, it moved a few inches over the concrete floor. She kept at it until the desk was positioned directly beneath the grate.

Holding onto the desk to keep her balance, she carefully stepped up into the swivel chair, then onto the desk itself to investigate the vent more closely. Four screws held it in place.

With a paper clip she found in one of the desk drawers, she was able to turn the screws until they were out far enough to grasp with her finger and thumb. One by one she removed them, then pried the grate out with her fingernails. Dust and fine litter showered down into her eyes. Blinking and pulling at her eyelashes until tears ran, she laid the grate down on the desktop, then climbed down.

A five-gallon can of joint compound sat in one corner of the room. It wasn't full, so she was able to lift it onto the desk. Standing on it, she could get her head up into the vent.

Metal ductwork stretched out in two directions. Did the ceiling have joists, or was it some kind of a false ceiling she'd fall through? Susan wondered. She ducked back into the room and looked at it. It didn't look like a dropped ceiling. These rooms lay beneath the concrete bay, the floor of which must be above her. Then there was a space for the mechanical workings of the place, then the ceiling.

There wasn't enough headroom in the duct for her to boost herself up with any force, so she climbed down and hoisted the swivel chair up onto the desk, then set the

five-gallon can on the chair. The chair swiveled precariously as she climbed up, but she gripped the frame of the
vent to steady herself, and this time slipped easily into the
metal duct.

The dark tunnel lay before her, a narrow passage just
slightly larger than her body. Where would it take her? A
blind alley? A shudder ran along her spine as she stared into
the blackness of the unknown. What might be waiting at the
other end? The irrational fears brought on by the dark had to
be fought. There weren't monsters at the end of this tunnel,
unless they were the human kind. Most likely there'd just be
another grate.

But that's not how it feels, she thought, suppressing
another shudder.

She edged forward on her belly, blocking what little light
was being thrown up from the room below. Her legs drew
up like a frog's and she went forward a few more inches.
The sticky gossamer of a cobweb coated her face and she
tried to wipe it away, but only succeeded in getting it on her
hands, too. With an inward shrug of resignation, she pushed
ahead.

Keep your mind on your purpose, she thought. *Don't
worry about spiders. No time for squeamishness.* As she
thought it, her hand touched a little cluster of something
hard, and she jerked back with a shot of adrenaline. It was
some animal's hoard of nuts, stored for the winter. They
rolled under her like ball bearings as she crawled on by.

She continued to work her way along, counting three
other openings to rooms below. Unless the ductwork
turned, she'd surely be to the end of the bay soon. A few
more feet, and her hands felt something soft. She fingered
it. Insulation. The fiberglass cut into her fingers like little
pinpricks. What was behind it? Why was there insulation?

She lay there a moment and thought, then pushed her
hands through it to a solid wall.

"You think of a wall as extremely solid," she heard Ted
saying again.

She gave a shove, but her arms weren't strong enough,

not with them stretched over her head. If only she could get turned around, but the duct was much too small.

With a reluctant sigh, she labored backward down the tunnel, pushing herself along with a different set of muscles, each one complaining sharply at this new attack on her much-abused body. If the first trip seemed long, this one seemed twice so. Finally her feet reached the open vent into the office, and she went down through it, teetering precariously on the can as the swivel chair tried to throw off its burden.

She carefully turned and got back in the tunnel with her head pointed the opposite direction from which she'd just come, and started once again through the passage, feet first this time. If her hands couldn't knock through the end of the ductwork, perhaps her legs could.

She soon had her doubts. Her muscles cramped with fatigue as she laboriously shoved herself through the darkness once again. The tiny bit of illumination became more and more faint as she pushed over a vent, then another, and another. And then she was there. Her feet touched the insulation and the solidness beyond.

She rolled over on her back and drew her knees up, wriggling her way close to the end. Then she thrust her feet out with all the force she could muster. Her legs crashed through into emptiness as the cover over the end of the duct went crashing downward. Where? She wished she knew. Her recollection of the end of the bay, from when she and Larry had approached the building, was that it just ended with a drop-off. That fit with the sound of the falling cover. One thing was certain, however: she wasn't going to take the time to go back to the vent, climb down, then back in facing forward so she could investigate. Her resources were about gone. She'd just have to take her chances.

She hesitantly edged closer to the end of the duct, shoving the remnants of insulation out. Once they were gone, the cool night air drifted in, and she realized her body was wet with perspiration. She briefly wondered what time it was. How long till nine o'clock Wednesday morning?

Feeling with her feet, she discovered that the concrete

wall wasn't bare. The grasping kudzu had begun an assault on the building. It massed here, tightly twisted together, and with only her legs and lower torso out of the duct, she tested the vines with one foot. They seemed sturdy. She put more of her weight on them and moved out of the security of the metal channel, clinging to the vegetation.

She began her descent, images of Jack and the Beanstalk playing in her mind, and was making good progress when one of the vines tore loose and sent her falling the last five feet into the mattress of plants below. She sank down into the mesh of hairy leaves and vines, frightened but unhurt. The aggressive plants engulfed her. Frantically, she struggled upward, tearing at the tendrils to break free of the snarl of leaves and twisting stems.

Surfacing, she stopped to get her breath and realized she was her own worst enemy at the moment. Fear was getting the best of her. *Calm down*, she told herself. *These are just plants. The danger is not here. Relax.*

Tentatively she stepped forward, and immediately her leg plunged downward through the tangle again. More calmly now, she drew her leg up and took another step, testing the vines. Each step was arduous and slow, but finally she struggled out of the deepest part of the kudzu and got to the road she and Larry had driven in on.

There were no security lights here; only moonlight illuminated the bizarre buildings. She supposed the Compound dwellers wanted to avoid detection from aircraft. There were no lights either in the barracks south of the building she'd been held prisoner in. Outside of the barracks there were still several vehicles. Maybe, just maybe, someone had left the keys in one of them.

Staying close to the outside wall of the bay, she moved along southward, peering both ways before she crossed the open area in front of the barracks.

Carefully, she opened the door of the first car, flinching at the click of the latch and the glare of the light. She found the manual light switch inside the door and pressed it with her left hand, while she felt for the ignition with her right.

No keys. She also briefly searched the floor, seat, and dashboard with the same result. Releasing her hand, she quickly but gently closed the door and moved behind it to the next vehicle, a pickup. She repeated the procedure. There were no keys, but her search under the seat revealed a box. She jerked and yanked until she could get it out from under the seat one-handed. It was a box of hand grenades.

No weapon could have pleased her more. She had seen enough television and movies to know how to operate one of these: just pull the pin and lob it—quickly. It seemed simpler than an automatic weapon. One-handed, she managed to thrust one in each pocket of her shorts. She could carry a third.

She was so intent on getting the grenades that she ignored the first noise, although she realized when she heard a cough that there had been an earlier sound; it was rattling around in her mind. She lifted her head slowly and saw the dark shape of a man coming around the barracks. She froze, her fingers grinding themselves into the button on the door-frame that was keeping the light in the truck off. The truck was parked at a slight angle to the front of the building, but even so, one look back and the sentry would be able to discern the half-open door of the truck and the legs protruding beneath it.

She watched, not daring to breathe, as he walked along the front perimeter of the building, then turned and crossed the road, not twenty feet from the truck she was searching, but now the car she had previously searched stood between the two of them. She couldn't turn to watch his progress for fear of his seeing the movement. So she waited, counting to a hundred. Then slowly, almost imperceptibly, she began to turn her head.

The sentry had disappeared, probably to walk along the other building's west side. She slipped out of the door of the truck in record time and moved to the west side of the barracks and squatted there behind some scrubby junipers, trying to decide what to do next. She ought to search the other cars, but the fear was acid in her mouth, and she didn't think she could do it.

Doubts begin to assail her as she waited. What if she depended on one of the grenades and they weren't even real? What did she know about this sort of thing? Maybe they were like blanks—for practice. She rubbed her head, gingerly touching the goose egg where she'd banged into the rock ledge where Lee had drowned. Behind her eyes there was a dull ache. She hoped it wouldn't turn into one of those siege headaches that practically immobilized her for a day every once in a while.

Finally, she saw the man's shape coming up the road she and Larry had driven on. He had apparently circled the building. Could she remain undetected in her present location? Probably not for long, but where else was there to go, especially now that the man was crossing the road in front of her? She scarcely breathed as he passed the bushes where she crouched. He abruptly turned eastward and went along the front of the barracks, then disappeared down the east side.

She had to make a break for it now before he came around the buildings. She wondered how far afield his route would take him. Would he immediately be coming back around this very building? She stood up stiffly and started to move to the intermediate cover of the vehicles.

Suddenly a light in the windows nearest her came on, and voices and the sounds of movement drifted out. A small voice. It was the bathroom and a mother was in there with her child. A toilet flushed.

Women and children? Here? It surprised Susan. She fell back into the shadow of a scraggly bush, her heart recovering its rhythm. She crouched there, listening. But the talk had stopped.

Her leg cramped, and she massaged the excruciating pain, trying to rub it away. The cramp subsided just in time. The sentry was approaching. She plastered herself to the shadowy ground. The lighted window distracted him and he didn't even look her way. "That you, Yvonne?" he asked.

"Yes. Tanya's up again."

"After you get her down, come out in back and meet me. Okay?"

The woman murmured something.

When he'd disappeared around back, Susan darted across to the building in which she'd been held prisoner, holding the hand grenades tight against her to keep them from beating against her as she ran. With the sentry and Yvonne somewhere behind her, she decided to follow the road back to the gate, always hugging the woods in case someone else came along in a truck or car. Once at the gate—well, she'd have to face that when she got there. Would she be able to launch a grenade, if necessary, to disable the gate guard, then another to get through?

It sounded straightforward, but she hadn't counted on the road diverging into two. In the dark neither looked familiar, so she took the left fork and figured the gate must be about a mile ahead. She knew her judgment would be way off concerning space and time, so she decided to count off steps. She thought the length of her stride must be close to a yard, so she began to count.

The counting helped the time pass, although it became so mechanical that once she lost track and had to try to concentrate on the words she was saying. At one thousand seven hundred and sixty there was no sign of a fence or a gate.

She went another of her stepped-off miles. Maybe it had been farther to the gate than she thought. A narrow track branched off to the right, and she reasoned that it would take her back toward the other road, although now she was thinking the track itself might run into the fence and border it.

She was right. Not three hundred yards down, she came to the telltale ridge of kudzu that was the fence.

The crickets and tree frogs were chanting, a comforting sound. Somewhere a dog barked. A summer night. The moon was dropping low and the stars were coming into their own with their brilliance. *Dear God,* she prayed, *please let me get out of this. I want to stop those madmen. This killing can't happen in a universe so glorious.* She was acutely aware of the feel of the grenades clumping against her as she walked.

Suddenly she realized someone was following her. Her heart leapt to her throat. She detoured quickly into the woods, and the noises behind her sped up, pursuing her. She was no sooner among the trees than she tripped over a kudzu vine and went tumbling down concrete stairs into the remnants of some kind of structure, now overgrown.

Before she could get up, a low, throaty growl met her ears. Her pursuer was a dog, waiting for her now at the top of the stairs. She wondered if a guard was close behind it somewhere. And why wasn't the animal already sounding the alarm?

Maybe it was just trained to detect people who came over the fence, and since she was inside . . . She hoped so.

Instinct led her down under the kudzu to burrow through the leaves and vines like an animal intent on survival, eluding the predator. Each noise was magnified as the stems of the plant broke and cracked at her passing. Another set of stairs rose from the opposite side of the foundation, and she crawled up them clumsily, clasping the grenade tightly, and emerged. There was no sign of the dog. A sigh of relief escaped her as she moved back toward the path.

But there the dog was again, behind her. She could hear it keeping pace. When she stopped, it stopped. If she turned ever so slightly toward the animal, it growled. She felt as if she were a sheep being herded.

She'd quit counting her steps, but she estimated it must have been at least thirty minutes since she'd turned from the road onto this path. Leaving out the time that she was in the woods, she'd walked at least a mile. The stars were beginning to fade, and she realized with a shock that morning was well on its way. Perhaps only four more hours.

The gate sneaked up on her. Before she realized it, it was there in front of her in the dim light. A sentry paced outside, facing away from her. Decision time was upon her. She turned to take cover in the woods, but the moment she made a move to the side of the path, the dog started barking.

"Katrina?" the man said as he swung around. Susan could tell he really didn't expect to encounter any surprise. She imagined guard duty was usually pretty peaceful.

He raised his gun, and she realized that she had no choice. With a sick feeling in her stomach, she pulled the pin on the grenade in her hand and lobbed it toward the gate.

At the same time she plunged into the woods and dived behind a tree. The dog came snarling after her but lost his drive when the explosion jolted him, throwing him onto the ground. The noise resounded through the woods, reverberating in her ears.

The gate had been blown apart by the grenade, and the sentry lay near it. *Maybe*, she thought, *he's just injured. Maybe I didn't kill another person.*

With that faint hope—but also with the fear that he would get up and grab her—she ran through the gate and past his still form. She had to get on her way quickly. The explosion would bring out the rest of the people from the compound.

She ran down the road, trying to ignore the aches and pains raging through her muscles and joints as she put as much ground between herself and the gate as possible. She hated to leave the roadway, the most direct path to help, but the woods offered the best cover, so once again she entered their shelter.

Wednesday Morning

19

THE SIEGE BY law-enforcement officials took exactly twenty-eight minutes. They'd approached the Compound stealthily, well hidden in the woods, and were waiting for the right moment to move in when they heard the explosion. One team moved forward, still with caution, and found the front gate to the place blown apart and a man lying in the wreckage unconscious. They managed to hide again, within the Compound, before two men came in a car from inside to investigate. The rest had been easy.

Deputy Emory Todd was surprised to see so few men in the Compound; he counted only five, and that included one injured man. There were fourteen women, ten of them pregnant, and eight children. Rumors around the area had reported the place to be at least a hundred strong.

Ted Morrow had been ordered to stay outside the mainstream of activity until everything was under control, so he was still in the deputy's car. Now Emory told him it was okay for him to join them.

"Did you find her?" Ted asked as he eagerly got out.

"She's locked in over there." Emory pointed at the concrete building. "We're getting a key." A few moments later, a state policeman appeared, urging one of the survivalists, a stoop-shouldered ox of a man who was carrying a bracelet of keys, and the four of them went across the road.

"Show us where Mrs. Morrow is," Emory said.

The survivalist glared at the lawman and ignored the order, until the state policeman prodded him in the back. With that incentive, he led them down the stairs and through the concrete corridor.

"Open it," the deputy ordered when they were in front of the room where Susan had been held prisoner.

Ted pounded on the door. "Susan, we're here. It's all right now."

Taking his time, the survivalist searched for the key, found it, and turned it in the lock.

Emory reached for the light switch. Nothing happened, but the light from the hall told the story. It exposed the hole between the two rooms.

"Looks like she ekscaped," the survivalist said with a grin. He seemed satisfied that the lawmen had met a deadend.

"Damn!" Ted muttered behind Emory, who was already through the hole into the office.

"Go through the door and turn on the light," Emory hollered back at the state policeman. There was very little illumination, but Emory was impatient and began to fumble around and ran into the desk. He felt along the top, knocked against the swivel chair that was precariously near the edge, unbalancing it, and just as the survivalist and the policeman got the door open and the light on, the chair and can came tumbling off the desk with a horrible din.

It gave all of them a start. The policeman drew his gun, and Ted cursed. Emory was the only one who anticipated the crash, so he just took a deep breath and said, "They were piled up here." He pointed to the vent.

All of them looked at the gaping hole in the ceiling, but Ted was already climbing up on the desk. "Hand me that can," he ordered.

When Emory handed it up, Ted stood on it and hollered down the vent. "Susan! Are you there?"

They all waited.

"Susan!" he tried again, then looked down at the survivalist. "Where does this go?

The man shrugged. "I guess just down to the end of the bay."

"I'm going through," Ted said.

"Wait a minute," Emory said. "Let's go out and find the end of it and see if it looks like she came out it."

Ted was already trying to climb into the vent, but Emory's words stopped him. "Okay. I guess you're right. That would make sense." He jumped down from the desk and started hightailing it back to the entry.

"You keep an eye on this guy," Emory told the state patrolman, indicating the survivalist. "And I'll try to keep up with him." A nod from the policeman sent him on his way.

Ted had already made it into the mat of kudzu and was gingerly picking his way across it when Emory caught up with him. "See anything?" he asked.

"Yeah, someone's been through here. The vines are broken down. Look up there! There's the end of the duct."

Emory saw it. The cover was gone and some of the vines had been torn away from the wall. "Looks like she came out there. Morrow, I'm looking forward to meeting this wife of yours. She must be some kind of woman."

Ted had his back to Emory, but even so the deputy could tell he shouldn't have said that right then. He struggled across the kudzu to the man's side and put his arm around his shoulder. "Hey, it's going to be okay. She got out. Hell, I bet she's the one who blasted through that gate." Emory could see a glistening around Ted's eyes. The poor guy was struggling to maintain control, had his bottom lip firmly between his teeth, and his eyebrows quivering. "C'mon," Emory told him. "Let's go find her."

The woods were peaceful in the predawn silence as Susan hurried away from the Compound. She'd worried for a while that someone might be following her, but she could do no more than she was doing, and that was to plod onward, the pink sky in the east her compass at first, then the sun itself. She was weary and hadn't the extra energy necessary for worrying. Her mind had switched into a gray area, her awareness dulled, her movements on automatic.

The long rays of the sun shot through the trees, bringing a sparkle to the dew-laden leaves. The condensation had puddled on one large grape leaf, and Susan stopped and tipped it to let the few drops of water run into her dry mouth. She licked the fine moisture from several others. Unsated but impatient, she started walking again.

The birds around her had started their morning chorus. They joined in, species by species—the early birds and then the not-quite-so-early ones—to greet the dawn. Her footsteps crackled noisily over the the deep layer of last year's fallen leaves as she picked up her pace. It was getting late.

Something flickered in her mind. She wondered about the man at the gate. Had the grenade killed him? And where was that dog? Had it been stunned? Maybe it was behind her. No, she didn't feel its presence.

It doesn't matter now. Just keep going. Keep going. Keep going. The repetitive words prodded her movements. A car. She heard a car. The sound sent her diving for cover. It was them. They were after her.

She lay there in the safety of the forest floor, hidden behind a fallen tree. She'd come this far through the nightmare; only a little farther. After a moment, she pulled herself upright, her eyes darting around, alertness returning.

The trees thinned ahead. A highway.

She knew it was silly, but she couldn't stop the short dry sobs that started erupting from her throat. Her shoulders were shaking. It wasn't over; she still needed to be careful. They might be out here looking for her.

Fearful of that, she stayed along the margin of the woods. She wanted to scrutinize any approaching cars before she flagged one down, but that proved to be impossible. The first car zoomed around a curve and passed her before she could even get a good look at it. Caution would have to go if she was to get to town in time.

Before another car appeared she rounded a curve and saw a country crafts store nestled in a wide spot on one side of the highway.

Her whole body ached, and her gait had become a hobble as she went across the road. Her destination was a public phone hanging on the outside of the building, but her heart sank as she got to it. Vandals had been there; the phone was gone. Just some wires hung limply from the wall.

"Damn it!" she said, hitting the plastic hood with her fist. She was certain the crafts store wasn't open because there was no car in sight, but she went up on its porch and rattled the door, realizing already that her time was running out. She peered in the window to see if there was a clock.

There was a phone on the counter. It would be simple to break in; much easier than breaking out of the room at the Compound. She limped down the steps to the parking area to find a rock.

As she headed back to the porch, a car swooped around the curve. It was a state police car. Her hands shot out to wave, but the driver didn't see her.

"Oh, no. Oh, no," she mumbled hurtling down the steps. "Don't go away. You can't go away." The grenades thumped against her legs as she ran down the steps. Quickly, her hand darted into her pocket and withdrew one of them. She pulled the pin and sent it hurtling into the middle of the road, then dropped down and covered her head. That should get someone's attention.

It did. After a few moments, she saw the state police car returning. Inside, two plainclothes officers were in the front, and in back were two dowdy-looking women and a little girl about eight.

"You've got to help me," she told the driver. She pointed down the way she'd come. "There are some white supremacists out there in the woods, and they're planning to blow up the federal building in Marshallville. This morning at nine. There isn't much time. I've got to get to a phone. Or you could radio in? You've got to stop them."

The words poured out of her too fast for him to comprehend. He made her start over again, then he told her he was coming from the Compound and that they'd just arrested the people there and were bringing them out. "Are you Susan Morrow?"

"Yes," she said. Relief swept over her, and her knees began to shake.

"Let me call the sheriff and tell him you're here." He picked up the mike and radioed.

Within three minutes, she heard a siren. A sheriff's vehicle careened around the curve and turned into the parking area. Ted leaped out of the passenger's side before the car quit rolling.

"Thank God, oh thank God! Susan, are you okay?" He hugged her tightly, and she relaxed into his bearlike grip. It felt so good. Tears welled up in her eyes, and she clung to him, but no words came. She was just overcome with relief to be with him again. How could she ever have doubted her feelings about him? Thank God she had a chance to continue her life with him.

"Oh, Ted, I'm so glad you're here. They—they're planning to blow up the federal building in Marshallville. Jen . . . we have to warn them." She shook her head. "I can't believe it—Senator Grindstaff—" Her voice broke.

"It's okay now." He patted her, rocking back and forth slightly. "The police have them all in custody. They won't be doing any blowing up anyplace."

The deputy who'd been driving the car, got out and wandered over.

"This is my wife, Emory," Ted said in a husky voice, still holding Susan in a bear hug.

"Glad you turned up. Your husband was in quite a state when we didn't find you back there."

There was another concern. Susan had almost forgotten. "What about Jan? Has anyone seen her?"

Ted pushed his glasses up and nodded. "She got back, but she's still in the hospital." He started to tell her the entire story, but Emory interrupted. "Let's get her into town; you can tell her about it on the way."

Ted nodded and began to hustle Susan into the car. "What's that in your pocket?" he asked.

She pulled out the grenade and handed it to Emory. "Do something with this. Please." She shielded her eyes to avoid the distasteful sight and climbed into the car.

Evan Grindstaff sat at his desk, his palms down on the blotter, fingers spread almost as if he were measuring it. The explosives had been set. He and Larry and another man had left the Compound just after midnight, allowing plenty of time to set the charges before anyone showed up at the federal building for work. Now the senator's cohorts had gone on their way, not back to the Compound but to a safe house in another state. He himself would go to his car in a short while and drive away. He was going to catch a plane to Washington. The reservation had been made weeks ago. Then, of course, he would hear the news on the radio and return to the scene of devastation. He rubbed his eyes. It would all make good press.

The phone rang. It was Emory Todd.

"I'm afraid I have bad news, Senator. It's about Maudie."

She was dead of course. That's what it meant when someone called and said he had bad news.

"She killed herself," Emory continued.

Evan was used to bad news. First it was his father, then one by one the rest of his family. He, Maudie, and another sister, Eleanor, were the only three left. Odd that he was among the last, with him the oldest. The oldest should go first if things were rational. He used to think he'd want to be the last to die, unlike some people who said they wouldn't want to live if all their loved ones were gone. But the reality was depressing. And now Maudie was gone. The youngest. His little sister.

A picture of Maudie as a little girl running across a field on their farm with her red hair streaming behind her appeared like a silent movie in his mind. What a little doll she'd been. Evan had been fifteen years older than her. When he was seventeen their father had come down with tuberculosis. He remembered it as a time of eating raw eggs and figs. The county health people thought that would keep him and his brothers and sisters from getting it. He'd finally had to take his father to the sanatorium down in the southern part of the state for treatment. For some reason his mother wasn't up to the trip; he supposed she thought she couldn't leave the younger children, so it was left to Evan to accompany his father on the journey. It was the boy's first train ride, his first adventure away from home. Two months later his father had returned and had spent his last months living on the back porch to take in the cold, healthful air. He'd died that December, and Evan became the father to his young siblings.

Well, he thought, *I did a pretty damn good job*. Four of them had gone to college, two to nursing school. He himself got a good education from life. Then there was Moore, who'd been retarded. Not much to do for him. He'd lived at the state hospital until his death at thirty-five. Lord, it had been so many years since Moore had died. Where had the time gone? How had it slipped through his fingers? Moore had been the first of the children to go. Next Ruby, then Earl. The hardest for him to take had been Ab, the brother nearest to him in age. Then last year Sybil had passed away.

And now Maudie.

He took in the details of her death almost in a stupor. She had killed a girl, and now she herself was gone. It was hard to believe. He wiped his eyes.

It was a shock about Maudie, but no more than what Emory told him next. He reported that state police, highway patrol from the neighboring state, FBI agents, and local law-enforcement officers—it sounded like an army—had gone into the Compound and arrested everyone on the premises and that Mrs. Morrow had escaped, but had later been picked up along the highway.

"Good thing we picked them up, Senator. They were gonna blow up your building! At nine o'clock this morning. We just got there in the nick of time."

Now why hadn't Mrs. Morrow said anything about his

involvement? Was it a trap? He felt perspiration pop out on his head. Lord! What was he going to do now?

His hand gripped the receiver for moments after he hung up, his bony knuckles white.

The sound of the outer office door jolted him back to reality. "That you, Jennifer?" His voice cracked. As usual she was early. Nice young girl. Quite a contrast to the unkempt women at the Compound. But they were hardy, used to being deprived, imposing the strictest disciplines on themselves. Good stock for the New Order, he supposed. It was hard for him, though, to rationalize some of their views. They considered themselves Christians, but they practiced polygamy. And they bypassed marriage and thought any child born of a healthy Aryan stock was legitimate. Maybe he was just old-fashioned.

He passed his hand across his face. The New Order. Was he ready for it? Some of them even worshiped Hitler; he'd heard Lee Newton talking about one group that wore swastikas. Well, he'd been in World War II and he couldn't quite get ready for turning Hitler into a hero.

Evan wondered about himself. He wasn't a religious man—that hadn't entered into his involvement with this rather odd group of misfits. He'd gone to Washington with a mandate from his constituents to do something about the insidious erosion of their rights. His platform hadn't been put in exactly those words, but that's what it amounted to. He was going to protect the rights of real Americans over those of the government. But how ineffective he'd felt against the enormous bureaucratic hydra. Back home, the people looked up to him; they thought he represented power. But if he didn't suck up to the right people in Washington, his effectiveness was zilch. And he had sucked in order to get things done—making deals, compromising. It made him sick.

But all the time he was looking for alternatives, for answers, and he'd found them in the guise of a man who wanted to make a campaign contribution on behalf of an obscure nonprofit organization the senator had never heard of. Its name sounded harmless, but one of the senator's aides told him it was a white supremacist group, and they shouldn't accept the gift. It would look bad. One of those things he'd find himself having to explain to the media or some committee. They hadn't taken the gift, but the man's name rattled around in the senator's mind until one day he ran into him at a social gathering.

After several meetings, the man had convinced the senator that violence was the only prod that would wake white people up. It would expose the ineffectiveness of the government. It would pave the way for change. What they needed to do was set up a training camp in this part of the country for a highly specialized corps, men and women who could then be sent out to make their random, thus terrifying, strikes.

The senator was fascinated and knew just the place—an abandoned rocket test site. He could pull the strings needed to take possession of it.

He'd been careful about his meetings, but it was damned hard to keep anything a secret, and somehow a rumor started circulating that he was involved with a racist group. His opponent had even made allusions to it, and the polls were beginning to show it. They'd started sliding. That's when the notion of blowing up the federal building had occurred to him. What a coup! Strike ZOG, and help send the senator back to Washington on the sympathy vote. On the surface it would pull him back from the fringe some of his constituents feared. And he could continue to work from the inside.

Jennifer Morrow appeared; her face looked drawn. "Good morning, Senator."

"They've found your mother, Jennifer. She's all right."

She sank against the doorjamb to steady herself. "Oh, thank God!"

The Senator looked at his watch. Twenty minutes and the New Order would begin its assault on the Establishment.

Jennifer came over to the desk and put out her hand, and he took it.

"Thank you, Senator," she said brokenly. "Thank you so much for everything." She clasped his hand in both of hers.

Maudie was dead. Pretty little girl running across a field. Maudie. Jennifer. Pretty little girl. He closed his eyes.

"Are you okay, Senator?"

He nodded and pulled his hands away and motioned her out of the office. When she'd gone, he looked up the building superintendent's number and started to pick up the phone, then changed his mind.

"Jennifer?" he called. "Are you in there?" He felt so very tired.

Emory left his office, checked with the sheriff, who was enjoying the flap with state policemen and FBI agents running all over *his* courthouse, then went into the conference room where Susan Morrow and her husband were waiting.

"Sorry that took so long. Have you had a chance to call your daughter?"

Ted shook his head. He had his arm around his wife's shoulder, and his hand rested on her knee protectively. "The lines are all busy." He smiled. "There are a couple of reporters, and all you law guys. This place is a circus." He adjusted his glasses.

"Yeah," Emory agreed. "I had to call Senator Grindstaff. He's been following this case, and I needed—"

Susan's eyes had been shut, but now they popped open. "Senator Grindstaff. But he's one of them."

"What are you talking about?" Emory asked.

"You didn't find him in the Compound? Oh, my God. Ted. Ted." Her arms and legs began to move in random jerks. "Oh no, oh no." She was in a frenzy. She grabbed Ted's left arm to look at his watch. "What time is it?"

He struggled against her agitation to look at his watch, and Emory could see he was reluctant to tell her. "Three minutes after nine."

Susan looked as if she'd been mortally·wounded as her face twisted in horror. Her heart-rending cry was probably heard all over the courthouse. "We're too late!"

* * *

Minutes ago an explosion rocked downtown Marshallville, destroying the west end of the federal building and the adjacent Walters Building. Police and fire crews are now on the scene and have found only one body in the debris thus far. The low loss of life is credited to the fast action on the part of the Building Superintendent Warren Smith, who received an anonymous phone call warning him to evacuate the building.

Jennifer was racing down the highway toward Breedlove much too fast when she heard the news about the explosion in Marshallville. Her very office building! She turned the radio louder, as she careened to a stop on the highway shoulder, shock charging through her body.

She gripped the wheel with both hands, her knuckles white as she remembered the senator's look when she'd stepped into his office. His face had been gray, the eyes moist.

"You'd better go over to Breedlove, Jennifer."

"Is there something wrong with my mother? Something you didn't tell me?"

"No. You just need to go to her. She needs you."

All at once he'd seemed impatient. "Now go on," he said. "Get out of here. I have to make a phone call."

Could he be the casualty? No, she assured herself. He would have gotten out when Warren told him.

She put her car in gear and eased back onto the highway. There was a town up ahead a few miles. She'd stop there and call Breedlove to let her parents know she was okay, in case they heard the news.

It was in a convenience store where she'd stopped to phone that she heard the rest of the news. Senator Grindstaff's body had been identified.

It was as if everything were coming from the netherworld of her mind: voices, telephones ringing, people moving around. The chief deputy was there in front of her. What was he saying? She tuned in.

"You're daughter's okay. She's on the phone. C'mon with me."

Susan plowed through the people in the hall to get to the phone.

"Jennifer?"

"Mom, are you okay?"

"Jennifer—I—I thought you were—you're really okay?"

"Yes, Mom. Really."

"They were planning to blow up your building."

"They did, but I wasn't there. I heard it on the news. But who . . . how did you know?"

"Jennifer, where are you?" She told her mother, and Susan said, "Why don't we wait until you get here to explain."

"Mom, the senator was in the building. He was killed. I heard it on the news."

Susan paused too long.

"Did you hear me?" Jennifer asked.

"Yes, I heard you. I'm sorry, honey." After a few more words, they hung up. Ted put his arm around Susan who said, "It was just too much to try to tell her on the phone."

Sunlight bathed the hospital room in brilliant shafts of light through the vertical blinds. Susan was slouched in a chair at one side of her friend's bed, drowsy from medication the doctor had given her for all her bites, stings, rashes, and aches and pains. She was still wearing the clothes she'd had on when she started the trip; the red-and-white shirt was now dirty and tattered. Ted was sitting on the marble windowsill. He too was dirty. Stubble was sprouting on his chin. Neal Lassiter was in another chair in the corner, sitting sideways on one hip, favoring his injured leg.

Jan alone looked clean, leaning against the starchy white pillowcases, propped up in the raised bed. "She put a bubble of air in my IV," she was saying, "but she didn't quite do the job, so she was trying it again. If Neal hadn't been looking in just then—"

"Shoot," he said, "you were taking care of yourself." He

grinned at Jan, then addressed the others. "I saw her fist draw back and—kerplooey—she let that woman have it in the kisser." He demonstrated.

"It was so hard to muster my strength, like running through mud in a dream. Have you ever had a dream like that?"

Neal nodded. "All hell was breaking loose around here about that time," he said. "The doctor had just found the clerk from the sheriff's office in cold storage, and Eugene Rice was on his way in there. When the doctor saw him coming in, he hollered at him. And Eugene took off running, looking guilty as hell."

Susan roused herself. "I'm having trouble following all this. The nurse wanted to kill you because you were going to press charges against her son? He was the one with the beard, right?"

Jan nodded.

"How'd the other woman get involved?" Susan asked.

"You mean Connie? She'd been raped by Eugene. In fact, she was pregnant by him. She came into my room, and I guess the nurse overheard us talking about her son. I was encouraging Connie to press charges." Jan shook her head. "I feel really responsible. Anyway, Eugene's mother didn't want him to be prosecuted. For more than one reason."

"What do you mean?" Susan asked.

"She was afraid it would hurt her brother's chances for reelection. I heard them talking about it when I was semiconscious."

Susan's mouth gaped. "She was Senator Grindstaff's sister?"

Ted nodded. "He was in for a tight race this fall— Jennifer told us that—and his sister didn't want Eugene hurting his chances."

"So she committed murder," Neal said. "Now that makes sense."

Jan shrugged. "She probably thought she could cover her tracks, that it was foolproof. It almost was."

"Ted," Susan asked, "did you ever have any idea what Senator Grindstaff was involved in?"

"Now I recall there was some talk about him, but to be honest I never paid much attention. I couldn't see anything wrong with Jennifer working for any senator. Live and learn—if you're lucky," he added.

As he said it, Jennifer appeared at the door, looking over the crowd until her eyes fell on her mother. "Mom," she shrieked, flying at her.

The two of them embraced, and Ted came over to hug them both. Then Jennifer began to ask questions. When Susan told her about the senator, the younger woman's eyes widened. "He planned that?"

Susan nodded. "He was running things."

"But why?"

Ted briefly told his daughter what he knew, then put his arm around her. "Maybe with some time we can sort some of this out. Right now, it's almost too much to comprehend. We're all tired."

Jennifer turned to her father and adopted a frown that resembled his habitual one. "That reminds me, how are you, Daddy? Did you know he'd been in the hospital, Mom?"

Her question inspired a series of questions about his hospital stay. "But really," Ted said, holding his hands up in front of him, "I'm feeling fine."

Jennifer smiled at her parents and then excused herself to go phone Marshallville. She felt guilty not being there to help.

"Do you feel like walking down the hall?" Ted asked Susan. "There's someone I want you to see."

Her eyebrows rose, but she got up. He took her by the elbow, and they went around the corner from Jan's room.

"Where are we going?"

"Right here." He ushered her into a room where an old man sat propped up in a bed. A couple sat in chairs by his side.

Susan's mouth dropped open. "Willy." She went over to his bed.

The old man squinted. "I remember you; you're the one with the army fella."

She nodded. No need to try to explain again that Lee wasn't an army fella.

Ted introduced himself to the two people in the room and explained what had happened.

"I'm Norm Burke; this is my wife Marge." He told Ted about their unfortunate encounter with Willy. "We're going to take him to his nephew's over in Marshallville to recuperate—as soon as he gets released."

"They're takin' care of my pup," Willy added.

Back in the hall, Ted told Susan that Neal had invited them to come out to his place to clean up and get some rest. Ted still refused to return to the only motel in town. "We'll stop at a general store and get some clothes of some sort. You'll feel better."

They walked slowly back to Jan's room, arm in arm, and started to go in, but Neal and Jan were wrapped up in what looked like an intimate conversation, so they went on by.

"A lot has happened," Susan said with a smile.

"Yes."

"You know, Ted, Lee Newton considered himself a Christian. He saw himself as a very moral person, armed with the Word. It was sickening to listen to him go on." She winced at the memory of his hatred.

Ted shook his head. "A crackpot."

Susan shuddered and felt her bottom lip quiver. There was a time when she'd have called him a crackpot. A week ago she'd have let someone else worry about the Lee Newtons of the world. But maybe there was no one else. Maybe it was the Susan Morrows of the world who had to fight the Lee Newtons.

Listen to me. I'm becoming quite a heroine, she thought wryly. It would be nice to put that sort of twist on the events of the past week. But she knew her actions had nothing to do with saving the world from the zealots, from the crackpots. Killing Lee Newton, injuring the guard—they were acts of self-preservation, not heroism.

But something else had happened on that Tuesday in July. She'd acted. She'd taken responsibility for herself. The aftermath felt like a little ember which had just caught a breath of air, glowing, almost ready to flame.

I've been through hell the last four days, she thought, *and I survived. I'm battered and bruised and awfully tired. But I survived.*